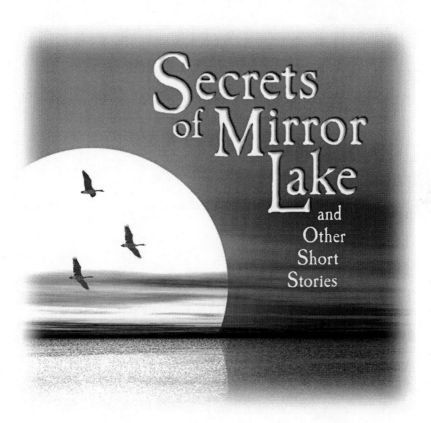

Secrets of Mirror Lake

and Other Short Stories

STEPHEN H. JANSEN

To Terry

Stephen H. Jansen

the *Tradewinds* company

D0228187

Copyright ©2009 by Stephen H. Jansen. All rights reserved.

No part of this book may be reproduced in any form or by
any electronic or mechanical means including information storage
and retrieval systems—except in the case of brief quotations
embodied in critical articles or reviews—without permission
in writing from the author. For information or addional copies
contact:

Stephen H. Jansen
www.stephenhjansen.com

First printing 2009

Although the author has exhaustively researched all sources
to ensure the accuracy and completeness of the information
contained in this book, he assumes no responsibility for
errors, inaccuracies, omissions or any inconsistency herein.
Any slights of people or organizations are unintentional.

Interior and cover design by
Wayne E. Johnson
WayneEJ@comcast.net

ISBN-13: 978-0-9799152-8-4
ISBN-10: 0-9799152-8-7

Printed by Publisher's Graphics
10 9 8 7 6 5 4 3 2 1

To my parents, Roni and Howard
who sponsored, believed and encouraged.

IV

Table of Contents

You Can See the Moon
From Heaven

The white, bright light of a full moon face shone in the window casting a subtle, gray stick figure shadow on the floor beside her. The jagged lines stretched across the room much longer, taller even than she. Fine lace sheers framed the window and hung limply without so much as the slightest trace of breeze. Yet the dark lines on the floor wavered like the black flag atop tall ships at full sail.

A golden cat's eye glint flickered in her hand. The tiny uniform bars caused her pause. Her sergeant stood tall stoically saluting fingers to forehead. His pointed cap covered a scar beneath the hairline he sustained when only three and a half years old. They'd lived in a three flat then just inside the city lines of Chicago. He'd brazenly decided to ride his tricycle down the outside stairs that led to the basement, one at a time leaning backwards like riding a bucking bronc. Only the second stair never came. He'd skipped it entirely while in midflight head over heels directly down where the bottom stair rudely greeted him awash in blood. Logical but foolish. Some things never change. Some people never change.

Suzanne Reichel never wanted her son to go to Iraq. It wasn't her war. It was a politicians's war fought in a far away land of sand for precious commodities far under ground. But he insisted, pleaded. Never much of a student he'd dropped out college and used the war to give meaning to his life. As if life at that tender age needed meaning.

Sergeant Jason B. Reichel died last September 22nd—when an insurgent sniper fired the bullets that pierced his neck. He had large, blackish-brown eyes you could see your reflection in. Smiling eyes that never saw a sad tear. The same eyes that swelled with joy as she breast-fed her boy.

Suzanne placed the shiny bars back in the box on the dresser and reached inside. The moonlit room provided little light but she knew right where it was. She removed a tiny flash drive she'd sent him from the box. It lay motionless, cradled in her hand like a wounded bird. This was all she had left of Jason. He had once been that small. Oh and how that boy could kick when he swam around inside her. Never when she walked or sat and rocked. Only when she sat still. Then Jason would get anxious almost as if he wanted out. It was hot that summer and like most Chicago summers you could wring the humidity out of your clothes. She'd spent most of her pregnancy trying to accommodate her restless son, most of it on her feet or rocking away the hours until he fell fast asleep inside her.

"Sitting in the dark again?" she heard his voice behind her.

"Robert, you startled me."

"How about some light so you can see what you're doing," He flicked the switch on. The moonlight and shadows disappeared from a room awash in light. On Jason's bed was bright orange blanket with a large blue 'I' on it, a souvenir from his first and only semester at the University of Illinois. There was a Spartan desk, a Michael Jordan poster and a National Geographic map of the middle east pinned to the wall. Above the dresser was a picture of Jason in full military dress against a backdrop of the American flag taken just weeks before he left for Iraq. He had proudly survived boot camp and was gung ho to see active service.

"I don't need light to see in here." She pocketed the flash drive.

Robert crossed the room to hug her. "Suzanne, we've talked about this before," he said quick-kissing her puckered lips. "Standing here in the dark isn't going to bring Jason back. Did you take your med…"

"Long day?" she cut him off as she had a habit of doing. Talking meant not having to listen.

"Yeah, New York branch came up with a new project this morning. Another high rise development on the outskirts of the city. Robert was an architect for Pert & Litton, a Fortune 500 Architectural Firm with offices in Chicago, New York and London. Urgent projects and a string of endless deadlines kept him busy these summer months.

"You?"

"Okay, I guess. I've had better days," she sniffled a little.

"You okay, honey?"

"My throat is dry like I'm catching a cold."

"Come with me. I have just the remedy." He placed his arm around his wife's shoulder and guided her out of the bedroom down the hall toward the kitchen.

"A glass of red wine?"

"How did you know?"

"That's your recipe for everything."

They sat outside each sipping from wine glasses as big as snifters. The soft breeze from the evening air nudged the tip of a napkin on the table. It still bore the heat of day. Robert had once again successfully diverted Suzanne onto the veranda for a drink together.

"What would you like for dinner, love?" Robert noticed the drawn look on Suzanne's face and answered his own question. "Pizza?"

Suzanne, her top lip well inside the wineglass covering her mouth bobbed her head in agreement.

"I'll order," he volunteered.

She smiled to herself. She loved pizza. The last pizza delivery boy had a mop of curly brown hair jutting out from underneath a tattered baseball cap he wore backwards. His wide, gap-toothed smile reminded her of her Jason.

Chapter Two

"Remember, I pick up Andy at 3:00 o'clock tomorrow," Robert said placing his glass on the fluttering napkin.

"Oh really, Robert. Is this a good time?"

"Suzanne, you said it was okay weeks ago. Now when he's due the next day you have second thoughts?" His voice deepened, grew louder. Suzanne was second-guessing their plans again, never able to make a decision.

"Yeah, but I just don't know. The house is a mess."

"Relax, Andy is a golf pro not a marine drill serg...bad choice of words,... the Inspector General." Suzanne didn't notice his inadvertent slip of the tongue. The wine and Zoloft made an apoplectic cocktail. The gleam of moisture in her eyes wasn't the emotion of tears but a film of indifference and isolation. Once the curtain closed Robert never knew what was going on backstage. He jerked loose his tie and stood to leave. "I'm going to change," he said taking his glass of wine and leaving Suzanne alone on the patio.

Their bedroom window looked down on the back patio. Shoulder high sawgrass and drooping tiger lilies surrounded the hand-laid brick. Robert watched her. He struggled to remove his tie. In his haste it had become knotted again. He tugged at the short end and then the longer end to no avail. Finally he yanked the loop over his head and flung it to the ground. Suzanne sat motionless. He watched for minutes and still no movement. Lifeless.

The cellphone on his belt buckle vibrated. The caller i.d. read 'Misty cell'. Misty Morgan was new to Pert & Litton, having recently been transferred in from the New York office. She was younger than he, mid-thirties and an exceptionally talented architect in her own right. Her office was right next to Robert's. She had taken to him and often sought his advice on company projects. He had become used to her popping into his office at any time of the day. Always prim and proper by day she wore business suits with her long auburn hair tied back. As project deadlines neared and they frequently worked longer hours into the evening she would loosen the band on her hair shake that long mane like a wild horse and remove her jacket to work more comfortably in her blouse. She had a habit of running her fingers through her hair when she stood in his doorway. Misty Morgan was hard to ignore.

For a moment he thought about not answering. He placed the phone to his ear and caught himself in the dresser mirror. The hair on his temples was just beginning show traces of gray. He'd debated touching it up but Suzanne insisted it was distinguishing. Robert moved back to the window and checked on Suzanne. She wasn't on the patio. He snapped the phone in its beltclip and let the call go to voice mail.

"Who was that?" Suzanne stood in the doorway, shoulder slumped against the frame slurping her drink.

Oh Christ. The shipwreck has disappeared over the horizon and here comes the flotsam. "Just Milt, honey."

Suzanne approached close enough to rub his five o'clock shadow with the back of her hand. "Did Miltie yell at you again, honey? She wet her fingers and smoothed down the cowlick in the back of his head. The glass in her other hand tipped precariously. Inside red wine heaved a perfect storm.

"Of course your friend can come. I'm sorry." His face was as red as her glass of wine. "Are you okay?"

"I'm fine. Maybe tired. But, I have just the remedy." Robert held her close. The warm vapor of grapes was sweetly seductive. He kissed her on the lips.

"Bed wrestling?"

"How'd you know?"

"That's your answer for everything." Suzanne backed away swallowing the rest of her glass. "Oops, empty again." She held her glass high for him to see and turned to leave. He removed his cellphone and placed it on the dresser as the ghost of his wife floated from the room.

Chapter Three

Suzanne always hoped to give Jason a brother or even a sister. Perhaps he wouldn't have been so restless then. Perhaps he wouldn't have left her for that damn war. She could never understand men and war. Like Icarus, the grail of glory overcame the risk. They all ended up flying too close to the sun. Some returned blinded. Some never returned.

Her first husband, Jeremy, left her. Not for someone else, just left her. Alone with Jason when he was three and still in diapers. She didn't stop him. Her career had begun to blossom. With the advent of blood and drug testing corporations, government and sports organizations were redefining employment. Registered nurses able to sell such services were extremely valuable. Within two years she had a company Lexus and a six figure income. Handsome and athletic, Jeremy seemed all she ever could want—then. She thought she loved him. No, she did love him. That's why she married him. Like her he was from a large Catholic brood in the same neighborhood. He used to play ball with her younger brother, Luke. Jeremy was five years younger than she. When they were in their thirties it didn't seem to make much difference. But when they grew into their forties the gap widened. He was struggling to build his law practice, still playing softball and coming home progressively later those evenings.

Quick to smile with a fun sense of humor, he was always able to make her laugh. She could still hear her mother's warning. That which endears you to someone can quickly become that which you detest the most. When the laughter finally stopped they began sleeping in separate rooms.

After putting Jason to bed at night she often sat alone. The nights became longer, lonelier. She stared at the moon for hours. Pristine and white, there for her every night. Soon Jeremy was gone. But blood trumped love, at least she had her baby Jason. Suzanne took to rocking him to sleep on restless evenings as the moonlight bathed his cherubic face. As he grew she would tell him about the moon and the stars he could see and the heaven he couldn't.

"Mom," he would ask, "can you see the moon from heaven?"

"Yes, I'm quite certain you can."

SUZANNE REMOVED THE tiny flash drive from her pocket and plugged it into the computer. After graduation Jason enlisted in the National Guard. Following September 11, 2001 he joined the regular army. He went to South Korea, Tikrit and eventually, Baghdad. He'd told her about the pictures. There were over five hundred of them, some taken by Jason some by other soldiers. He couldn't wait to return home and deliver the stories of the pictures. Without their narrator the pictures on the monitor seemed one-dimensional, lifeless.

Suzanne had always found expression in "craft-type" things like cross-stitched hand towels, Christmas ornaments and knit scarves. Eventually she decided to paint the photos. She knew a little about the world of oil and canvas having minored in Art in college. But that seemed a different life ago so Suzanne joined an informal ladies' painting class through the local library. An upstairs bedroom once converted to an office now served as a small studio. The afternoon sun bathed the small room with rich, ambient light. The warmth provided sanctuary for her other self. Here her persona, her ghost, her shadow melded into one soulful artiste. She would paint what the soldiers saw, an alien world of washed out sand hues and strange faces. The paint was smooth, cool. Its sharp scent jarred her back to childhood, to the smelly cans and scattered rags of her father's basement workshop. Suzanne peppered her father with endless questions. To keep his curious little girl busy he let her paint the three-legged milk stool he'd just built. Little did he know the affinity for paint and brush he'd bred. She still had that stool buried somewhere up in the attic.

Numerous paintings adorned the walls. A recently completed one sat drying on an easel. The painting depicted a solitary soldier in silhouette. In the background a helicopter was suspended in the night sky. She called it "The Sentinel".

ROBERT WAS LATE picking up Andy at the airport having stayed later at work than expected. But his old college roommate knew him well and had told Robert to pick him up at 6:30 p.m. knowing that he'd be there right on time at 7:00.

It had been years since the two had seen each other. Andy had moved away over five years ago to become head golf pro at the Ishnala Golf Club on the Gulf side of Florida just south of Fort Meyers. Ishnala was the Winnebago Indian name for "one alone." At the time Suzanne and he laughed at what an appropriate name it was for Andy to have landed there for their old friend was certainly unique, an island unto himself.

"Sorry I'm late," Robert offered as he hugged his friend.

"Nonsense, right on time—Robert time." They laughed together as Andy slung his golf clubs over his shoulder and Robert wheeled his small carry-on luggage out to the car. Minutes later they were out of the bustling airport on the freeway home.

"How is our resident golf pro?" Robert asked.

"Don't ask. I'm not at Ishnala anymore."

"I'm sorry to hear that, Andy." Robert's tone showed no surprise only heartfelt sadness for his friend. Part of the reason Andy had left for Florida besides the great opportunity it afforded golf pros, especially a talented one like Andy, was the fact that he'd had trouble holding down jobs. He'd worked at three golf courses in three years before leaving for Florida. The last one he was canned for indiscretions with a couple of the member's wives. Apparently he'd been giving private lessons on the side. Women had always found Andy attractive. In college he always had a sock hanging on the handle of their dormitory door. The sock was code for "do not disturb—entertaining." Often times

Robert had to bunk with a friend on the same dormitory wing. He'd get so mad at not being able to sleep in his own bed that he'd steal the sock off the door handle. One of Andy's professors asked him if he weren't color blind as he always wore mismatched socks.

Andy hadn't shaved in days. Robert never went one day without shaving. Yet it looked good on Andy. With his tanned skin and athletic build it looked like he'd just jumped down from his horse after a long cattle drive.

"Don't be sorry. That was a dead end job anyways. All the damn people at the club were family—Jewish family, tougher to infiltrate than the Mafia. You know how you could tell the Gentile members' wives from the owners' wives? The members' wives were the ones with the fake furs and real orgasms!"

"You'll never change, you schmuck."

"How's your family?"

"You know Jason was killed in Iraq."

"I heard through the grapevine. I'm so sorry, Rob. I know you loved him like a son."

"Like the son I never had."

"How's Suzanne taking it?"

"It's been tough. They were very close. She finally took a leave of absence from work three months ago. We've been sleeping in separate bedrooms for like, seven weeks now."

"I'm sorry to hear that, pal. Perhaps I should have come later..."

"Thank you, but not at all. It's been nine months since he's been gone. We're allowed a life now, I think."

"She's his mother, Rob. Things are different with women, especially mothers."

"So I've found." Robert changed the subject to dinner.
"I hope you're hungry. Suzanne made your favorite."

"Fried chicken?!"

"No, Matzoh Balls with Mogen David wine."

Andy slid down in his seat. "Oh yi vay, enough with the ethnic cleansing."

The sharp ring of Robert's cell phone punctuated their merriment.

But the ring tone was different than the regular call tone. He knew by the jingle he'd programmed who it was.

"Hi Misty."

Andy turned with raised eyebrows to give Robert a purposefully inquisitive look.

"Oh no! Not tomorrow. I've got out-of-town company. He needs us both? I understand it's the Whiteshire Tower project, but...Yeah, yeah. Okay I'll be there. See you tomorrow."

"Don't tell me. No golf tomorrow?" Andy said bobbing his head pretending to understand.

"I'm sorry, Andy. It's this Tower project..."

"That's a catchy name."

"Whiteshire? He's a megamillionaire in..."

"No, Misty."

Chapter Four

"Andy," Suzanne said warmly, hugging their guest affectionately, "how are you?"

"I'm fine. He embraced her warmly then withdrew to look her over closely. "You look marvelous."

"Oh please, stop." Suzanne had always liked Andy. He looked good. The hot Florida sun bronzed his skin, adding creases to his forehead and thin wrinkles outside his eyes. When he smiled thin slivers of virgin white skin that never saw the day's sun opened like the crack of an oyster shell. His hair hadn't yet begun to gray like Robert's. He was handsome and fun-loving, but not the marrying type. Robert was more the marrying type.

"We're not shaving this week?"

"Not until I get a job."

"Oh Andy, not again."

"Suzanne, please. Andy's had a long trip. Leave him alone."

"It's okay, Rob. I don't mind." Andy took her hand in both of his. "I'm so sorry to hear about Jason."

"Thank you, Andy."

"He was very brave, you must be proud of him."

"We miss him. Not a day goes by that I don't..." her voice grew weak and trailed off.

"Why don't we have dinner," Robert interjected, escorting them to the dining room.

AFTER DINNER THEY sat outside on the patio so Andy could enjoy a fine cigar. He rolled the fat stogie around in his fingers peering at it intently as if it were a kaleidoscope, changing prisms of color with each twist. Suzanne and Robert had quit smoking years ago. A feat only made possible by the mutual pact they made with each other. A weary inch long ash leaned precariously from the tip of Andy's cigar. When he rocked his head back for a swallow of wine they watched the ash sever, plunge to the ground, crash onto the patio bricks, and splatter like a bird dropping. This scenario repeated until Robert found him an ashtray. Andy continued to puff away oblivious of the gesture. Cigar ash continued to carpet bomb the bricks below.

"Nothing makes a man feel the lap of luxury like a good cigar."

"I always liked valet parking."

Andy pointed his cigar at Robert, "Close second."

"Quite frankly, I prefer a 1985 Chateau Dionne," Suzanne chimed in raising her glass in a toast.

"Here, here" the two men said echoing each other and acknowledging her toast.

The sounds of laughter resonated in the evening air giving the household a cheer long not seen. Suzanne enjoyed Andy's company. His dark brown eyes widened when he laughed. Jason's were like that too. When he got excited his eyelids rolled back like blinds. You could see your reflection in his eyes like the outside of an automobile window, but you couldn't see in. When Andy spoke his lips curled themselves around his teeth the same way Jason's did when forming words.

"So what's on the agenda for tomorrow? Are you boys golfing?"

Robert leaned forward in his chair. A slight rumble emanated from his chest as he cleared his throat. "Andy's going golfing. I have to work tomorrow."

"On a Saturday? You never work Saturdays."

"It's the Tower Project. The deadline has been moved up. It's all hands on deck."

"Well, you've never worked Saturdays. Everyone is working?"

"Yes, unfortunately."

"Then I shall begin a new painting tomorrow. Andy, please feel free to use my car for golf." Suzanne rose to leave. "Now I suggest we get some rest." As she left Suzanne looked back over her shoulder at her husband making sure her last remark wasn't lost on him. "Some of us have a big day tomorrow."

THE BRILLIANCE OF an almost full moon shone into the small studio bathing the room in a milky translucent light. Suzanne lay the 'Sentinel' painting in the corner and placed a new canvas on the easel for tomorrow's project. The interlude between paintings was always a special time, a kind of pregnant pause that would soon give birth to a new creation. She had hoped to paint him one day. There were plenty of pictures of him on the flash drive. Still, she couldn't bring herself to attempt a sketch of Jason's portrait.

The moon waxed fuller than last night. She hoped that where he was he could see the same moon she saw. There was comfort in that. The sky's luminous orb was theirs to share, a portal to the soul. She recalled Jason's terrible scream echo throughout the house that day. It sounded like it came from upstairs. Suzanne ran up the stairs two at a time then down the hallway toward the master bedroom where the screaming seemed to be coming from. Sure enough there was Jason underneath his father's tall boy dresser. Fortunately it had fallen against the bed. Instead of crushing him each one of the drawers had opened up pinning him down. When she got there all she could see was ankles and wrists wriggling underneath socks, shirts and underwear. Apparently Jason had been captivated by a crystal dish overflowing with coins his father kept atop the dresser. He pulled each drawer out just far enough that it formed a stairway to the prized dish. Later they would laughingly call the doomed effort his 'stairway to heaven'. By standing on the bed and methodically pushing the top couple of drawers closed she was finally able to push the chest upright. Jason kicked the bottom two closed and scrambled out. Later they sat in the kitchen as Jason held ice cubes wrapped in paper towels to the bruises on his forehead and chin while sipping chocolate milk through a straw.

Suzanne smiled at the memory. For a moment she thought she could see a smile in the shadows of the distant moonface. The temperature in the room warmed. She was no longer felt alone.

The squeak of a loose floorboard startled her. She wheeled around toward the doorway. "Robert, is that you?" But there was no answer. A cursory examination of the hallway revealed nothing. Perhaps a mouse. They'd trapped one in the kitchen just yesterday.

Suzanne covered the easel with a sheet so as to keep the canvas pristine for tomorrow's project. Her bedroom was down the hallway past the room Robert slept in and the guest room Andy occupied. She passed Robert's room and paused to listen. His telltale snoring reverberated through the room. Andy's room was across the hall. A sliver of moonlight peeked out underneath the door. Nothing but silence.

Chapter Five

Robert left about the same time as Andy the next morning and agreed to meet back around six for dinner. He eased the powerful V-8 Cadillac onto the expressway toward his downtown office. He missed Suzanne. He missed the old Suzanne. Not a day went by he didn't think of ways to snap her out of her daze. The psychiatrist told him it was just a matter of time and gave her a prescription for the anti-depressants she took like vitamins. The offer of a weekend getaway fell on deaf ears. When they went out for dinner it had to be somewhere close. Suzanne got anxious after eating and always wanted to return home as if the light of day was sunburn. A vase of red roses sat in the living room until day thirteen when the water turned filmy and the weary petals gave up their vigil fluttering to the floor one by one until there were none.

Misty had been great the whole time. She sat with him. She listened to him. Her eyes grew moist when he described with anguish his dilemma. Then she'd run her hand over his and tell him that things would get better. What she didn't tell him was that things usually got worse before they got better. That she was counting on.

THE BRIGHT RED numbers on the studio clock indicated it was past noon. She'd been staring at a blank canvas for over an hour unable to sketch more than the vague outline of a man's head, neck and shoulders. A picture of Jason taken by a fellow soldier filled the computer screen. Like the other soldiers he wore a multi-colored desert camouflage uniform. His helmet was tipped back a bit most likely due to the heat. Beads of sweat ringed a small childhood scar in the middle of his forehead. His eyes were hidden by sunglasses but his strong jaw and protruding chin depicted a soldier's determination. Suzanne turned from the computer and slammed down her sketching lead. She still couldn't do it. The half-empty glass of wine gave her solace. A single shiny tear slid down her nose into the glass. It may not be the body and blood of our Savior but she too partook of her own bitter blend of blood red wine and tears.

The garage door chugged open as Andy pulled her car into the garage. Moments later he clamored noisily into the kitchen. Just like Robert. Never quietly. She dabbed at her eye with a Kleenex careful not to smear the eyeliner.

"Hi Andy, there's cold beer in the refrigerator."

"Thanks, Suzanne. Just what I needed. Anything for you?"

"There's an open bottle of merlot if you would."

Upon entering the room he took one look at Suzanne and knew something was amiss. "You okay?"

"Yes. Now. Some days are worse than others."

"Perhaps I can help," he offered.

Suzanne managed a weak laugh. "Why is it men always think they can help?"

"Because you want us to."

"Think you can help?"

"Yes. Or letting us think we can."

"Okay then, I think you can. Would you be a dear and sit over there. Talk to me while I sketch."

He sat, took a swig of the cold Heineken and struck a pose. His square chin bore a cleft partially hidden by his week-old beard. A rich Florida tan deepened his olive skin, evident of a Mediterranean heritage. His straight nose looked smallish with high cheekbones and long face. Jason had a small nose with prominent cheekbones. As a baby he had more of a roundish face, like hers. He was always boyishly handsome. Andy was more rugged-looking, especially with that damn beard, kind of cowboy handsome. Deep set eyes drew you to them if only to search the dark for light.

"You're having a difficult time, aren't you?" Andy asked.

"Meaning?"

"You are having a difficult time painting him."

"What makes you say that?"

"There are no paintings of Jason in the room."

"You've been in my studio?"

"Couldn't sleep last night so I went downstairs for a nightcap. When I came up this room was bright with moonlight."

Suzanne recalled last night's 'mouse in the house.' Andy sipped the cold beer and belched, not loud enough for an 'excuse me'. Not that he would anyway. "I'm thinking this studio is good for you. A place where you can let your hair down. You look peaceful here, Suzanne, almost regal."

She was willing to let him go on. And on.

"I like this painting over here," he pointed to the recently finished painting near the wall.

"Yes, I do too. Just finished it. I call it 'The Sentinel'." She continued her busy work as they chatted.

"Very intriguing. We all need something to keep us going. Sometimes life is too much Swiss cheese. The holes will kill you. For me, golf fills the holes."

"I like your logic. Better than your metaphors."

"How is Rob taking this whole thing?"

"Good question. Sometimes he's such a dear. I think he's trying to grab the ghost and hold it close until it becomes real again. Then he comes home late from work days in a row or works on a Saturday. I don't know who he really is any longer."

Suzanne began sketching with more fervor the longer she talked. Her hand danced across the canvas with panache heretofore unseen. The sketch was the outline from which a vibrant oil painting might soar. Tomorrow the oils. Tomorrow the heart's rendition of color that breathes life into this embryonic miracle. She wiped her brow with the back of her wrist and finished with a sigh.

"May I see?" Andy asked.

Suzanne stood back to better gauge the sketch. Andy came around to see her work.

"Oh my God," he exclaimed. The portrait bore a squarish jaw, high cheekbones and dark eyes. But high on the canvas near the hairline a scar creased the subject's forehead. This wasn't him at all. Suzanne had sketched her son, Jason.

Andy grabbed Suzanne and hugged her tightly. "You've done it. You've done it!"

She wrapped her arms around his neck forcing his head closer. "Not without your help."

Below the garage door groaned as Robert's car swung into the drive. High above in a second floor window two silhouetted figures grew close becoming one.

Chapter Six

Robert brought Suzanne's favorite, sausage pizza topped with sun-dried tomatoes. The threesome devoured dinner quickly washing it down with a couple bottles of inexpensive Chianti. After dinner they retired to the patio. The summer air at dusk hung heavy. Their quiet mirrored the balmy stillness. Neither words nor breezes blew. Robert filled their glasses with wine, finishing one bottle and uncorking another. Andy tooled his cigar around his fingers creating anthills of ash at his feet. Suzanne glanced at Andy then peered sullenly into her glass. His shiny visage appeared while she sipped. Her lips rippled the wine. A wavy image of Jason now floated across the sea of red. She glanced about to find their moon but cloudy skies prevailed.

"How was your round of golf today, Andy?" Robert asked, breaking the awkward silence.

"Fine, and the Whiteshire Tower Project?"

"Coming along fine. Very busy day."

"And Misty?" Suzanne inquired.

Robert choked down a swallow of wine. Andy's cigar rolled out of his fingers onto the patio bricks.

"Excuse me."

"You heard me. How's your playmate, Ms. Misty?"

"Misty Morgan? From the office? How could you…?

"Oh please, Robert," Suzanne forcefully stamped her foot while walking over to refill her empty glass. "I read the caller i.d. more than once when you left your cell phone laying around. How long have you and that slut been sneaking around with each other?"

Robert enraged, stood to face her. "I've never touched that girl."

"Oh girl, excuse me. She's younger?"

Andy had seen enough and jumped to his feet. "Suzanne this isn't necessary. Rob explained the whole thing to me in the car yesterday. If anything, Misty's been stalking him. He'd never have anything to do with her."

Not listening Suzanne raised her hand to slap her husband but Robert saw it coming and caught her wrist. He took this moment to seize the initiative. "And what are you two doing sneaking around second floor windows?"

"Oh come on, Rob. That was nothing." Andy had barely gotten the last word out when Robert sent a fist in his direction but missed badly. His momentum carried him into Andy sending them both crashing to the ground with Suzanne in tow. They scuffled like little children before rising to encounter each other faces reddened from the rushing blood of anger, flushed with wine.

"I don't know what the hell is going on here." Suzanne said dusting herself. "But I know this; one of us must leave here."

Chapter Seven

Suzanne rose early the next morning. Her breakfast consisted of multiple cups of coffee followed by numerous Tylenol finally assuaging the pain racking her head and the lull in her step. She'd been painting Jason's portrait most of the morning. Inspiration came piecemeal as the events of last evening rolled out to sea like a bad morning fog. Perhaps she'd been wrong about Robert. Andy certainly felt so. But he'd been severely mistaken about her and Andy. One of them had to go. If neither of them, then her.

Jason's face gleamed against a nightfall background of tiny lights from a sandy town somewhere outside Baghdad. High above the lambent light of a perigee moon burnished his resolute profile. Suzanne's painting captured her son's boyish spirit and a soldier's strength.

So enraptured was she that the sound of a car pulling in the drive went unnoticed. The backdoor slammed followed by a rustling in the kitchen. The refrigerator door creaked open, followed by the clanging of bottles. Heavy footsteps plodded up the stairs one by one. Six, seven, eight—she counted each step silently. The soft scuff of shoes on carpeting emanated from the hallway. Suzanne sat stiff-necked before her painting. A shallow-lunged pant approached from behind. She felt a moist kiss on the back of her shoulder near the neck.

"Good morning," he said.

"Good morning. You're up and about early."

"Andy and I had breakfast. Then I took him to the airport. He explained a lot of things and apologized. He offered his apologies to you also." Robert stared at his feet. "I'm sorry, Suzanne."

"I'm sorrier," she offered. "I'll miss him."

He took his hand in hers. "I've missed you."

"It's nice to be missed."

"Andy said you were working on a portrait of Jason."

Suzanne stepped aside so her husband could see the painting. "Oh Suzanne, it's magnificent!" He peered closer. "That's our son alright. This is wonderful." Robert kissed Suzanne on the lips lingering a moment to savor their perfect fit, then put his arm around her shoulder to again admire the soldier's portrait.

"I'm going to call it 'Night Watch'," she said. They stood together, with their son standing guard beneath a resplendent moon. Suzanne pulled at the hand hung over her shoulder, held it close and looked up at her husband, "Do you think you can see the moon from heaven?"

Popanse Creek

Down near the railroad tracks on the far side of town ran a swiftly moving creek. Local folks say that once upon a time or back when men traveled by horseback it was actually a small river or tributary of the Popanse River that dissected the county from the northeast to the southwest. Legend has it that the Popanse Indians used the river to irrigate their cornfields. Tribes from the north navigated it down to the plains here, their canoes laden with hides of caribou and bear. Here they would trade for corn and deerskin and then head further south to trade their valuable hides. On many a summer morning the cool waters of the river mixed with the humidity of the day to usher up dreamlike steamy vapors that hid the movement of the swift canoes. But if you listened closely you could hear the precision paddling of oars gently dipping into the waters or the dulcet tones of a native songs rumbling down the channel only to be lost in the fog.

Across the creek was an ancient willow tree with droopy, thin leafed branches that hung over the water like an old woman washing her hair from shore. Young boys would hang a rope from one of the sturdier branches and tie a large knot at the end so as to be able to stand up while holding the rope in one hand and a knife made of whittled sticks in the other. Then they would sail across the great divide hair rustling in the breeze and bloodcurdling war hoops cascading down on the enemy below.

First to lead the charge for his band of warriors was Bip Mullen. Occasionally he would find a feather lost by a wild goose or duck, place it in his red bandanna and creep along the banks, stick held tightly like a fine bow, ready to hunt down that evening's dinner or protect his tribe from invaders. He would hold his whittled stick of a knife in his teeth and with one hand held tightly on the rope, urge his band on. Then he would circle his free arm in the air, violently stirring a pot of emotions within his braves.

Bip wasn't the biggest or the fastest or the most skilled of the bunch but he always went first. Asthmatic since birth, he was tall for his age and rail thin. You could count the ribs on his chest like rungs on a ladder. Perhaps his condition prevented him from being the most athletic but it never diminished his fearless nature. And his closely knit band loved him for this. Who else would lead a band of twelve year-old savages across the swirling waters of Popanse Creek to fight the insolent intruders.

As Bip was always first then little Timmy O'Shea was always last. Timmy had suffered and beat leukemia as a small child. He was very young then, barely three years old when diagnosed. But by age five he had beaten the dread disease and was able to live a somewhat normal life. As a result of his battles or possibly a result of massive dosages of chemotherapy and radiation his growth at this formative age had been stunted. No matter how quickly he endeavored to keep up with the other boys, little Timmy always trailed behind.

Oftentimes they would go down to the small local grocery store for pop or candy or sweet rolls. Timmy never seemed to have enough money with him. His father was a butcher at the meat market the next town over and his mother did sewing for the ladies in the neighborhood. Even with insurance Timmy's medical care had been extremely expensive. But the O'Shea family, had prayed together and stuck together. They were very close and very happy.

Not having enough money ever bothered little Timmy. Often Bip would 'lend' him enough for a chocolate candy bar, his favorite. Other times, Timmy just helped himself. Not being very tall gave him the perfect cover he needed when in a small crowd and Timmy learned early on how easy it was to just help himself to a candy bar or two. After all his pockets were only two feet off the ground and who looked at peoples' shoes anyways. Sometimes he would just stand near a couple buying their groceries chocolate bar in hand and the clerk would just ring it up on their tab figuring he was with them.

That was when Bip tagged him with the nickname Chocolate Timmy. And whenever he heard his nickname a shy smile would bless his freckled face. He was one of them.

Not having the weight or momentum to swing himself across the creek, Chocolate Timmy found himself swinging aimlessly only halfway over the creek. Somehow he lost his grip, dropped his homemade weapon and fell what was thought to be twenty to twenty-five feet from the rope but was probably more like ten to twelve feet into the fierce waters of Popanse Creek. A tuft of red hair appeared on the surface and then his face redder than anyone had ever seen and cheeks puffy as a blowfish popped out of the water. His arms thrashed wildly amid the rough waters which had begun to sweep him downstream. His band led by Bip ran along the banks hopping tree branches with bows and knives high in the air in an effort to keep up with Chocolate Timmy.

"Help, help—I can't swim," his head disappeared underwater momentarily and then surfaced again. None of them knew Chocolate Timmy couldn't swim. They had practiced their archery on homemade scarecrows, refined horseback skills on overturned tree trunks and caught an occasional fish on safety pins but had never thought about swimming events.

"Hold on Timmy, I'm comin'," Bip, already short of breath from the frantic run, dove into the creek and swam out to his friend. He paddled hard as he could but his wheezing turned worse and he began struggling for air. Gulps of air alternated with gulps of water as his oxygen-starved lungs betrayed him. By the time he got to where his friend had been he had almost drowned himself and Timmy had floated even further downstream. Two of the other boys helped pull Bip out onto the bank.

His burning chest heaved against closing lung passages. Droplets of water fell from his hair onto his face and mixed with his tears. He raised his head in agony to look at his band of friends. Their frozen faces shared the same tears. Their friend had not surfaced again.

"I could--n't reach him. I could--n't save him," Bip gasped. He lay across a large boulder wheezing and heaving and spewing mouthfuls of water.

Not far away the shrill truncated call of a whippoorwill pierced the air. Bip left the creek that day for perhaps the last time. His bare feet padded along the bank tracing footsteps left long ago by Popanse braves returning home, their band smaller with each treacherous campaign. The screams and wails of deerskin clad mothers and lovers rose from the village like smoke from smoldering campfires ascending above the clouds to be heard throughout the plains.

The next day at the spillway downriver in Kishwaukee the body of little Timmy O'Shea was found. It was not the first time Popanse Creek had given up its dead.

Covet Thy Neighbor

At first glance the house was rather non-remarkable. It was a two story Georgian, red brick with tall white pillars and white framed windows. A curved road wound its way up to the home which sat back from the road about the length of two football fields. Of more interest though was the carriage home or guest cottage behind the stately Georgian. It had been advertised for rent by the month.

Joshua Clark, aspiring writer, had been looking for just such a quiet retreat to begin his work on a story for a popular magazine. His small condo in the city was both too noisy and cluttered to do his work. A quiet place in the far suburbs might be more conducive to writing he thought.

The carriage house was much older than the main home maybe, a hundred and forty or fifty years old he guessed. It was a long white frame building with a green roof and appeared to be in immaculate condition. The midday sunlight reflected off the second floor windows on the west side of the building like welcome lamps. There were few windows on the bottom floor save for those at either end. Three large garage doors stood closed.

Mrs. Amanda Pennington, the same woman he had talked to over the phone, stood aglow in the bright of day. The brilliance of her fine gold necklace and teardrop earrings sparkling in the sun obfuscated her facial features. She paused to open the door for him to enter. Extremely thin, she seemed all arms and legs. Her perfectly coiffed sandy hair belied a recent trip to the salon. She wore cream slacks and a silk, copper colored blouse.

"So, you're a writer," her soft brown eyes twinkled with each vowel that dripped from her wide red lips. He thought he noticed a slight southern drawl in her sugary voice.

"Aspiring," he smiled shyly.

"Perspiring?"

"That too."

Josh followed Amanda inside. The main floor had obviously once been a stable that quartered horse drawn carriages and their steeds. Hired hands once polished the black leather coaches to a fine shine. The large draft horses snorted loudly and pawed the floors with their hooves while being bathed and groomed. Hay once stored above had to be pitchforked down and then piled up in the stables. An almost indiscernible scent of cracked leather lingered in the air. Nowadays the carriage house served as a garage and storage facility. An old silver Mercedes sat at the far end.

"That was my husband's. This one here is mine," she pointed to a white Cadillac sedan that was probably new five or six years ago.

The upstairs was clean and well lit by the numerous windows that wrapped around the building. The dark wooden floor had been sanded smooth. There was a kitchenette at the far end and four-poster bed and dresser nearest the stairway they ascended. In the middle of the long room was a simple wooden table and chairs. Opposite it and underneath a couple of windows stood a desk. It offered a view of the back lawns and across a short hedgerow a large two-story home and swimming pool.

Joshua looked around the spacious quarters and was impressed. He would be right at home here. The carriage house would be a perfect place for him to write in peace.

"Hemingway would have loved it," he said absent-mindedly.

"Promise no drunken brawls or boxing matches, Mr. Hemingway." Amanda said playfully. She took her leave and walked toward the stairs. "Oh, and Josh, please feel free to park your car underneath. You may use my spot. I will be leaving for a few weeks to visit my sister upstate." She paused sometimes as if short of breath or just to let the syrup drip off her words. Josh thought he smelled cornbread baking.

He watched Amanda glide across the room and slowly descend the stairs. Her white hand and sculpted nails rolled over the banister and disappeared. Josh shook himself out of a stare. Amanda Pennington was as lovely and classy a lady as he'd met. Perhaps it was best she was leaving for a while. He had work to do. If she continued to linger in his consciousness, she'd have to be a character in his story. That's all the pleasure he could afford. A good writer should know his weaknesses. He wondered if Hemingway did.

Chapter 2

He opened up his laptop and finally set to work. The piece he was assigned was commissioned by a local magazine wanting an historical overview of the Chicago River and the locks system employed to connect the River to the second largest of the Great Lakes, Lake Michigan. Weeks of research in the library and on the internet had left him with copious notes which filled his nearby yellow legal pad.

Using the morning sun as a reference, the double windows before him afforded what he calculated to be a northerly view which was nice since the sun would rarely be directly in his eyes yet the scenery below would be awash in sunlight on nice days. An expansive lawn spread as far as he could see to the sides and maybe a hundred yards to the rear of the property. A long row of peony bushes separated another large yard of green sweeping up to a massive house with what he counted to be five gables and seventeen windows. The brick was not the red brick of the Pennington Georgian but rather a light, creamy colored brick. Its array of light brown pitched roofs gave the structure a much more modern look than the other homes in the area.

Between the small hedgerow and the house was a rectangular lap pool connected to its parent building with an expanse of cement. Poolside were various chairs, chaise lounges, umbrella tables and a cabana. The late morning sun shone from behind the cabana. A slender pair of feet with lofty arches as if formed by high heels protruded from underneath the shadow of the cabana. One foot lay prone with the other crossed over it. Each was very tan as if they'd been lying out there for weeks unattended. Josh continued with his writing busily tapping keys on his laptop and shuffling through pages and pages of notes. He also continued his poolside vigil. Occasionally one foot would rise in the air and switch places with the other. But it was the only sign of life. Hopefully there was some at the other end.

An afternoon stretch and scotch always refreshed him. He swilled the elixir like mouthwash and threw his head back. After swallowing, with his head still tipped, Josh belted out his best Pavarotti imperson-ation complete with sweeping arms and upraised scotch. Although not sounding to bad to himself, it sounded like Pavarotti done by Tarzan.

The expanse of green lawn below him lie swathed in the after-noon sun. The poolside figure was now exposed all the way up to the dark recesses of the cabana itself. Slender tanned legs lay motionless in the baking sun. One lay prone while the other was upright bent at the knee. That leg supported a book held by an equally tanned hand. There was no movement at all save the infrequent turning of a page from inside the shadowy cabana. Slow reader. Just my type he mused.

Chapter Three

The midday sun overhead beat mercilessly on the backyard pool. Ripples of heat rose from the cement patio which had become so hot you could cook raw meat well done on it. Petunias encased in clay pots wilted as if taking their afternoon siesta. A silent ripple of waves cascaded outwards from her smooth entry into the cool pool water. At the far end of the pool the swimmer's graceful summersault and push off the wall made a quiet splash. Her arms, elbows upraised, alternatingly cut through the surface with precision while flapping feet beat in unison. She pulled up after a few laps, shook her dark hair vigorously and stopped to poke a finger in one ear and did the same with the other.

"Howdy, Josh Clark. I'm staying at the Pennington's. May I help?" he extended his hand downward.

Not impolitely, she swam toward the ladder and exited the pool on her own.

"My, we are friendly, aren't we?"

Rita Marzo stood legs apart. She wore an aquamarine bikini that made her tanned body seem as dark as the heritage conjured up by her married name. Her wide shoulders and arched lower back gave her the appearance of a body builder. Shiny beadlets of chlorinated water dripped from her long black hair racing each other down her athletic body.

"What are neighbors for?" Josh offered her a nearby towel. She accepted it with a slight grin. "Was that a smile?" he asked.

"Call it what you want. How long have you been watching me?"

"Today?"

"So you have been watching me."

"I'm staying in the Pennington's carriage house working on an article for a local magazine. I couldn't help but notice the pool from the window and you were in it."

She tilted her head and looked up at him with a furrowed brow and eyes barely visible underneath the hooded towel.

"To answer your question, a few days."

"I see. What do you write?"

"Whatever I'm commissioned and whatever pays."

"So you're not a real writer, yet."

"What a magnificent home. How long have you..." he hesitated for Rita to fill in the missing information.

"That's too bad about Mr. Pennington."

"Mr. Pennington?"

"He was a very nice man, always tending to the flowers, always a nice thing to say. Died only a few months ago."

"Yes, Mrs. Pennington pointed out his car in the carriage house. I didn't realize he was dead. I thought maybe they'd been divorced or something..."

She turned her back on him and dried herself with one leg raised on a nearby chaise lounge. "To answer your question. My husband and I—that's what you're looking for—have owned Marzo Greens for close to seven years now."

He took 'Marzo Greens' to mean the whole estate unless of course her husband was in the produce business. "It's beautiful. What does Mr. Marzo do, if I may ask."

"Sam is an envoy to Mexico. He works with our government, travels a lot and tells me very little. Only that it is confidential, top clearance. That type of thing."

Josh shook his head as if he understood. They stood a few feet away from each other in a span of silence for what seemed minutes. Josh baked in the afternoon heat. He shuffled his feet not from nervousness but because his sandals were melting.

"I must go now," she said hesitating as if to recall, "Josh."

She'd used his first name. Compelling.

"Do you swim?" Rita asked him playfully.

"No but I can float and am adept at splashing around a bit."

"Come by tomorrow afternoon, if you'd like."

He watched as she left him sweltering on the patio. Rita Marzo was both captivating yet brusque. Returning to the carriage house he wondered about Mr. Pennington. He was also curious about Rita's husband, the mysterious Sam Marzo.

Chapter Four

Why hadn't Amanda Pennington mentioned her husband's death? After all it had been fairly recently. Josh searched through the local newspaper obituaries on his laptop beginning four months ago and worked his way forward. It didn't take long for him to come across the name of Lowell Pennington, survived by his widow, Amanda and two children from his former marriage that now lived out of state. He had died of an apparent heart attack though only fifty-two years old. Lowell had obviously married a much younger woman his second time around. Amanda may have seemed older with make-up and the over-load of gold jewelry but she couldn't have been more than forty.
Rita liked Mr. Pennington but never indicated how he died. Perhaps she wasn't aware of the cause of death.

Josh stood his notes up on the desk easel before him and resumed work on his magazine assignment. He'd been making sufficient progress save for yesterday when he visited Rita. There was something about her. He couldn't get the picture of her sashaying away in that aquamarine bathing suit and turning around to ask him over for a swim. She moved with the grace of an animal, strong and svelte, each step carefully planned and executed perfectly.

She had mentioned her husband, not fondly he recalled, and noted that she really didn't give much detail as to exactly what he did. Josh placed an e-mail to his friend in Chicago, Lieutenant John Evoy. Evoy had been a detective for seven years on the Chicago police force and recently been promoted to chief of detectives. They had worked many cases together back when Josh was a reporter for the Times and had developed a professional regard and kinship. He'd helped him out with important case information and later served as an expert on the stories he wrote. At the same time Josh also kept sensitive information out of the paper so as to not impede investigations. He asked Evoy if he knew anything about Rita's husband, Sam. Josh also inquired about Mr. Pennington and whether he knew of his death.

The sun shone brightly on the greens below his window. The peonies that served as a hedgerow between the Pennington's property and the Marzo's had grown to their full height of two and a half feet and were in full bloom. Large balls of white-petalled flowers resembling popcorn balls bobbed in the wind. When still, they hung down heavily on long thin stems. The next breeze acted as conductor and with a wave of the baton an orchestra of brightly flowered peonies arose and busily played the beat.

Poolside, the painted toes and well-defined calves of Rita Marzo protruded from the shade of a cabana. He poured himself a scotch and water and resumed his work. Two scotches later the sun had swung around to his left enough to reflect on her olive thighs. A tall drink glass with a long straw sat close by the cabana. It was another hot afternoon in paradise.

Josh slipped into his swimsuit and sandals and donned a white tee shirt that was too small for him but made his chest look bigger. He was in good shape and it showed, not Rita Marzo shape but still pretty good.

"Where have you been? I've been expecting you," Rita peeked out of the cabana, removed her sunglasses and dabbed a beadlet of perspiration from her forehead..

Josh peeled his tight tee shirt off above his head. Rita placed her sunglasses back and watched him closely. Taut chest muscles rippled above his well-defined stomach and thin waistline. He pulled up a chair facing Rita so he could see into the shaded cabana.

"So, shall we swim or chat?" he asked her.

"Oh, thank you, Josh, but I swam my 40 laps this morning. I find it cooler in the morning. It's much too hot to do anything outside today. Would you like a drink?"

"It's a little early," he feigned, "but why not."

Rita emerged from the cabana and grabbed her empty glass. "Feel free to get wet while I make us a drink." Rita slipped her sandals on and made her way to the sliding glass doors of the kitchen. He watched her from behind as she bounced toward the kitchen. It was hard to distinguish at first because her skin was so dark, but slightly above her low-slung aquamarine bikini a butterfly tattoo danced as each of her ass cheeks rolled from side to side.

Josh dove into the glassy pool water, surfaced and paddled his way to the far end. Even with the heat of the midday sun searing its cement collar, the water was cool, almost chilly. He placed his hands on the hot cement only briefly before rising out of the pool gracefully, toweling off and quickly donning his sandals. Rita still hadn't returned. Josh wrapped his towel around his dripping bathing suit and walked toward the sliding glass doors. From somewhere behind his reflection in the glass he could see Rita motioning him to enter. Once inside the air-conditioned iciness slapped his face.

"I'm sorry, Josh," she placed the cordless phone in its cradle. "That was Sam."

"I see. Perhaps I should go."

"Oh don't be silly. He just called to let me know he'd be home tomorrow." She offered him a tall vodka lemonade with a lemon slice perched precariously on the side of the glass.

"Cheers, neighbor."

He smiled bashfully and returned the toast with a clink of his glass. Like her skin, Rita's eyes were dark, almost black. This was the first time he'd really been close enough to notice. He peered deep into her eyes as if searching the abyss of a cave.

"And the reason you're staring at me is…" she didn't pull back from him but instead held her ground.

"I was thinking about your husband," he said.

"Josh," Rita paused to sip her drink. "Sam is Sam. His work is his secret and I don't really give a damn. When he's around he's the show. And when he's not, which is most of the time, I keep myself busy."

"And that would include exercising."

"Among other things," she smiled coyly.

Josh considered the bait. What would Ernest Hemingway do? Hemingway was a man of conviction and action. But he didn't live long enough to ever say no to anything. Josh hated making decisions. But Rita Marzo had already made hers.

Raising his glass up and to the side as if inviting his partner to dance, he slid his arm around her supple waist and kissed her. Rita didn't stop him. She broke only to rest her drink on the counter. He leaned into her hard body and kissed her passionately. Her head fell back, long dark ringlets of hair lay on the counter behind her. His hands ran up behind her bikini top loosening the strap and letting her top fall to the ground. She tugged at the towel around his waist and it fell to his feet. They stumbled a lover's dance toward the den.

"Your bedroom..." he managed between hurried breaths. His hand circled underneath her hair and brought her neck to his mouth.

"Too far..." she gasped.

They fell onto the comfort of the den's plush carpeting, never making it as far as the bedroom.

Chapter Five

The same cloudless skies that burned in the day brought bright evening skies lit from overhead by a panoply of shimmering stars. Josh sat at his laptop, scotch in hand admiring the starlit skies and pondered the voluptuous Rita Marzo. When the cat's away the mice will play. But what was with this cat? Not even his own wife knew what he did other than mentioning something about being an government envoy to Mexico.

The ubiquitous 'you've got mail' message droned from his laptop. It was from Lieutenant Evoy. He had contacted the local authorities and found that although Mr. Lowell Pennington's cause of death was listed as an apparent heart attack. That was only for lack of more concrete findings. Apparently the Penningtons were not on good terms, to say the least. Mrs. Pennington had wanted a divorce but Lowell didn't want to grant her one fearing the fallout would make a man of his distinction look bad. That's all anyone knew.

The information on Sam Marzo was more interesting. Evoy had called in a marker with a longtime friend of his who had been with the CIA. Your Sam Marzo is well-connected. He is suspected of heading up their 'extraordinary rendition' program. This program is responsible for the abduction of suspected terrorists abroad and then shipping them to other countries for interrogation. These countries house covert prison systems set up by the CIA four years ago. This hidden global internment network, or so called "black sites", is a central element in the CIA's unconventional war on terrorism. There, unlike here, they can hold prisoners as long as they want and interrogate them without restrictions imposed by the U.S. legal system. This secret detention system was conceived in the chaotic and anxious first months of the 911 attacks on our country.

Josh remembered Rita telling him that Sam was an envoy to Mexico. Could Mexico be one of those 'black sites'?

He pushed himself away from the desk and stared at the screen in horror. Sam Marzo was a ruthless government agent with a license to abduct suspects anywhere in the world, possibly torturing them for information and he had just left his home after a roll in the rug with his wife! He steadied himself and went to the kitchen to make another scotch and water. The bottle of scotch shook so badly in his hand he didn't need to mix the drink.

Just a few moments ago he couldn't believe his good fortune at having held the fabulous Rita Marzo in his arms, her tongue winding its way down his neck and onto his shoulders. Now he couldn't fathom crossing a member of the CIA with obvious discretionary powers beyond the scope of his imagination. And, of all things, Sam Marzo would be returning tomorrow. Josh wished his story was finished and could leave now.

He dashed off a quick e-mail reply to Evoy asking him to update him with anything he heard on the suspicious death of Lowell Pennington. He also informed Evoy that he would meet this mystery man, Sam Marzo, soon—sooner than he wanted.

Chapter Six

The late morning sun awoke with a vengeance, its' bright of day' powers wilted flowers and bent back blades of grass.

Another day in paradise had turned into another day in limbo for Josh Clark. He couldn't get Rita out of his mind. He wanted to see her badly. The information Evoy had sent over on Sam was alarming, especially in light of his impending arrival. Setting foot on Marzo Greens had now become precarious. In the end, as it usually did for him, his more visceral emotions won out. Josh decided that although visiting Rita was a dangerous proposition he needed to see her again and she needed to be told the truth about her husband.

When he arrived on the patio he bent down to check the cabana and felt the stifling heat rising from the cement. Rita wasn't inside. He made for the house but noticed something dark at the far end of the pool. As he approached it looked like a dark towel or shirt was floating on the water.

"No, God, no!" Josh saw a mass of black hair, silent and unmoving. He dove in the water fully clothed and pulled up the limp body of Rita Marzo. Her once dark skin was now a pallid blue. She'd been dead for hours. He laid Rita's body on a towel poolside and hurried to the kitchen. The sliding glass doors were unlocked. He placed a call to 911 and waited for what seemed hours for the authorities to arrive. A ray of sun glared through the windows drawing a bead in the center of the den where the two had tangled. The rug that had seemed like wild prairie grass when they rollicked was now a barren wasteland. Outside the kitchen doors poor Rita lay prone. What once had been a bright playground of fancy and seduction was now a horrible picture of iciness and gloom.

WHEN THE YOUNG detective with mousse in his hair finally finished questioning Josh of the gruesome details in finding Rita Marzo drowned in her own pool he paused for a moment and looked up from his notepad while his partner combed the area closely.

"What were you doing over here, Mr. Clark?"

"I'd come to visit. Sometimes I swim," his words were devoid of emotion.

"How'd you know where the phone was?"

"As I said, officer, I've been over before."

"Where's her husband?"

"CIA," he mumbled sheepishly.

"Excuse me?"

"MIA, you know, missing in action."

"I see, Mr. Clark. Thank you very much. Please don't go anywhere in the next twenty-four hours. We may have more questions," he handed Josh his card in case he thought of anything else. Josh winced as the paramedics placed Rita on a white-sheeted gurney, covered her body and whisked her off the patio.

THE CARRIAGE HOUSE that had been home to him and provided his window on the Baltic now seemed like a cold cell. The ice cubes in the tall scotch he made tinkled in his unsteady hands. The last twenty-four hours had been a whirlwind for Josh. Sam Marzo was some kind of CIA pariah that was due back soon. Death stalked the Penningtons house. He had taken the gorgeous Rita Marzo. And now she was dead. Josh had cared for Rita. Somehow out of some sort of carnal closeness or just plain guilt, he felt responsible for her being dead.

The ring of his cell phone startled him. It was the young detective with the fancy hair calling.

"Mr. Clark, we found fingerprints all over the kitchen and den area. You need to come in and fingerprint for us," he insisted.

"Detective, I told you I'd been over there before, " Josh repeated.

"There's something else. The coroner's office confirmed that Ms. Marzo had sexual relations recently. Although we didn't find any semen in her bed we did find a pair of ladies panties underneath a chair in the den. We also found semen on the rug in the same room. We need you to submit a DNA sample also."

Josh almost dropped the phone. "I will be there promptly, detective."

He couldn't believe he was now a suspect. Shit, how would this look. He'd been caught with his pants down, literally.

In a panic Josh placed a call to Lieutenant Evoy. He informed Evoy of Rita Marzo's death and that he had become a suspect. Evoy agreed to meet him at the station. But before hanging up Evoy had some important information. New findings on the death of Lowell Pennington indicated foul play. After Evoy's call the local police had turned up the heat in their investigation of his death. A reexamination of body fluids and tissue samples saved from the as yet unconfirmed suspicious death of Mr. Pennington had turned up trace amounts of antifreeze in his system. Antifreeze administered slowly over a period of time in the guise of say, for instance, Gatorade or some like-type of sports drink becomes a lethal poison. Mr. Pennington had suffered an atrocious death. Mrs. Amanda Pennington was being sought for questioning as they spoke.

In addition, Mr. Sam Marzo had recently gotten himself in hot water with top war department officials. There was indeed a CIA 'black site' in Mexico headed up by Sam Marzo. Secret inside photos of prisoner abuse and severe torture had made their way into the public domain. The press had published some of the photos. Even worse, some had made their way onto the internet. The prison had become an embarrassment to the government. Sam Marzo was being called on the carpet by officials in Washington D.C.

Josh thanked Evoy for offering to meet him at the station. The situation had become grave. His idyllic retreat had become his hell.

Chapter Seven

The room was ten foot by twelve foot with a solitary metal table and three chairs with a large rectangular two-way mirror on the wall facing him. The detective who had originally questioned him, the one with the salon hair, had momentarily disappeared to get coffee at his bequest. Josh wandered aimlessly over to the mirror and looked at his reflection. Dark bluish circles rested underneath his weary, bloodshot eyes. His lips were cracked as if he were alone in the desert dying of thirst. Alone he was in his room of doom.

He had come to this sleepy little town to finish his article for the magazine and instead delusions of grandeur and visions of the great Hemingway had danced before him like false gods. Perhaps he was mere mortal. Perhaps he wasn't the next Hemingway. His next great work now would be written behind bars like Hitler's *Mein Kampf* or Dostoevsky's *Crime and Punishment*.

Subconsciously he heard the door open behind him. The slick looking detective had returned.

"Josh!" a familiar voice rang out.

"Evoy!" Josh said, shaking his hand vigorously. Evoy still wore the crew cut flat top he had in the military.

"I have some good news for you."

"My novel has been published and is in its' third printing?"

"Always the joker, Josh. It's even better than that, sit down."

Evoy rested his elbows on the table and folded his fingers together. "You are free to leave. You've been cleared of all charges."

Josh looked at Evoy in complete surprise. "But Rita Marzo, Mr. Pennington..."

"After the findings on the poisoning of Mr. Pennington, I had the local boys bring in Mrs. Pennington for questioning. I remembered you saying she was upstate visiting a sister. We finally tracked down this sister and she said Amanda left her yesterday and was headed back home. Her car was spotted parked in the Eaglewood Spa & Resort not far from here."

"She was here last night? But why not return home?"

Evoy leaned forward "It gets better. Our boys find the room number at the front desk, barge in with badges and guns blazing and there is Amanda Pennington but she's not alone. She's with none other than Sam Marzo! They're both getting dressed to go somewhere, somewhere far away. Their suitcases were already packed and the both of them had airline tickets to Mexico. They question her on the spot and she breaks down crying that she didn't mean to kill him, that it was all Sam's idea and so on. To make a long story short, Amanda admits to poisoning poor Lowell Pennington. Sam Marzo is trying to choke her to death. When they finally get them separated, Amanda comes clean with the whole story.

Amanda and Sam had been having an affair for a little over a year. He comes up with the idea to poison Lowell because he won't give Amanda a divorce. Then after they thought all had died down, he comes home last night from Mexico, they get the room at Eaglewood. This morning he gets up early and knowing his wife's morning swim routine sneaks over to their home and drowns her in the pool."

"Poor Rita, she deserved better than him," Josh said.

"Not only that but the whole idea of renting out the carriage house was a well conceived plot. They hatched the whole scenario. Apparently, Sam knew Rita couldn't be trusted and would eventually…" Evoy hesitated, shifting in his seat uneasily.

"That's where I come in," Josh offered. "If she couldn't be trusted, then I became the perfect frame up man."

"I'm afraid that's right, Josh. Sam and Amanda were going to retire in Mexico as his days with the CIA were over in light of the mess at the 'black site' prison and all. He wouldn't have faced charges as the place wasn't supposed to exist at all. But he was due to be unceremoniously dumped. That's what initiated the whole sordid plot."

Josh thanked Evoy as they both left the stationhouse together. He returned to the carriage house to pack up his laptop and belongings and finish his article at his own home. He took one long last look at Marzo Greens. He pictured Rita Marzo lying in the steaming sun, her long tanned legs and painted toes protruding from the cabana. Turning from the window, he smiled to himself whimsically.

Later that same year, Anderson's Book Shop, had a book signing for the public. A long line wound its way from outside the store inside to a crowded table. Behind the table Josh Clark sat beaming, busily signing his latest work, "Covet Thy Neighbor." Hemingway would have been proud.

Mrs. Nikki's Cats

S he loved to plant flowers. Lilies and petunias and pansies, geraniums and hydrangeas surrounded her house. There was no particular order or sequence, not even a grand scheme for the landscaping she did. She would just plant and plant and when she was tired she'd plant some more. She created such a beautiful array of color and textures that her house was the talk of the town. The old widow, Ms. Nikki had the most striking house on the block, maybe even in town, even if it was a little busy looking. Some folks would stop by thinking the wild assortment of flowers was a greenhouse. They'd park their cars on the street and walk all over her property as if they were at market. When Mrs. Nikki would come out on her porch, her tattered apron billowed in the breeze. Thin wisps of grey hair swirled about her head as if charged with electricity. She'd raise a broom in hand and chase them away with ancient Celtic utterances that frightened even the largest of men. But still they came.

But it wasn't the flowers so much that she loved, although she certainly found enjoyment in them sitting on the front porch rocking away the latter years of her life. Mrs. Nikki loved to get her long bony fingers into the soil beneath the ground. She loved the smell that came not from the first couple inches of topsoil but the dirt below, the deep dark moist ground way down. The earth there smelled like the charred wood of a smoldering campfire. Her fingers prodded about and stopped momentarily to enjoy the coolness that radiated upward through her body on hot summer days. Perhaps that's why the dead slept so well. They'd been given a cool, comfortable resting place for their last nap.

She ate mostly macaroni and cheese. It was a simple meal, one she'd never forgotten how to prepare. When the water bubbled ferociously like a witch's cauldron she'd dump in the elbow macaroni and watch them play tag like kids at the pool. Then when she'd strained the noodles and put them in a large bowl she'd add the yellow/orange cheese-milk coating. All the while a few of her twenty-seven cats would purr and rub against her ankle-length nylons. They could smell the cheese-milk coating, the earthen fingers that stirred it and the dry flakes that floated to the floor from her cracked, wrinkled skin.

She'd open a can of tuna fish and scoop some out onto the rose-petaled china plates her mother had passed on to her. Those that were hungry would come and surround the bowls like birds to a birdbath. Others would stare aimlessly out the slits of light where long, dark, window drapes shuttered the day. The shears behind filtered the light giving it the same hue as the stale clouds of cigarette smoke floating throughout the room, imprisoned forever by closed windows, even in the summertime.

All too often, another cat would show up on her front porch. Some were just alley cats tired of life in the streets or too weak to fight for their food any longer. Many happened by and stayed because they were lonely. Others came because they knew of her. She took them all in.

On Friday nights Mrs. Nikki would play jazz records on the hifi in the front room. There she'd sit in her velvet-lined rocker, glass of sherry in a multi-cut crystal glass and a cat on her lap. All the cats gathered around, rubbed up against each other and swayed to the hifi's magic sounds. Their ears peaked straight and tall, their fur bristled and their tails flip-flopped the beat like a tick-tock clock. And if the jazz singer hit a high enough note all the cats would meow in unison to croon the moon. After another sherry and the jazz songs were over, Mrs. Nikki would rock to sleep. A faint smile crossed the lines of her peaceful face. The needle on the hifi bumped tirelessly against the spinning record label over and over and over.

Night passed and morning came as if they were one and the same. She replaced the tone arm on the hifi and shut it off. Then she gathered up her empty crystal sherry glass and placed it on the counter to be washed, next to the one from last Friday and the Friday before that. She almost tripped over what she thought was a rumpled throw rug.

Below her feet one of the older cats had passed away overnight. Bending down to pick it up, she stroked its soft furry head and without a tear, ran her bony fingers down the length of the body. Mrs. Nikki placed the cat into a shoebox and took it outside.

Once outside she dug a small deep hole near the side of the house. Her fingers felt good down deep in the cool soil. She breathed in the earthen smell and gently placed the shoebox into the hole. Next she brought out a tray of bright yellow marigolds and planted them on top smoothing the dirt flat with her rough hands. Then she stood and tamped down the dirt around the flowers with the toe of her shoe.

Later she sat on the porch rocking. Another car pulled up and a couple got out to approach her. But she was in no mood for strangers. Today was a day of mourning. She stood and uttered a guttural Gaelic curse learned long ago as a child. The couple frightened, retreated and left. As the car pulled away from the curb the passenger door opened and a kitten was left by its lonesome. It sauntered its way up to the porch suspiciously. Mrs. Nikki picked it up and placed it on her lap and stroked the kitten gently behind the ears. Its purr was faint. They went inside for macaroni and cheese and tuna. Come Friday they'd have some jazz music and a glass of sherry, or two.

Subject of Interest

I t had been a good year for Charlene Katz. All her diligence and hard work had finally paid off. She had finally begun to sell enough of her work to rent out a studio in the center of Clifton's downtown business district. Katz Studios was a cozy working place with skylights that let in the natural light of day. They also had shades that closed electrically should one need to invent their own choice of lighting. An array of lights atop solid metal supports stood around the studio like robotic Cyclops. A shiny strobe light, a tripod with camera body perched on it and a translucent umbrella faced a painted backdrop. All stood guard over a snaky black sea of cables.

Proudly displayed behind her desk hung the one that had recently been published in the Chicago Herald. Soon afterward, the Associated Press had called and paid a handsome royalty for its syndication.

The photograph, an old man alone on a park bench feeding a stray dog part of his sandwich, had been shot in black and white. Char enjoyed the austere realism of black and white photographs and the way it made its subjects come alive. Although the scruffy dog stood on its hind legs begging, it was no taller than the man's knees. His wrinkled, age-spotted hand held the elusive treat inches above the dog's nose. The hungry little dog turned a marvelously executed pirouette. It balanced itself perfectly by extending its front paws outward patting the air. The tired man's look was not one of excitement and glee. The glare of his yellowed eyes seemed demanding, as if he were the dog's trainer.

Char had snapped the shutter the exact moment the dancing dog opened its mouth in anticipation of reward like a baby bird awaiting a worm from its mother and just as the old man stood and looped his other hand in the air orchestrating the difficult movements.

It was if the old master had released his grip to send his dance partner on a wonderful twirl. He even displayed a look of approval, the kind of look you took for appreciation not glee. A half smile could be seen growing on the dog's muzzle as if the playful pooch knew who the real master was.

The old man and dog locked in dance was titled, 'Astaire and Rogers'.

Just recently Char had been awarded an exclusive showing at the Clifton Museum of Art where her works would be displayed for two weeks. The Clifton Museum of Art although a metropolitan museum, had last year been named to the top ten small city museums in the state. An exhibit at the museum especially by a local talent was unheard of. A busy schedule of afternoon shoots at the park and long hours in the evening editing and then carefully preparing her selections had sapped her energy lately. But the excitement of the impending date overrode her weariness.

Single and childless, Char had often spent her quiet times thinking about love but a long line of unsuccessful relationships had eroded her energy. Her parents had enjoyed a long marriage. Why hadn't she been able to sustain a relationship? Unlike her photography work, love was so elusive. Unlike relationships, her works of art gave her a chance to wrap herself around something tangible. They opened a door she could walk through, pour all her heart into and walk back out of dripping wet and cleansed as if from a rainshower. She uncovered a little more of her self each time she sat with them. And although it sometimes made her feel guilty, she had her favorites.

One such favorite appeared on the computer screen before her. She had just shot it at the park this afternoon. It stood out from the others quite prominently. Char edited busily cropping and playing with light variations until she thought she had something remarkable. As much as she appreciated the somber qualities of black and white, this photograph was full of majestic color.

The subject was a young girl lying in the grass and front lit by a strong afternoon sun. Char had placed the camera only a few feet in front of the girl but down in the grass.

The girl, a young friend of hers in her late teens had that innocent playful look one finds on faces in the park. She lay on her stomach, elbows spread wider than her body and her head resting gently on her hands. The shot was taken at a slight side angle so as to catch the full effect of the bottom of her legs which were bent at the upward at the knees. The untied laces of her tennis shoes hung lazily in the air like spaghetti. In the background and slightly out of focus because of the depth of the picture, stood a grove of trees.

The true marvel of the photograph other than the young subject's playful pose was the green blades of grass inches from the camera lens. A warm grassy translucence served as window sheers on a sunny day. This brilliant sea of green combined with the blurry background greenery of grass and trees was the portal to a dreamworld. She would call it 'Girl in Grass'.

Chapter Two

As often happens Char had lost track of the hour with her enthusiasm over the new work. She had found the perfect combination of lighting, exposure and sizing and began to print it out.

"Hi Char, you hungry?" came a voice from behind her. Char swiveled around in her chair to see Brenda Gillum.

"Oh Brenda, I'm sorry. I completely forgot..."

"It's the showing again, isn't it? You forgot our dinner date."

Brenda whisked her long hair over her shoulder with the snap of her head. She leaned forward and the two hugged and kissed each other politely. Brenda Gillum owned a picture framing shop in town. Her mother and she had run it since Mr. Gillum passed away. Brenda knew many 'artistes', as she liked to call them. She framed all of Char's works and took a genuine interest in them. Char was talented. This Brenda knew. Even when Char had her doubts, which were often, Brenda encouraged her not to despair. Char worked too much. A 'photoholic' she called her. She needed to get out more. She needed a pet or a boyfriend or something.

"Where shall we go, tonight?" Brenda asked.

"You pick. I haven't even thought about dinner yet."

"Oh please let's go to Milagro's. I have such a taste for Italian."

While Char readied herself Brenda walked around looking busy. She scooped up a photograph from the printer tray and studied the 10 x 12 picture. "This new?"

"Oh where is my purse? What? Oh that, yes. I haven't seen the printed copy yet." She tore apart the workshop looking for her purse.

"How did you shoot this?

"I placed the camera in the grass and laid on the ground to snap it."

"You're so talented. Gosh, it's beautiful."

"Thank you Brenda, you're a sweet."

"No, I mean it, Char. The colors are overwhelming. It's just… Who's the girl?"

"Nadine, from the College. You know, the Young's daughter"

"Who's the boy?"

Char had found her purse and approached. "What boy?"

"I think it's a boy."

"Let me see," The two of them shared the photograph for a moment, examining it closely.

"You're right. There is a boy behind the subject. I hadn't enlarged and printed the photo out yet before you came by. But I see it now. My goodness, I don't even remember seeing a boy at the park."

There was a young boy in the photograph. He was in the background but because the camera had been placed on the ground the boy was up toward the middle of the picture and obscured by the girl's sneakers. He wasn't far enough to be out of focus but far enough to be missed in smaller versions of the picture. His head rose slightly over the top of the girl's sneakers while his shoes and socks stuck out from the bottom. Unless you looked very closely you would never notice him in the picture. The girl's playful pose amongst magnified colors caught one's eye primarily.

"Is that bad?" Brenda inquired.

"Well a subject behind the subject is usually not acceptable but one can hardly notice him. I didn't."

"Well, I like it, Char. Will it be in the exhibit?"

"I think so."

The two walked out of Katz Studios and down Cass avenue towards Milagro's. As close friends often do while thinking of the same thing, neither of them mentioned the young boy again.

Chapter Three

Glos Park was always busy no matter what time of day. Two little girls rounded a swingset while being chased by a young boy. A couple of attendant mothers exchanged lively conversation while their kids took turns riding down a slide. Occasionally a jogger would roll past on the asphalt track that ringed the park.

Char sat at a park bench changing lenses on the body of her camera and aimed her camera at nothing in particular focusing the lens. The new telephoto lens enabled her to shoot objects across the park. As she panned the park she snapped a few photos. She swiveled slowly on bench and stopped to focus on a subject walking by a stand of trees. Surprised, she lowered the camera. Across the park was the boy from the photograph. Quickly she raised the camera and zoomed in on the subject. She wanted to snap a shot but he was obscured every couple of steps by trees as he walked. Char immediately packed her camera into her case and walked briskly across the park toward him. Red cheeked and out of breath, she finally caught up with the young boy as he was leaving the park.

"Hi there young man, my name is Char. I'm a photographer," she held up her camera case to display. A mop of thick black hair hung over his dark skinned face. He looked quizzically at the strange woman before him.

"I have a picture of you," she smiled. Still he said nothing.

"Do you have a name?" More silence.

"Name," she pointed to herself, "Char".

"Name?" she pointed to the boy.

He smiled shyly, "Amir".

"Well, I think Amir is a fine name for such a nice young man."

Amir looked at the strange woman before him. She was bending down, her face slightly closer to him than he preferred. He backed up a step. Her mouth was moving but he understood little. She seemed friendly but his parents had warned him about strangers, especially in this country. The dark skinned boy turned and left the park. A few steps away he looked over his shoulder and smiled. Wide, olive-purple lips framed his small gapped teeth. Then he was gone.

Char watched him cross the railroad tracks turn west and pass the YMCA. Unaware he was being watched he turned north on Evergreen street. Char found herself tracing his steps just far enough out on to the railroad tracks so she could see north down Evergreen. The boy climbed the steps to a gray frame house in the middle of the block and disappeared inside. That he didn't talk to her was disconcerting. The fact that she hadn't gotten another photograph was even more disappointing.

Chapter Four

The next morning Brenda prepared to frame each of the photographs Char had carefully selected for the exhibit. She had only a couple of days to finish. Each photograph had its own unique persona. Each needed its own special dressing. Painstakingly she matched shades of mattes to a picture then chose a specifically textured frame to complement it.

Her mother got to the shop mid morning. Usually cheerful, Mrs. Gillum walked in quietly and laid her purse on her desk. Brenda didn't hear her cheerful 'good morning'.

Mrs. Gillum turned to her daughter. Her face was drawn and a tear appeared in her eye.

"There's been a bombing at a train station in Chicago."

"Oh mother, no." Brenda rose from her desk.

"Many are dead, more are injured," she fingered a crumpled tissue. "It happened at the height of rush hour this morning."
Brenda sank to her seat. "How terrible. Are they sure it was a bombing?"

"A suicide bombing the news said. It's struck the very heart of our country this time," she reached out her quivering hands and Brenda took them. "I wish father were here now."

"So do I mom, so do I." They sat comforting each other as much as two who lost their strength could. Had he been there Brenda knew he would have wrapped his arms around them both and said something comforting. The tone of his voice, not so much his words, stilled their hearts.

BRENDA DROPPED WHAT she was doing and accompanied her

mother to St. Catherine's Church. On the ride the drone of the radio detailed the disaster in staccato bursts. At 8:00 a.m. that morning, at the height of rush hour, a suicide bomber detonated a bomb in the crowded terminal of the Burnham Train Station. The death toll had reached thirty-seven. Fifty-six people were critically wounded. Countless others were injured. Mercy and Children's Hospital were flooded with bodies. The Red Cross had sent scores of volunteers. Mayor Singleton would address the media in an hour.

After prayer service Brenda returned to the shop to finish her work. Her mother had stayed behind with some of the other women from the parish. She would get a ride back later.

The various frameworks that lay about the shop reminded her of the bombing chaos she had seen on television. What is wrong with this world? How much can you destroy before you have to build and what would be left to build on? These people offer you a ring—a ring of dynamite around your waist. Then poof—everlasting happiness for them and theirs while widows and orphans weep in the street collecting the teeth and brains of those they used to know. Whatever happened to protest movements, marches and sit-down strikes? Some get hurt but none die.

Brenda forced herself to concentrate on the work at hand. She tapped together a metal frame that encased Char's 'Girl in Grass' photograph. She found herself mesmerized by the brilliant greens of the park and the young people in it wondering what kind of world was being left them.

Chapter Five

The next day the Chicago Herald estimated the bombing death toll at forty-six. The injury count had risen to seventy-four. A temporary morgue had been set up at the train station to identify the remains of the dead. Mayor Singleton decried the terrorists responsible. He called in the National Guard for assistance.

Brenda entered Katz Studios with three more of Char's photographs framed and ready for the showing.

"S'pose you heard about the bombing."

"Yes, how terrible. Who could be that sick?"

"Not only that but now I hear the suicide bomber was just a child."

"That's so sad. Brenda, can we talk about something else, please." She wrung her hands together in nervousness. Brenda watched her closely as if her friend had something on her mind more serious than the upcoming exhibit.

They sat down together and turned their attention to the task at hand. Brenda set the photographs on easels for Char to see and flipped on the small television set in the corner. Char studied each photograph in its new frame.

"Oh, Brenda you've outdone yourself. They're wonderful. Each one of them."

"It's easy to frame genius."

"Please don't give me a big head, especially not the day before my showing. I'll be a bitch all day then."

A news update interrupted them. They turned and watched the horrible scene at the train station. Photo surveillance cameras had caught the suspected suicide bomber. A grainy black and white photograph appeared on the screen. Brenda's jaw dropped as she turned to Char and covered her mouth with her fingers. They both looked from the television to the framed 'Girl in Grass' and back to the television. The boy on the news was the same one in the background of Char's photograph!

Chapter Six

Char related the story of meeting the cute little boy, Amir, in the park the day before yesterday.

"He couldn't have been more than eight or nine years old," she said.

"Are you sure it was him?"

"You're doubting my trained eye?"

"I'm sorry, Char, it's just that he's so...young."

"Obviously, these people will stop at nothing."

"What did he say?"

"Nothing, other than his name. I don't think he spoke English at all."

It was then that they realized the grand plan for the poor boy who shied from strangers and spoke no English. Brenda contacted the information hotline number the news station had provided. Char contemplated the park picture and reflected how the boy's half smile resembled his smile when she met him. Within the hour FBI agents were at Katz Studios comparing the news photo of the young suicide bomber with that of the young boy in 'Girl in the Grass'. Char had enlarged the photograph on the computer and digitally enhanced it for the agents. They all were sure that the boy was one and the same.

FRANK CLEARY WAS the FBI agent in charge of the train station bombing. Actually it was a division of the FBI called the Anti-Terrorist Task Force that did the investigating in these types of cases. The ATTF had been set up in 1980 in response to bombings at that time. Cleary was one of the original agents hand-picked for the force. At fifty-five he was the senior officer. Cleary didn't know how many more 'bombings' he had in him at this late stage of his career. He had passed up the offer of a cozy desk job in New York. Some days a pension sounded even better. Some days he still had a passion for this type of work.

He ran his hand through his thinning grayish hair. "Ms. Katz there's no doubt you have a picture of our suspect here. How did you say you came about this."

"It was quite by accident. I didn't even know he was in the photo until I blew it up and printed it."

"I see. Well you've given us significant break on this case. The only question is how cold is the trail. These people move quickly."

"I know where he lives—lived," she corrected herself.

"How is that?"

"Well, I sort of followed him home from the park one day."

"Can you show us where this home is?"

"Certainly."

With that Cleary organized his task force and was out the door in moments. They jumped in the charcoal ATTF sedan and screeched away from Katz Studios with sirens blaring. He notified the local Clifton police and called in a SWAT team he'd had on standby just in case. Within minutes they all arrived at the gray frame house on Evergreen that Char had seen Amir enter. SWAT men crept around the house until it was surrounded and then on Cleary's signal they broke down both the front and back doors and stormed inside. Sixty seconds later Cleary heard the words "secured" and "all clear" over his radio. He told Char to stay put and for a man of fifty-five covered the distance between his car and the house in record time.

Char waited nervously. The whole morning had been a blur what with her and Brenda recognizing the photo of the boy and then the authorities arriving and now this whole home invasion. The morning had taken on a sort of surrealism. As the gray frame house before her began to melt down she retreated into the photograph in the park. It had been so warm and colorful, a portal to a dream world. She was trapped inside the photograph like Alice in Wonderland and nothing seemed real.

Fifteen minutes later Cleary and his agents and the SWAT team emerged from the home with a computer and a couple of cartons of evidence. His face was red and was wiping his brow with a handkerchief. As he entered the car the police cars and black sedans sped away with the evidence. The SWAT wagon followed behind them. It had been just over twenty-four hours since the bombing yesterday morning.

"They were there all right," he said to Char, confirming her worst fears.

"From the information we found on the computer they took a flight from Chicago to New York. From there they switched airlines hoping to get a flight out of New York to Amsterdam. Our boys picked them up as the plane was about to leave New York. Fortunately, there were a couple of Federal Air Marshals on the plane who detained them while the plane was on the runway. They're in our custody now, thanks to you, Ms. Katz."

Char's head dropped. She didn't feel like a hero. "And the boy," she asked.

Cleary had seen a lot in his twenty-five years on the Anti-Terrorist Task Force. But nothing had prepared him for what he was about to tell Char. He inhaled deeply and rubbed his chin. "I'm sorry, but there is no easy way to put this…we found evidence that three of these people had entered the country from Germany originally from somewhere in the Mideast. But only two tickets were purchased for the flight to New York. Apparently the child and the man and woman were all unrelated. It appears that we have found a cell or cells that specializes in child bombers. We may have not seen the last of this type of thing."

Char said nothing. All along she had hoped she was wrong about the young boy. Cleary knew she took little solace in cracking the terrorist cell. He put his beefy arm around her.

"Ms. Katz, I know this isn't what you wanted to hear." He offered her his dirty handkerchief. Char dabbed her tears, blew her nose and gave him back the handkerchief. Cleary pocketed it oblivious of the sweat, tears and snot they'd left together on this case. He hadn't had much stomach left for these bombings anyway. The case had been broken but he hadn't taken his usual pride in solving it. That pension was beginning to sound better.

As the charcoal sedan pulled away, the two of them sat in the back seat slumped together against the side door, their heads barely visible.

Chapter Seven

Char had titled the exhibit at the Museum, 'Windows of the Heart'. Opening night was always a nervous affair for an artist. The harrowing events of the last two days had also taken a toll on her. Every time she found herself alone her mind wandered to the little boy Amir and the senselessness his death. He had seemed such a nice happy child. She recalled his large gap-toothed smile in the park. To calm herself she spent part of the afternoon at Angelo's Day Spa. She had an hour long Swedish massage complete with aromatherapy treatment that made her feel like Cleopatra. If only they'd had milk baths. Later she went to the beauty salon and had her hair styled and highlighted. Her nape of the neck length soft brown hair looked dazzling with light blonde streaks.

Char had also bought herself a new outfit for the occasion. It was a black knee length cotton dress. Double straps highlighted the otherwise bare shoulders while a similar double strap cut across the bottom of the v-neck cut giving the dress a formal but very modern look. She wore gold earrings and a simple gold chain so as to not take away from the appeal of the dress.

Her proud parents were there along with many artist friends whom Brenda had invited. Char had asked Cleary to keep her involvement in helping solve the train station bombing out of the news. She had not wanted to attract undue attention to herself.

Over twenty of her favorite photographs had been chosen for the occasion, including 'Astaire and Rogers'. Clifton's own dignitary, Mayor Wagner, began the celebration with a short speech about the importance of recognizing local talent. Following that he invited the throng to join him in a champagne toast to Char Katz and the show opened.

LATE THAT NIGHT after all had left, Brenda and Char sat together with each other.

The exhibit had left them both spent. Brenda offered to drive Char back to the studio to pick up her car.

"Well, now that you are Clifton's most famous artiste, how about stopping at Milagro's for a glass of wine?" Brenda offered.

"Oh, Brenda, thank you but I'm exhausted. I feel as though I've just given birth."

"That's fine, I understand. You've had an exciting couple of days."

"To say the least."

They sat in silence for a couple of blocks before Brenda opened up about what had been on her mind all evening.

"I wish you had put 'Girl in the Grass' in the showing."

"I couldn't, you know that."

"But, it was important to. Others need to know about the viciousness of these kind of zealots. They need to know what they don't stand for instead of what they do stand for..."

"Brenda, we've been through this before. I am an artist not an activist. I just can't be what you want me to be."

"Okay, okay. I understand. I just wish somebody would...never mind"

Brenda pulled her car up in front of Katz Studios. Char gave Brenda a hug and a kiss. "Thanks for helping with the showing, Brenda. You're such a sweetheart."

"It was nothing. You were the star. Now get some rest tonight."

Brenda pulled away and Char instead of getting into her car and driving home went into the studio. She opened the door slowly and entered the chilly darkness. A small nightlight guided her way until she found the light switch. Once the studio was bathed in light she found the easel with the cover draped over it. She flipped the cover over the picture and sat down.

It really was exceptional, as good as if not better, than any she had selected for the exhibit. There was something more to it than the brilliant colors and its dreamy netherworld appearance. The playfulness of the girl in the grass and the innocent look of the boy in the background gave such life to the picture. She wouldn't let herself believe that the little boy in the park with the shy smile who called himself Amir could have known what he was being used for. Char touched the girl's smiling face then slid her fingers over to trace the figure of the young boy. They were all so precious, her pictures. And this one had been her favorite.

Below the picture in the middle of the frame where it had once been titled, 'Girl in Grass' hung a new title card Char had asked Brenda to install. She covered the picture, turned off the lights and left the studio. One day she would display the picture she had retitled, "Children in the Park".

Secrets of Mirror Lake

The Cape Cod cottage sat atop the highest point of The Island, or what the Wisconsin natives called the round outcropping of land jutting into the south side of the lake. In reality a peninsula, it was attached to the shoreline via a winding access road running alongside Simmons Feed Farm. On the other side of the road was lowland water and tall reeds that grew like cornstalks. The high land mass overlooking the lake was almost completely surrounded by water save for the access road from which grew the theory that it at one time could have been a true island. With time came electric, water and seventeen single family homes.

The grey Cape Cod with the red front door was the first house on the right of a circular drive that ran up hill from the access road around The Island. The place had been empty for nearly seven years now. Then on a recommendation of a fellow island resident, Royce Wendell purchased it as a summer home. Often he would sit on the end of the pier that stretched far out into the lake and admire the view.

The island sat majestically above a serene body of water known as Mirror Lake. It was small in size, a mile at the widest point and shallow, only twenty feet at its deepest point. The fact that it had no marina kept it more private and free from the ubiquitous, motorized boat traffic that crowded other nearby lakes. Surrounding hills peppered with forests of tall White and Norway Pines stood guard against the winds. The peaceful lake took its name from the stillness of its waters at dusk and dawn. Long rays of morning sun or evening moonlight shone across the still waters reflecting their brilliance like that of a mirror. One had only to look into Mirror Lake to see their image.

Out in the lake a pontoon boat floated by lazily.

Royce heard a splash beside him then another as small finger fish snapped up insects skirting along the water's surface. The pontoon boat became larger. Bright blue and white canvas trim made it look like a tub toy. It appeared to follow a rhumb line toward his his pier.

"Ahoy, mate. Are you the new owner?" A woman stood up from behind the wheel to acknowledge him. Her tee shirt was tied inches above her waist. Most of her light hair was scrunched up under a long-billed baseball cap.

"I am," he returned proudly. Word travels fast up here. "Are you alone?" he inquired, afterward feeling strange for having asked the question.

"You're lookin' at it, ship, captain and crew."

She pulled close, put the engine in reverse and gently nudged the boat up against the tire bumpers hanging on the pier posts. He helped her onto the pier and offered her a cold beer from the cooler that doubled as a footrest.

"Mind if I tie up?" she asked. He looked at her quizzically. "My boat. Mind if I tie up?"

"My pier is your pier."

"Grab the stern line. I'll take the bow."

While he took what he supposed was the stern line she grabbed the line at the front of the boat and began circling the rope around the pier post like she was roping a calf. He looped the line around and tied it in a knot. She came back and undid the knot showing him how to loop the line around the post a couple of times then yank it tight as a drum without a knot. Royce was sure she'd spent time with the local rodeo.

"Sarah Olsen," she said extending her hand.

"Royce. Royce Wendell," he guessed she wasn't much older than himself, mid-forties maybe.

The midday sun poured over her like a milk bath. She removed her cap emptying a bucketful of hair that bounced on her shoulders. There were faint touches of red, muted like wild rhubarb in her blonde hair. Beneath her eyes the very lightest of freckles sparkled like sea salt. Sarah tipped her head back and drank from the bottle. He couldn't remember ever seeing a woman drink beer from the bottle like that.

They drank beer with each other until the setting sun cast long shadows on the silvery lake. Sarah told long, flowing stories about the origins of Mirror Lake, how after the War the Army Corps of Engineers displaced the levee that ran alongside the Fox River which then spilled and filled the lake from the northwest corner. Royce listened intently, sharing little about himself, considerably more fascinated by this woman and the history of Mirror Lake. She stopped only for a swig of beer. Her smile was thin yet different from the narrow-lipped smile the locals gave you when sliding your purchase across the counter. "Flatlanders" they called the folk from Illinois who came up with fistfuls of dollars to spend in this once upon a time bastion of American automobile manufacturing. A decade ago the Chrysler plant in Kenosha employed over twenty thousand workers. The aged plant dated back to the forties when it used to spew such grand automobiles as the Nash and the Rambler. Shuttered years ago by more modern facilities, the building currently housed a long string of weary warehouses. The region was jobless and depressed. Its people wore long, stoic faces. Although the Flatlanders' money was welcome, they would always be like fur trappers come to the Indian village.

Sarah and Royce met again for dinner the next evening. Later they walked the private beach on the island where moonbeams reached out across the flat water to lap at their feet. The next day, Sunday, he called to say goodbye before returning home for the weekend.

"I do think we'll be seeing more of each other, Royce Wendell."

"I'd like that. You've fascinated me. The history of this lake, the whole area," Royce said.

"There's so much more you don't know. Will you be coming back soon?"

"I hope to get back next weekend. I've got a lot more work ahead of me to spruce up this old cottage."

"Kindred spirits never wander far." She smiled to herself, recalling the phrase from her childhood.

Sarah found him unusual for a Flatlander, rather genteel and urbane, more willing to listen than expound—unusual for a man. Thinking about the past was something she disdained but in meeting him found it hard not to. He was different from the men she was used to, bored to death with and long had suffered. It had been a long time

Chapter Two

Beadlets of sweat dripped from his forehead as he dumped out the bucket of dirty water, squeezed the mop clean and hung dirty rags on the clothesline to dry. Royce had not anticipated the work it would take to ready the long empty cottage for habitation.

Thanks to Bernard Macklund, the accountant for his printing business, he'd been able to afford the fix 'er upper. Bernard's wife, Grace, had spent her summers at the small cottage on Mirror Lake that her father purchased in the early 1950's. After their marriage the Macklunds bought a cottage on the island themselves. When talk turned to Royce possibly buying a summer home Bernard insisted he drive up to Mirror Lake to look at his father-in-law's cottage that had been up for sale since his death.

"Howdy neighbor." A square-shouldered man with thick glasses smiled at him extending his hand forward.

"Oh, hi Bernard." Royce quickly becoming used to people just dropping in on him any old time, shook his meaty hand.

"How's the old place shaping up?"

"Well, okay I guess," he said wiping his brow with a red kerchief. "I've decided to take a couple of weeks off if I'm to get this place ready for the summer."

"Sweat equity, Royce. Be an asset on the books one day,"

"The sweat part I've got down."

They both chuckled and took a seat on patio together.

"Can I offer you a lemonade?"

"Can't drink plain lemonade. Got any vodka?"

"Oh that's right, we're on vacation." Royce wiped his still clammy forehead again. "One vodka lemonade comin' up."

Against his better judgment, Royce joined Bernard as they clinked glasses in a toast to the new summer home.

"This place has a lot of good memories for me," Bernard swept his arm drink in hand in a wide circle. "Grace and I were still in college when we began dating. Spent many a summer weekend up here, boating, fishing..."

"Drinking," Royce chimed in.

"Among other things," Bernard flashed a sly smile.

"Grace's old man, Dean was his name, always liked me. Liked having me around. Company for him and Grace I guess. His wife had passed years before her time from a brain aneurism."

"Why was the place vacant so long? I mean this is a great location, only an hour and a half from Chicago, a beautiful quiet lake."

Bernard sipped from his glass, stared into it and snared a lemon wedge. He squeezed the juice from the wedge in his thick fingers until dry and then plopped the fruit back into his drink stirring it with his forefinger which he then sucked clean.

"Well, initially the place was stuck in probate for a couple of years. The house was paid off, Dean paid cash for it. He also left a trust fund that invested in municipal bonds generating enough income to pay the real estate taxes every year, so there was no hurry."

"Yeah, but five years?"

"As you'll learn, the folks here on the island, we're a tight group. We didn't want to sell to just anyone. I mean, there were some prospects but no one ideal."

"Thanks for making me feel special," Royce raised his glass in salute and finished the rest in one long gulp.

"Did you say her father paid cash for this place? Was he that well off?"

"Not rich, rich, but he did well for himself. He was the county assessor for Chicago for over thirty years. For some reason or another..." with this Bernard raised a single eyebrow in knowing silence before continuing, "he always had a lot of cash at his disposal. Dean was a wonderful man, started the High Council here at the Island."

"The High Council?" Royce asked.

"Yes, that's what us old windbags call the Board of Directors for the Island. It's made up of five homeowners who basically do all the policymaking and handle business matters for the Island. All homeowners are welcome at the monthly association meetings. You'll want to join us later this month." With this Bernard stood to put his heavy hand on Royce's shoulder. "After all, you're one of us now."

"That's fine, I'd like that."

"By the way how is Gina?"

"Fine, fine." Royce had hoped that Bernard wouldn't ask. His wife had been up to the cottage a few times now but found it boring. 'Nothing to do there' she would say. She was more at home on the sandy beaches of South Florida where her folks had a winter home than the grassy shores and long-piered cottages of Wisconsin. There she could lie for hours at a time the sun baking her tanned skin until it cracked. The narrow fissures made her appear years older than he. Sometimes he wondered if it was the daunting task of fixing up the old cottage that scared her away.

"Oh was that the Olsen girl I saw down by your pier last week?" Bernard tipped his head down to look over his glasses at Royce.

"Yes. Nice young lady. She…"

"Can be a handful," Bernard finished pushing the center of his glasses up with his forefinger.

Chapter Three

Big Bob's Tap was located a mile west of the Island at the lonely intersection of Route 13 and Highway B, not to be confused with Highway BB. All the roads in the southeastern part of the state seemed a jumble of numbers and alphabet letters. Often times for no apparent reason and with plenty of letters from the alphabet left, they'd name a highway AA or BB as if to deliberately befuddle out-of-state travelers with their cryptic coding.

Behind the bar was a bear of a man called appropriately enough, Big Bob. He had played for the Green Bay Packers when helmets lacked face masks. As a result his face bore the telltale flat nose that went both east and west. A jovial man, Big Bob was far less intimidating than his presence. He'd bought the old Roadhouse Tap when a knee injury ended his career and after long thought, renamed it after himself. A large glass case behind the bar housed one of his game jerseys. If you looked close enough washed out blood stains could be detected in the white of the numbers. On any given night you might find a group of wide men with booming voices—old Packer players—sharing maudlin memories over pitchers of beer and the best hamburgers in Racine County. Big Bob's Tap served two burgers and two burgers only, the Big Bob and the Little Bob. The Big Bob was a half-pound of freshly ground sirloin, the Little Bob a third pound of the same.

"Big Sarah, how are you?" Everyone was big in Big Bob's Tap. "How's the house going."

"Fine, thank you Bob. The frame is up already and they just finished putting on the roof," Sarah said, removing her baseball cap. Having their attention, she combed her hair with her fingers then shook her head. "Say hello to Royce. He just bought the old Russell cottage on the Island."

"Big Royce, welcome to Big Bob's Tap." Big Bob's wide smile was one tooth short.

"Nice to meet you," Royce managed as the gentle giant took his hand in his and smothered it.

"'Bout time someone bought that place. Big Dean was quite a character. Spent most every weekend on his sailboat. Won bunch of regattas. Drank like a sailor too." Big Bob lurched back in laughter. A mouthful of silver glinted down at them.

"We'll have one Big Bob and one Little Bob," Royce said.

"All the fixin's?"

"Drag it through the garden."

Big Bob laughed heartily again. "City boy, eh? I like that. One Big Bob, one Little. Drag 'em through the garden," he bellowed to the cook while moving down the counter wiping the bar clean.

"Drag it through the garden?" Sarah asked Royce.

"Yeah, cityspeak for load it up with all the veggies."

"Well, seems I learned something new." Underneath the counter Sarah dropped the flip flop off her foot and surreptitiously began running her toes up and down the inside of Royce's leg. He'd told her he was married but she didn't know how married. She watched closely for his response.

But Royce seemed unflappable. "About time I'm the teacher," he said with a straight face.

"I like that." She stopped her toe touching but wasn't dismayed for often the planted seed took time to sprout.

Royce sipped from his beer mug leaving a moustache of white foam above his lip. "What did Big Bob mean when he asked you about your house?"

"Oh gosh, it's a long story. I grew up here. Worked most my adult life as an administrative secretary for a v/p with Johnson & Johnson.

"Your family was from around here?"

Sarah paused for a brief moment as if her story were being interrupted. Her childhood wasn't worth talking about. Usually she was able to glance over it quickly with oblique references but now could see that Royce was genuinely interested. Her voice dropped low and she spoke softly as if trying to summon distant memories long ago repressed. "What family? I was orphaned when four years old. My mother died in a drowning accident on Mirror Lake."

"Oh my God, I had no idea," Royce said.

Sarah shook her head not to worry. "I still have a picture of her. Grandmama named her Angela because she was her little Angel. My mother had shiny black hair that ran halfway down her back and a complexion that turned copper in the summer sun. She was part Potowatomi Indian and proud of it. But folks around here didn't care much for Indians.

"And that's the sad part. They were the natives, until we took over," Royce added.

Sarah bobbed her head in agreement. "Many couldn't hold a job and drank too much. Her family ended up being pushed north toward to the reservations where the casinos are now. Often she told stories told to her by her mother and grandmother, my great grandmother, Wai-kee-shaw. She lived back in the times of the great, Waubonsee, war chief of the Three Fires Confederacy—the Potowatomi, Ottawa and Chippewa tribes. Later Wai-kee-shaw married an Indian trader by the name of David Laughton. After his death she moved north to Wisconsin where our ancestors settled. Waukeshau County is named after her. The women in our family were always very close. My mother was fond of saying that we would always be together for 'Kindred spirits never wander far'. After her death I spent a year and a half in an orphanage and later raised by foster families."

"You'd never know it, Sarah," Royce said laying his hand on hers. "What about your father?"

"Never knew him. She never mentioned him. It was just us two until she…"

Big Bob delivered their burgers and another round of beers. Sarah took the opportunity to shut the door on her past.

"So two years ago I bought some of the last land available on Mirror Lake, over on the northwest end of the lake where the Fox River feeds in. It's mostly all marsh there but there I did some research and found a small lot firm enough for building. I got a permit and started building but ran into some legal problems with the DNR."

"DNR?"

"The DNR—Department of Natural Resources—is God up in these parts. You can't as much as fell a tree on the shoreline without their approval."

"How'd the DNR get involved?"

"High Council at the Island."

"Excuse me! My High Council! On my Island?"

"I'm afraid so."

"But why?"

"The land next to mine is the old MacNamara Lodge. They let me dock my boat there temporarily. That place has been in the family for three generations. Kathleen and her husband have four young kids. He lost his job at the auto plant years ago. And business at the Lodge has been slow. Now the bank in Racine is trying to foreclose on the place. Used to be you could miss a payment in the off season and make it up come vacation season."

The Racine County Bank was the bank Bernard had recommended to mortgage the cottage. He never expected approval what with his printing business only recently beginning to take off. Then there was the matter of Gina's credit card debt. He was shocked when the loan officer mentioned the thirty-five thousand dollar debt. When confronted by her husband his wife feigned surprise at the amount and promised to watch her spending. But the business was doing extremely well she reminded him. Fortunately Bernard knew the bank President and the loan was quickly approved

"Why does the bank want the lodge?"

Sarah sipped her beer then adroitly licked the foam from her lips, savoring the tasty bubbles. "It's very valuable property. More important, its got lake access rights for thirteen piers grandfathered with it. Hard to come by these days."

"You mentioned the High Council?"

"They want to buy the place in bankruptcy court. I've heard they plan to tear down the MacNamara Lodge and develop the property into pricy vacation condominiums."

Royce took a bite of his burger and chewed thoughtfully for a moment. Bernard had invited him to an association meeting in the future. He'd mentioned the High Council but didn't really say much about it. Apparently their influence had a long reach.

"The DNR is attempting to block my lake access rights and building of a pier because it's too close to the marsh and the river. Something about ecological balance." The muttered words echoed in a mug of cold beer. She took a long gulp then another.

"How is the High Council involved?"

"Royce, don't you know who is on that Council? Some of the most powerful men in the state. They run the DNR."

"I know Bernard. He suggested I buy his father-in- law's cottage."

"Bernard Macklund? Royce, he's the President of the High Council!"

Royce recalled Bernard's comment about Sarah. How had he known she was visiting on his pier? Sarah stared into her beer. Lumps of foam swirled around inside as she circled the mug in her hand. On the counter her Little Bob burger sat untouched.

Royce put his arm around her. Sarah's glassy eyes reflected his image, his hidden desires on fire. Nudging close to the side of her face he whispered, "I've known Bernard a long time. I'll see what I can do."

Sarah felt his warm breath on her face, the tender concern in his voice. Somewhere lower, between her knee and shorts his fingertips singed her skin. But there was little he could do for her. After all, the High Council was connected and powerful. Yet there was something about him she hadn't seen in the faces of men from these parts—beaten, downtrodden men with long faces, reddened by the sting of alcohol and awash in self-pity, many without jobs, too many mouths to feed, and desperate wives beseeching them constantly. There was something different about Royce Wendell. Sarah wrung her hands together as she often did when deep in thought. Nine years was a long time—much too long.

Chapter Four

Royce couldn't imagine his old friend being behind such a power play. At the same time he thought it strange that Bernard knew Sarah visited his pier. The Macklund summer home was four doors down from his. Even if he'd walked by his cottage his pier wasn't visible from the road. The pier was a good hundred feet below the house down the side of the hilly Island.

The old cottage had two bedrooms and a full bathroom upstairs. The east bedroom didn't have a bed yet and overlooked a stand of tall oak trees. The west bedroom, where he slept faced the circle of homes on the Island drive. Both bedrooms were in need of a fresh coat of paint but needed a good cleaning first. He began in the narrow, dormered closet. Barely large enough for one to enter, it was impossible to turn around in. Working on his hands and knees he scooted a bucket of suds along as he cleaned the floor by hand, backing up carefully in the tight quarters.

In doing so his foot banged up against the far wall, knocking something over. He backed out of the closet to see what he'd bumped into. A small section of the wood wall had fallen off. Royce inched closer chiding himself for having left his hammer and nails downstairs. Before he could replace the loose wall board he noticed something inside the dark hole. He reached inside and pulled out a cardboard shoebox. Royce backed out of the closet on his hands and knees dragging the shoebox with him. Once out he wiped a heavy layer of dust off the box with his wet rag and sat on the bed. His heart pounded heavily as he removed the lid of the box. Inside was a manila folder and a bunch of envelopes. He peeled open the folder to find two stacks of money rubber-banded together. Each stack had a hundred one-hundred dollar bills—twenty thousand dollars! Royce bundled the money back up while deciding what to do about his find.

His attention turned to the stack of letters. The letters were addressed to Dean Russell, none had a return address. He pulled one of the letters out and thought he detected the faint sweet scent on the paper. A woman perhaps? A love interest? He felt awkward reading someone else's private letters. But Dean was dead some seven years now. The old cottage was his now. He had bought it 'as is'. And 'as is' meant 'was his'. Opening the top letter, he read on.

> Dearest Dean,
>
> Not an evening moon passes by these eyes without my soul rising up to peer out this lonely bedroom window, searching for you, thinking how meaningless my life was before you built the fire that called my soul home. Before the Great Creator guided you to me I spent many seasons drifting above the fertile plains not knowing, but never fearing that one day you would ride out of the horizon bathed in rays of sun and extend me your hand.
>
> Together may we ride into the last sunset until the clouds call our spirits home.
>
> My heart, my spirit
> Wakipi.

Royce stared at the letter in his hand its scrawl obviously not that of an educated person yet the sheer elegance of the words was powerful and moving. Who was this Wakipi? It sounded native Indian. But, there hadn't been Indians in these parts for decades now.

The doorbell shocked him out of his trance and he ran downstairs with the letter still in his hand. From the windows alongside the door Royce could see three men dressed in white shorts and shirts holding tennis rackets. *Damn, he'd forgotten completely about their tennis date.* Shoving the letter into his back pocket, he opened the door still wearing his dirty work clothes. Bernard smiled knowing Royce had forgotten about the tennis match. He introduced his new neighbor to his fellow Island residents Ted Teagle, President of the Racine County bank, and Chuck Edgerton, Chairman of the State Dairy Association. Royce promised to be down to the Island courts in five minutes. Changing into his tennis whites he put the love letter and piles of cash back in the box and returned the box to its hiding place where it had been safe for years.

Lost in the excitement of his new discovery was the fact that he'd just shook hands with three of the most powerful men on the Island and the State of Wisconsin, all members of the High Council.

Chapter Five

Royce picked up a pair of binoculars on sale, figuring it might be nice to watch the multi-colored sailboats that dotted Mirror Lake on the weekends. Come nightfall his back was sore from all the repair projects and his legs were tired from tennis. Helping himself to a cold beer from the refrigerator he plopped down in his favorite recliner to play with his new toy—Bernard wouldn't be the only one doing some spying.

Sarah's predicament and his promise to help her perplexed him. She was not only concerned for herself but also for her friends and neighbors, the MacNamaras. After tennis Bernard stopped over to see the improvements he'd made. Ted Teagle and Chuck Edgerton were members of the High Council he informed him. He recommended joining them again for tennis. The DNR was the High Council's puppet. They not only ran the state waterways, they walked on them. Ted Teagle was President of Racine County bank which held the mortgage on the cottage and was also trying to foreclose on the MacNamara Lodge. It all seemed overwhelming to him. Without moving from the recliner, sleep came quickly this evening.

It was past midnight when his cellphone woke him. It was the familiar ring he'd programmed for his wife, Gina.

"What are you doing?" she asked this question frequently. He was never sure if she was really interested or just checking up on him.

"I was sleeping."

"I'm sorry. Are you going to spend the whole month up there?"

"Gina, do you know what time it is?"

"When are you coming home? The grass needs cutting. Bill and Emily invited us over for a barbecue next weekend. I told them I'd talk to you. Why don't we go honey. It sounds like fun. You love Emily's cooking."

And you love Bill's stupid jokes. "Do we have to talk about this at this hour? I'll call you tomorrow."

"Come home soon sweetheart."

Royce assumed dinner out meant yet another outfit for Gina, possibly some new earrings and a fresh credit card bill.

He took himself and his binoculars upstairs to turn in for the night. From his second floor window he could see the Macklund home four doors down. It was late, almost one o'clock. Bernard's front door swung open and a woman with blonde hair lighted down the stairs. Grace Macklund was a brunette. She hadn't bounded anywhere in years. Royce trained the binoculars on the woman. She was blonde all right and attractive. He pushed the zoom lever on the binoculars for a closer view. They were worth every penny of the two hundred dollars he'd spent. Bernard's late night visitor had sweaty, bleach blonde hair matted to her forehead and smeared circus clown makeup. She scrambled into a dark blue Mustang and took off quietly without headlamps. Royce closed the bedroom blinds. So old Bernard had his fishing pole in another fishing hole.

UNABLE TO SLEEP, Royce once again removed the secret box from its hiding place in the closet. He still hadn't decided what to do with the twenty thousand cash. The pack of love letters piqued his interest. He opened another and again was immediately enticed by the sweet scent of lavender. It reminded him when he was little how he used to watch his mother primping herself at her vanity enveloped in a fog of delicious scents.

> Dearest Dean,
> Our journey together has made our hearts one. Today a hawk crossed my path to warn me. I cannot bear to see you leave my side. Your precious

touch soothes me at day and quiets
me at night.
   I know now that you may never
return. Our lives are as different
as the colors of our skin. But I am
at peace for I shall always have a
part of you inside me.
   Kindred spirits are never far
apart.

My heart, my love.
Wakipi

'Different as the colors of our skin'? So he was right. Dean's lover was indeed a native Indian. And it seemed, about to part ways. The bittersweet love note bore faint ringlets of water stains. Royce closed his eyes and held the letter close to his face. It smelled like the salt of ocean water. These were the salty stain of tears. Yet even in the face of abandonment it seemed hopeful. What had she meant by 'a part of you inside me'? Was Wakipi telling her lover she was with child! And 'Kindred spirits are never far apart'. Where had he heard that before?

Chapter Six

Royce threw a pair of grungy shorts on over his swimsuit. A crumpled laundry bag made a convenient beach bag which he loaded up with sunblock, towels and a half pint of blackberry brandy. It being Saturday, Sarah had invited him out on her boat for his first fishing trip on Mirror Lake. He wasn't sure yet whether he'd tell her about the box or the love letters, certainly not the cash he'd found. But first, he wanted to review the mortgage documents on the cottage. Ted Teagle's bank was behind the attempted foreclosure of the MacNamara Lodge. That along with the swift processing of his mortgage made him suspicious. A cursory examination of the documents showed everything in order until he got to the fourth page. His income was grossly overstated. Furthermore, it looked as though the line entry for Gina's credit card debt had been whited out. Sure enough, the Racine County Bank had forged his mortgage application. Why had they wanted him so badly?

ROYCE JUMPED FROM the pier onto Sarah's pontoon boat. She had on the same long-billed baseball cap he'd seen her in the first day they'd met. A long reddish blonde ponytail stuck out the back of the cap, swinging playfully. She wore short shorts and a bikini top. Royce greeted her with a kiss on the lips for what seemed a long time. She seemed pleased by this and bore a saucy smile the rest of the day.

"Are you going fishing or to the laundromat?" Sarah teased him.

"Oh this?" He asked hoisting up the old laundry bag. "It's the very latest in beachcomber fashion. Sunscreen?" he offered rubbing lotion on his pale skin.

"Just a little bit on my shoulders, please." Sarah too was light-skinned but had been in the sun enough to cook her skin russet. They headed out onto Mirror Lake she guiding the tiny vessel while he stroked her slender shoulders. The queen of the Nile sat stiff-backed trying to ignore the goosebumps as her manservant tended her.

It had been a long time since...

"This is it. Drop anchor, mate."

Royce found the anchor near the back of the boat, tossing it into the flatwater with a splash.

"Royce dear," she started.

"What?"

"Lash the anchor rope to the boat, please." He bent over and began a series of loops with the rope. Sarah couldn't help but notice the how muscular his legs were. His rear stretched his shorts tight enough to show the outline of his swimsuit underneath. She wondered what it might be like to be in his arms. Would he caress her? Would he kiss her behind the ear, her soft spot. Royce turned to catch her staring at him but she averted her eyes forward to watch for boat traffic. A shame he's married. But why is he up here alone so much?

She showed him how to bait the hook by sticking it through the worm a couple of times corkscrewing it in the figure of an 's'. Royce begrudgingly went along dropping the slimy worms more than once. The sunlight highlighted freckles on her chest and top of her breasts, cousins to her lightly freckled face but larger and a shade darker like pennies. Her markings were as unique to her as she was a woman. She showed him how to cast with a sweeping arm and flick of the wrist. Soon they both had lines in the lake.

Royce took a swig of the blackberry brandy, swishing it around in his mouth. Its licorice taste helped kill the oily stench of fish onboard. "Sarah, I don't know if I should be telling you this..." he hesitated, "but I've found some love letters in the closet of my cottage."

"How lovely. I never thought of Dean Russell as the romantic type."

"These were written to Dean. Apparently by his lover, who I think was a native Indian woman."

"And you know this, how?"

"The imagery in the letters and a reference to their different colored skin." Royce was holding back some information, cautious in his approach for truth.

"Who wrote them?"

"They were signed by a woman called—Wakipi. I thought maybe you'd heard of her."

Sarah dropped her rod and covered her mouth. Royce's quick reaction saved the rod from falling overboard.

"Wakipi was my mother," she said, hand over her chest, fingers splayed.

"But you said your mother's name was Angela."

"Her given name was Angela. Her true Indian name was Wakipi."

"She had a love affair with Dean."

"She couldn't have. That man was despicable."

Royce put his arm around her. "I'm so sorry, Sarah. She said in the letter 'Kindred spirits are never far apart'."

Sarah dropped her head. "That would be my mother."

"There's something else." Sarah lifted her head to look at Royce. "She may have been pregnant."

"No, no, no!" Sarah began flailing her arms at Royce in an effort to quiet him. He grabbed her arms, stilling them and looked into her eyes.

"He planned on leaving her unaware, I believe, that she was pregnant. This note was to let him know."

"That bastard." Sarah slumped in her seat. "No, I'm the bastard."

"Stop it now. This doesn't change who you are. You're better than that." He dabbed her tears with his towel.

Sarah leaned over the railing to reel in the fishing lines. Her reflection bobbed lazily in the sun-baked water. The image of a woman with long dark hair and copper skin melded with hers until the two were one. 'Kindred spirits' it whispered, then rippled away until Sarah saw only herself again.

After she composed herself she brought in the fishing rods. They headed the boat back to Royce's pier. The pontoon boat floated slowly like a funeral pyre, carrying her heavy heart, leaving nary a wake behind.

"ROYCE, ROYCE, COME quickly—it's burning." Sarah gasped.

Royce rushed out from the back door onto the patio.

"Oh my god. Quick give me your beer." Sarah offered her bottle.

There was so much smoke coming from the gas barbecue grill he could barely find the handle. He grabbed a mitt, reached into the bluish white plume and threw the top open dumping the beer in to extinguish the fire. The smoke began to clear. "Whew! That was close. I'm sorry, I was making our salad."

"Let me help. I'll finish the salad. You watch the chicken." After dinner they sat together at the picnic table watching the boats crisscrossing the lake, pinballs on the water, scurrying home to beat the sunset.

"That was some crispy chicken." Sarah said.

"That wasn't crispy. That was cowboy style." He replied with a polite smile.

The brilliant sun faded below the western edge of Mirror Lake illuminating its still waters with elongated prismic strands of burning beams. Windows on the lake houses reflected the dazzling yawn of day like campfires on a hillside.

"Sarah, about today, maybe I shouldn't have…"

"You should have. Now let's change the subject. Tell me about your wife," she leaned back swallowing the last of her beer.

"Well, there's not much to tell."

"When men don't talk about their wives it's usually for good reason."

Royce smirked at the comment. "I discovered, or the bank discovered, she had thirty five thousand dollars in credit card bills."

"Wow. What was she buying?"

"I don't know. Clothes, shoes, jewelry. Frankincense and myhrr."

"Really now."

"Since she has her own credit cards, I'm not really sure yet but she may have a problem with Internet gambling. Friend of mine had the same disease. Ran up thousands on his credit card. I've got Bernard looking into it as we speak."

"Is she lonely?"

"I bought this place because I thought it might help us. You know give us a getaway hideaway. A place to be alone together. Nothing I do seems to work."

"You like it here, don't you?"

"I do."

"You've got to be a special person to like it here on Mirror Lake. It's quiet, peaceful. That's why my people settled here. They believed that if you could see back with one eye and forward with the other, you were in your destined place."

"How about you, Sarah. Are you lonely?"

"I was married once. Seems like a long time ago. He still owns the place we operated on Brown's Lake. Little place with six cabins and a bar. I caught him with one of the waitresses one night. Left and never looked back."

"That's sad."

"Don't be. The jerk will never outlive his liver anyway. Never met a drink he didn't like."

"And since then?"

Sarah paused to take a drink. Her eyes followed a black ant on the ground bumping along busily, looking for crumbs. She watched his path, never straight always off in many different directions. Neither one of us seem to have found a path yet, little fellow.

"Nine years ago I had breast cancer. The doctors removed a malignant cyst. Then I underwent nine months of chemotherapy."

His troubles paled in comparison to hers. Especially in light of the news he'd sprung on her earlier in the day. She deserved better.

"I haven't been with someone since, so I haven't had to explain." Royce took her chin gently in his thumb and forefinger. Turning her face toward his, he let his lips drift toward hers. She hesitated at first then met him better than halfway. Once was not enough. With the second kiss they looped their arms around each other, their bodies touching. He pressed tightly against her chest. For a moment he feared hurting her breast. But she remained firmly in his clutches. He stood to take her hand. Sarah rose to meet him. Again they kissed.

"Oh Royce, please..."

"You'll never have to explain again," he said stroking her satiny pumpkin-hued hair.

Royce led Sarah to his spartan bedroom. Before entering he scooped her up in his arms, carried into the room and gently laid her down on the bed. It had been such a long time. She'd suffered a lifetime of dreams waiting for this moment. The small of her back arched up off the bed twisting, writhing in his firm grip. They spent most the night learning each other. Underneath cool sheets, soft words, gentle cooing and rhythmic movement permeated the night. Moonlight crept through the windows cutting jeweled rectangles on the floor. A cacophony of chirping crickets, rustling branches and other ominous night noises stopped momentarily, as if interrupted.

Afterwards, the lovers lay exhausted, clinging to each other. Sarah enjoyed a peace she hadn't known. Tomorrow she would cut a daisy from her flower garden and wear it in her hair. She would bake for him. Everyone adored her dutch apple pie.

A cool breeze swept by causing her to pull the sheet up. My little Sarah, soon we will be reunited. You will not recognize me. I will come on eagle's wing. Kindred spirits are never far apart.

Sarah fell asleep holding fast to Royce so her spirit wouldn't wander the night.

Chapter Seven

"Let's see what she can do." Bernard pushed down hard on the throttle. The nose of the twenty-one foot Bayliner rose like a hungry shark. The captain's thin, grey hair flapped mightily in the wind. Royce, having almost spilled into the back of the boat, clung to a seat with both hands. The boat trimmed out nicely reaching top speed within a minute. Across the lake a man wearing a khaki shirt and shorts trained his binoculars on the speedboat. He turned on the ignition and the black hundred and twenty horsepower Mercury engine whined. It spewed bluish smoke and spit a stream of water. The letters on the side of the boat read—Marine Police.

Bernard turned north shooting a tidal wave of water starboard side. The great white hunter wore yellow aviator glasses with prescription lenses. Droplets of lake water spotted his face and glasses. Coming out of the turn he sped into the straightaway, the longest stretch of Mirror Lake—almost a mile long. "Bandit, two o'clock high," he yelled down to Royce who'd ended up on the deck at the last turn. The flashing red lights of the Marine Police approached swiftly. Bernard motored down to a stop. Royce scrambled to his feet.

"Howdy Sam," Bernard said. The khaki man wore green teardrop sunglasses that made him look like a big bug.

"Oh, it's you, Bernard. Sorry, didn't recognize you. How's Grace?"

"Fine thanks. Beautiful day for a run."

"Yes sir. We've been getting complaints about kids drinking and speeding, so just checking."

"No problem. Say hello to Royce Wendell. He just bought the old Russell place."

"Pleased to meet you. Old Dean loved to sail out here. How about you, Roy—you sail?"

"Royce. And no, I don't own a boat—yet."

"Well you two enjoy." Sam swung his boat around to leave. "Bernard, keep it under a hundred."

They laughed as the police boat trailed off.

"Beer?" Bernard offered.

"Sure," Royce said accepting. They were out in the middle of Mirror Lake alone with each other now. He watched Bernard closely, suspiciously.

"How's the Olsen girl doing?"

"Fine, thanks for asking."

"Saw you two out on the lake yesterday."

If he'd seen them out on the lake then he also knew that Sarah's pontoon boat had been docked at his pier overnight. "We went fishing but didn't catch..."

"Royce, there's something I've been meaning to ask you. The Olsen girl..."

"Sarah. Her name is Sarah."

"Yes, well she has been involved in a lawsuit with myself and some business partners. Since you and she have become friends as of late," Bernard removed his aviator glasses and began cleaning the lake sprayed lenses with a beach towel. His thumb and forefinger worked meticulously like a tailor. "We are willing to make her a peace offering."

"A peace offering?" Royce played dumb.

"Yes. A very substantial peace offering, if you know what I mean. Enough to make her go away."

The information he'd pieced together so far was like brushstrokes on canvas. Bernard had just painted the picture for him. Royce placed his empty beer in the cooler. "Can I think about it?"

"That a boy." Bernard patted him on the shoulder. "Hey, would you like to drive the boat?"

The Bayliner cut across the smooth waters effortlessly. Royce sat atop the seatback one hand on the wheel the other on the throttle his head just above the windshield. Bernard's friendship and offer of a great deal on a lakehouse was all a ruse. He and his pals wanted him to make the 'Olsen girl' go away, just like their predecessors did with

Wakipi. Anybody that stood in the way was fair game, like the MacNamaras.

"How about another beer," he asked Bernard.

Bernard headed back to the rear of the boat. He steadied himself with one hand on the gunwale and reached down to open the cooler. At the same instant Royce threw the boat into a sweeping turn. The sheer force of the sudden turn pitched Bernard over the gunwale and off the boat. Royce took his time completing the lazy turn and headed back. Bernard had lost his glasses and was waving furiously for help.

Royce circled the boat around his prey just out of Bernard's reach. "Who's the little blonde midnight delight visiting you the other night?" Royce yelled. Bernard glowered at him. He tried to swim to the boat but it kept circling away from him.

"Sonfabitch!"

"Now, now, Bernie Boy. I thought we were friends. Would you like to tell me why your buddy Teagle down at the bank forged my loan application? Did you need a liaison to Sarah that badly?"

Bernard flapped his arms wildly, disappeared underwater for a moment then popped back up. His large roundish head bounced on the water like a bobber. "What the hell is wrong with you?" he blurted.

"Who's Wakipi? What about her and your father-in-law?"

Bernard's eyes went big on the last question. He disappeared underwater again but reappeared in moments. "Get me out of here, dammit. What do you want?" Bernard's pleadings came in short rushes of breath. He'd become less animated. He was tiring. "What do you want?"

"The truth, first of all!"

"Yes, yes, the truth."

"And your promise to leave Sarah alone."

"Anything you want. Get me out of here!"

Royce pulled up close to Bernard. He was too weak to climb up by himself so he helped pull him into the boat.

Once onboard, Bernard leaned over the gunwale coughing up water, trying to catch his breath. His red-faced reflection in the shimmering water resembled the devil. The ghastly sight caused him to recoil. Droplets of water fell from his wet head causing the image to waver then disappear until he saw only himself.

"My glasses, they're gone," he panted.

"You haven't been seeing well for years. Now, talk to me, Bernard."

"Yes, you were our way to get to the Olsen girl. Sarah, I mean. Your troubles with Gina paved the way. The rest we just left to Sarah."

"Ted's bank falsified the loan documents."

"The same bank that is trying to foreclose on the MacNamara Lodge?"

"Yes. That property was to be our 'retirement plan.'"

"What about Wakipi and your father-in-law, Dean?"

"She was his cleaning lady. Once Dean's wife passed the Indian…"

"Poor choice of words, Bernard."

"This Wakipi, she was all over him. Got herself pregnant. Dean offered to pay for a, you know…"

"Yeah, yeah. Go on."

"But the Ind…" he coughed, "Wakipi, wanted to keep the child."

"Sarah Olsen?"

"Yes. Sarah is their daughter." Bernard squeegeed the water from his hair with both hands. His temples throbbed. "So he paid for her to go away. She returned with her child and lived in the area for a few years but was constantly demanding money from him."

"Don't tell me he…"

"She drowned. Boating accident."

"And since she was native Indian no one really investigated that hard?"

Bernard nodded his head. Royce picked up a towel and threw it at him. "Here's what you're going to do. Unless of course you want Grace to find about out your little blonde girlfriend and the Racine County Bank to undergo an embarrassing audit."

Chapter Eight

Gina called the next morning. "When are you coming home? I've got some boxes I need to get down from the attic and I can't do it by myself. What about dinner at Bill and Emily's? Should I tell them we can make it? Royce, the grass is ankle-high already. What's keeping you? Aren't you done working yet?"

Royce finally relented, agreeing to come home tomorrow then called Sarah at work, suggesting they meet up at Big Bob's after work for a bite. He'd picked up the phone twice yesterday to call her but feeling awkward put the phone down. For the first time in his life he didn't know what to say. In a short time Sarah had become a good friend. Saturday evening came along so fast. Too fast?

Then Gina called this morning. Sometimes she sounded suspicious. She was calling him every day now. What kind of debt was she piling up now? He made a mental note when he got home to check the computer history of websites accessed. That way he could tell if she'd been using internet websites to gamble on. Or was she astute enough to delete the history? If it was deleted wouldn't that imply guilt?

BIG BOB THREW a bar rag over his shoulder. His booming voice could be heard throughout the bar. A group of bar patrons surrounded him. "So then Donaldson gets the ball, I clear out the middle linebacker, Herm something…Herm McElroy that's it. Big sonofabitch for a linebacker. Hit 'em low while our tight end, Billy Adams come across and hits him high. The double high-low block was legal back then, not today. They got sissy rules today."

His audience shook their heads in agreement. "Well, McElroy does a complete flip in the air, like a cartwheel. His head is where his feet used to be and his feet are up in the air. This guy must've had size fourteen shoes. When he stood on the chalk yardage markers we couldn't tell what yard line we were on. His damn shoes covered the whole number!"

This drew a roar of laughter from the patrons at the bar who hung on Big Bob's every word.

"So while McElroy's feet are in the air the metal cleat on one of those gunboat-sized shoes cracks Billy Adams right in the mouth. There's blood all over the place. Billy Adams goes to the sideline for a play. Next play he runs back into the huddle and wants to know what the count is. Only we can't understand what he's saying. He can't say 'count'. He opens up his mouth to ask again and we see he's lost three teeth. He couldn't even repeat the snap count let alone the play. Damn if he didn't catch the winning touchdown in the fourth quarter for us though."

"Later that evening at the bar, I asked Billy if it hurt." He says, 'only when I dwink cold beah.' The whole place went crazy with laughter. Here's this giant of a man, tougher than a mile of Wisconsin backroad, talking like a baby!"

There was a lot of guffawing and slapping each other on the shoulder. A few of the old Green Bay Packer players raised their beer mugs in salute to Billy Adams. Others wiped tears from their eyes they were chuckling so hard.

Amidst the commotion Sarah entered. Spotting Royce in a booth she slid in next to him, kissing him on the lips. His return kiss was not as inspired as days ago.

"Something wrong, Royce." She could tell there was.

"Nah, just Gina."

She's lonely again. "When are you leaving?"

"Tomorrow," he said rearranging the salt and pepper shakers. "I'll be back though," he promised.

"When?"

"When I get the grass cut." With this they both broke into laughter.

"Royce," Sarah became serious. "Did we ruin our friendship?"

"God, I hope not."

The only man she'd ever cared for in a lifetime of longing was about to leave her. She couldn't bear to hear his story. The reasons he must leave. The lies about coming back.

A little girl approached their booth. She stopped a couple of feet short of the table. Her long straight hair hung just over her shoulders on the sides, longer in the back. She wore jeans and a pastel tee shirt with a floral design on the front. Bending over to pick something up off the floor, she rose with a shiny quarter.

"Excuse me, but did you lose this?" asked the little girl not more than five years old. Sarah was taken with her simple, pretty looks. She had soft brown eyes, friendly looking. Sarah felt as though she may have seen her before. "What's your name?"

"Anne," she said.

"Anne, what a pretty name. My name is Sarah. Come sit with me and let me see that quarter."

Anne jumped into the booth and sat next to her new friend. Where did she know her from? "No I don't think that's my quarter." Sarah said examining it closely. "But since you found it you may keep it." A cool breeze swept by the table, yet her body felt hot, clammy. But she wasn't sweating.

Her mother's name was Angela. This little girl's name is close to that—Anne. The girl spun the quarter on the table top. They both watched it spin its way around the table, a dazzling hypnotic dance, a momentary trance. Kindred spirits are never far apart. You will not recognize me.

By the time the quarter stopped spinning she realized someone was addressing her.

"I see you got a new friend, Anne," Big Bob said. "This is my grand-daughter," he said to Sarah and Royce.

"I'm sorry," Sarah apologized. I must've been daydreaming."

"Don't apologize. Anne has a way with people."

"Grandpa can I stay with Sarah for a while longer?" Anne asked Big Bob. He loved to see his granddaughter happy and smiling in spite of all that was going on in her life.

"She is a very pretty young lady," Royce said.

"Thank you. She's visiting grandpa for the week. My daughter is getting d-i-v-o-r-c-e-d."

"She's getting divorced," Anne said.

"If it's okay with your Grandpa, then you must let me take you for a pontoon boat ride on Mirror Lake." Sarah wanted to see more of Anne.

Little Anne left reluctantly and only after Big Bob agreed to let Sarah take her for a boat ride later in the week.

"Cute little girl," Royce said.

"Darling," she replied unable to erase Anne's image. Sarah was certain she had felt the spirit of her long lost mother, Wakipi. She needed to see Anne again, just to feel her presence—to realize their destiny together.

"By the way, good news."

"What Royce, what." Was he coming back next weekend? Going to stay another week soon?

"Bernard and the High Council have dropped their lawsuit against you."

Sarah looked at him in amazement. He smiled, the smile she loved.

"You are free to build your pier on Mirror Lake. The DNR will not bother you any longer."

"Oh my god. Royce how could you…"

"Let's just say I had a talk with one of the influential members of the High Council."

Sarah threw her arms around his neck and kissed him not once but twice.

"Whoa, whoa. That's not all. Your friends,the MacNamaras. Their lodge will not be foreclosed on. They may make this month's mortgage payment now and will have until the end of the year to make up any missed or late payments."

Now Sarah was in complete shock. How had Royce done it? She remembered his promise to help but never really thought it possible. He had gone from friend to lover to hero in short time.

Royce explained to Sarah about Bernard's confession.
The High Council did indeed try to strong arm both Sarah and the
MacNamaras so they could build their condominium development on
Mirror Lake. The mortgage on the old Russel cottage had been fixed
so Royce would get the place. He would then be persuaded to inter-
cede on their behalf to make you disappear—one way or the other.
The affair her mother had with Dean Russell had gone bad, very bad.

"Royce, do you think my father could have been responsible for
my mother's death?"

He paused for a moment thinking of how to best answer her
question. "Not that I can prove."

Sarah's complexion went dark with hate. She stewed for moments.
Little could be done without proof. But she was convinced.

Royce removed a box from a bag on the floor. "I want you to have
this."

Sarah took the box in both hands. Could this be the love letters
Royce spoke of? She opened it cautiously, carefully removing one of
the letters. A faint scent of lavender brought a smile to her face. Her
mother had been fond of filling sachets with the dried, pale purple
flowers. Indeed a few bits of the spiked leaves fell from the envelope.

It had been a long time since Sarah had seen that handwriting. The
scrawled signature read—Wakipi. Tears welled up in her eyes. After so
many, many years. A part of her mother would be with her forever. She
pressed the letters to her heart.

"That's not all. There's more."

Sarah opened up a thick manila envelope. She pulled out two
stacks of hundred dollar bills. "Royce, I can't accept this. Who's money
is this?"

"Let's just say it's an inheritance. Should help build your pier and
make those legal fees go away."

Sarah returned the letters and bundles of cash to the box and
closed it. Her fingers lay gently on the box. For all her good fortune
she wore a frown.

"What?" He asked.

"Now I know you'll be leaving."

"Don't be silly. I'll be back," he promised kissing her on the forehead. She thanked him again. He took her hand in his. Royce couldn't help but feel that perhaps Sarah was right, somehow their friendship had forever changed.

Chapter Nine

The next couple of days were busy ones for Royce. His printing business had grown so that just a few days away meant days of overtime ahead. He had adequate help to assist when he was up at Mirror Lake but his customers valued his expertise and knowledge. Who'd have thought that ten years ago when it was just Royce, Gina helping with the books and one employee that the business would expand into larger buildings twice and now employ a dozen workers.

Then there were the never ending homeowner duties he'd come to dread now that he had his cottage on the lake. He came home from work mid-afternoon one day just to cut the lawn. Gina was right. The grass was ankle-high. The lawnmower quit on him a number of times choked by the sheer height of overgrown lawn. Royce promised himself to call a landscaping service the next day. Once finished he went inside for a cold beer. Since Gina had gone shopping for the afternoon, Royce took the opportunity to check the computer's history. To his dismay the history had been deleted. Why Gina? What were you hiding? He decided that rather than confronting her directly it might be better to wait until Bernard had audited their credit card bills. Then he would have proof positive that she was indeed gambling away his hard earned money on the internet.

"Hi honey. The lawn looks beautiful. Did you take off early today?"

Gina said, walking into the kitchen from the attached garage. Thanks to the local tanning spa she'd been able to keep her signature Florida tan year round. Her dark hair was pulled back in a short ponytail. Despite her weathered facial features she still had a great smile and warm brown eyes that drew one closer.

As husband and wife often did, they chose to answer each other's questions with a question of their own.

"No packages. I thought you went shopping. Or is that the UPS truck I see outside?" Royce asked.

Ignoring him, Gina gave her husband a peck on the cheek. "Honey did you call Bill and Emily to let them know we're coming tomorrow night. We've got to get a nice bottle of wine to take with. Emily is making that veal dish of hers you love so much. Oh god, I've got nothing to wear."

"Nothing to wear!?" Royce seemed incredulous.

"Oh nothing fits anymore."

He'd noticed that since he'd been away more lately Gina had put some weight on. She placed her purse in its usual spot, on the chair in front of the computer. "Oh the computer is on. Working from home again, honey?"

Royce seldom worked from home. His business was only three and a half miles away. "No just looking for an outfit for you for Saturday at Chico's online website."

Gina untied the arms of the light cotton sweater she wore over her shoulder, tossed it on a kitchen chair and wrapped her dark arms around her husband. "Now I remember why I married you." She began to kiss him but his cellphone rang.

"Uh, excuse me, I should get this."

"Oh honey, not the office again." Gina retreated to make them some margaritas.

"What! Oh my God! When?" Royce exclaimed.

Gina dropped three ice cubes into the blender but hesitated turning it on, listening intently.

"It's the Racine County Fire Department. My cottage just burned down."

"Oh no," Gina exclaimed. "Is anyone hurt?"

"No, no one's been hurt," Royce repeated the words from the other end to his wife.

"Well, I'll be up right away. What do you mean? There's nothing left?"

"Nothing left?" Gina gasped.

"I see. Thank you Captain. I understand. Yes it is insured. Tomorrow morning then. Thank you. Not as sorry as I am. Thank you again."

Royce sank slowly onto a kitchen chair. "Oh my God. I've lost the cottage. By the time they got there the whole place had burnt to the ground. There's nothing left."

"I'm sorry, Royce." Gina rubbed his neck with her hand. "I know you loved that cottage." She paused for a moment to let her concern linger in the air. "I heard you tell the Captain it was insured, right?"

"Yes. But it will take months and months. The fire department needs to do a routine investigation. The insurance adjustors need time to prepare a claim. Then it'll take months to rebuild it."

Gina approached Royce from behind and began lightly rubbing his temples with her fingertips. "Anything can be rebuilt—in time," she whispered, gently massaging the words into his head until he relaxed. Gina knew how to make him feel good even in the worst of moments.

"So you're going up there tomorrow instead of tonight?"

"The Captain said there is little I can do now. It'd be dark by the time I got there. Tomorrow is fine he said. He's certain the fire has been struck. They've soaked it real well so it won't restart."

"Honey, I don't feel like cooking now. Let's grab a pizza out, okay?" Gina offered him a margarita.

"Yeah, I don't feel like cooking either."

"Good, I'll go change. Give me five minutes."

The margarita tasted good. He wondered about the fire at the cottage. Was it an accident? Or was it the High Council? Bernard sure would have motive. So too would Ted Teagle. But his bank held the mortgage note on the place. Why would he destroy it? And neither Teagle nor Bernard could afford to have him expose them. Was Sarah that upset with Dean Russell that she'd burn the old place down in her mother's memory?

Royce got up to top off his drink. Noticing the computer still on, he walked over to turn it off. Something red glinted in Gina's purse when the monitor flashed off. He reached into the open purse and pulled out a bright red book of matches. On the cover it read, 'Big Bob's Tap—Best Burgers in Wisconsin'.

Train Dreams

The silvery Sky Chief burst through the darkness of the covered bridge into a brilliant pastiche of crimson, orange and golden rays of autumn light. The deafening whistle of the train horn echoed off the mountain walls and rumbled down the tracks announcing its arrival. Inside a motionless engineer guided the train as the cool seasonal wind rustled the short-sleeved shirt arm he casually hung out the window.

At the sound of the horn Mitchell removed the brush from the canvas dipped it into solvent and began wiping it clean on his apron. His paintings hung on the walls of the wealthy, corporate offices and even in some of the smaller galleries that dot the art world. Most were nature scenes awash in brilliant colors, some were young, attractive scantily clad models in Rubenesque poses while others were scenes of sport captured in a slow motion still at the crowning moment of glory. Mitchell Mannion was a burly man, Hemingway-like in stature, with a booming voice and full beard just like Papa, save for the baseball cap he wore to hide his balding head. He'd painted since he was a young boy. He could paint any subject or any scene. Revered as much for his talent as his versatility, all his paintings had one common theme—they celebrated that which was alive. Wherever portrayed, once finished his works took on a life of their own.

But now many once bright primary colors ran together to form a muted brown lagoon—a final resting place for weary shades of pigment. There the oils would harden, resembling the topographical map of a scorched earth state like Texas or Nevada.

"Mitch, gotta run dear," Melba stuck her freshly caked lips out inches from his face. He kissed her automatically on the cheek so as not to mess her paint. "Turn off the heat when you leave, close the blinds and remember to turn off the kitchen light." She'd already retreated toward the front door but continued to address him over her shoulder. "It was on last night again when I got home..."

"Come again," he smiled to himself knowing she heard him but would pretend not to have, not because she didn't want to but because she didn't have time to.

Chapter Two

The clock on the wall read 10:36. Should be at the Centerville Depot in seconds. He glanced out the studio window and saw the Sky Chief riding the shiny rails down from the hills following the bend right below him toward the Depot. Car windows flashed by like stills from a movie camera filled with passengers reading newspapers but never turning a page. Some faced each other as if in intimate conversations but never uttered a word. Others stared out the window with frozen faces.

Model railroads were so much more predictable than real trains. Arrival and departure times were measured not in hours and minutes but in seconds. Mitchell loved precision.

The G-Scale model railroad (G for Garden Scale) outside his studio window took up about 160 square feet of backyard space, all his wife would let him commandeer at this point, and ran on two separate levels. Each rail car measured approximately six inches tall by eleven inches long. The upper level Burlington Northern freight train ran through hills and forests tediously sculpted with his own fingers. It crossed lakes filled with real rainwater atop bridges meticulously crafted from hundreds of tiny brown timbers. Unlike his paintings, the railroad gave him the opportunity to work in a different medium, a different world. The Sky Chief passenger train ran on the lower tracks and was just emerging from a dark tunnel soon to stop at the rustic burgundy colored depot complete with miniature hand-painted passengers glued to cobblestone walks. The train slowed to a stop at the station beneath a semicircular sign, letters yellowed with age that read 'Centerville'. 10:37—right on time, again.

Mitchell dropped his brushes and scurried outside onto the brick patio next to the enormous garden train system. He crept closer and knelt down beside the railway. Midday sun reflected brilliantly off the stainless steel cars. He squinted through the bright light and carefully examined his train. There was something strange about the last passenger car, something wrong. Mitchell carefully lifted the top off car number three and leaned forward to peer inside. Everything looked fine on the upper deck observation seats. All the stiff-backed passengers were still in place and all seats were taken as they usually were since the observation deck afforded such a breathtaking view of the landscape. Removing the upper deck seats, he stuck his nose into the crowded passenger car. Oddly, there was an empty seat at the rear. He peered closer inside.

Mitchell gasped in horror at the scene below him. In the rear where two seat backs faced each other a young woman lay in the aisle. Her legs were akimbo as if broken. A fatal head wound pooled bright blood beneath her. Still, glassy-eyed passengers oblivious to the grisly scene stared aimlessly while others held cellphones and newspapers aloft.

"What happened here?" He reached into the cabin and removed the toy figurine. The woman was young, mid-thirties perhaps, and well-dressed. Her head wound was toward the rear of the skull. Drying blood caked her blonde locks. One leg was broken near the kneecap, as if from a fall. Mitchell wiped the sticky blood from her head with his handkerchief. "This is not good. Not good at all." He hurried into the house and ran the figurine under warm sink water until it was clean. Grabbing a soapy cloth and towel, he cleaned the blood from the floor of the car by sticking his forefinger inside the rag. He toweled the floor in the same manner until it was spotless.

Mitchell sank to his knees holding the lifeless blonde he'd created in his hands. Sad gray eyes stared up at him. Before they had been a steely shade of blue like his father's '56 Buick, a color they didn't make any more.

From somewhere nearby a voice trailed into his consciousness as if a television were on in the background.

"Sorry, Mr. Mitchell. Didn't know about it myself until one of the passengers notified me. We were just outta Turner Junction and almost through the Hillard Tunnel."

The Hillard Tunnel. The words bounded about the synapses of his brain like sparks from a flopping live wire. A tunnel he himself had designed from scratch out of molded fiberglass to withstand the rain and cold. Later painted with earthen shades of browns and greens and decorated with ersatz flora and arbor, it would take the Sky Chief almost thirty seconds to pass all the way through from engine to last passenger car.

"Never shoulda built that tunnel, Mr. Mitchell. First the old man last week and now this poor young woman."

Mitchell snapped his head in the direction of the engine. But the engineer sat motionless eyes focused straight ahead on the tracks in front of him.

Still holding the lifeless blonde figure in one hand he used his free hand to remove a remote control from his shirt pocket. Mitchell squeezed and the train began to pull away slowly from the Centerville station.

A bubble rose in his throat soon to burst. Just last week an elderly passenger had died from something sudden, like a stroke. He could still see the man's pursed lips and bulging eyeballs as he removed him from the train. Now this.

He bent down and pried one of the patio bricks up with his pocketknife. He scooped out a little dirt and laid the blonde woman inside. His fingers trembled as he carefully replaced the brick and smoothed out the surrounding dirt. She would be at peace now. She would find comfort lying next to the old man who had died on the train last week. Mitchell stepped on both the adjacent bricks and with the toe of his shoe brushed away some dirt.

Something was terribly wrong on the Soo Line. In the distance the faint whistle of the Sky Chief rose skyward as the train rounded the bend out of sight.

Chapter Three

"So what are you painting now, dear," Melba said between long drags on her cigarette.

"Please, Mel, I asked you not to smoke in the studio. It corrupts the oils."

She picked up a glass ashtray and smashed her cigarette firmly so he could see it die. He had met Melba in College twenty years ago. They dated for a short time. He'd not dated many women and Melba was by farthest the cutest. She was petite with thin reddish hair that flew about in even the slightest of breezes. A wide mouthful of small but perfectly shaped teeth crinkled her face when she smiled making her narrows eyes seem like slits. Her pale Irish-white skin was lightly freckled. The freckles on the side of her neck formed an unusual pattern. Arranged like a constellation of bright red stars they resembled the shape of a butterfly in flight. Mitchell would kiss her there telling her how beautiful she'd look in his net. Melba insisted the butterfly was elusive and suggested he keep up his attempts. They were married before they graduated.

"It looks like a brown mess. Are you going abstract now?"

"It's not a mess. To have light you must start with dark. The contrast provides the quality of real light."

She placed the ashtray down and fumbled aimlessly inside her purse. "You should've seen all the police and ambulances at the mall today." Her husband silently focused on his work. "Apparently a woman died there this morning."

Mitchell dipped his brush in the wrong oil color and quickly wiped it clean. "Died? How?"

"Fell to her death from a third floor walkway," Melba revealed. "There was a picture of her on the news, blondish hair, kind of pretty.

Thirty-seven years old. Can you imagine?"

"How sad." He kept cleaning the paintbrush.

"Is something wrong, honey? You seem preoccupied."

"No, I just feel uninspired." He rested his brushes and removed the smock he wore. He'd been uninspired for months now. And he found it even harder to work under the glare of Melba.

"Maybe you got painter's block."

"It's writer's block, not painter's block! And how many times have I told you there is no such thing?" Sometimes conversation with Melba left him with a hangover—without the fun of intoxication.

"Suit yourself. That poor girl. This just after that elderly gentleman passed away in Church last week." Melba found her cellphone and left the room. Still rummaging through her purse she grumbled something about needing a larger one. Mitchell muttered something about Samsonite luggage.

They had been at 10:30 Mass last Sunday when a load groan sounded near the rear of the Church. A man collapsed suddenly and died of a heart attack right in the presence of the Lord.

Mitchell's hands shook as he folded his smock. He had forgotten about the old man at Church. How terrifying to die in the Lord's house. "One must be prepared mustn't one?" he'd remembered thinking. And now that young lady at the Mall falls to her death.

He couldn't help but think of the blonde woman on the train. It did appear as though she'd died from a fall. Mitchell decided not to tell his wife that the Sky Chief had departed the Centerville Train Depot one passenger short this morning.

Chapter Four

Melba wasn't happy about having to smoke outside but the patio afforded a comforting view of her flower garden. She had hand-picked each one and coordinated their placement with specific instructions to the landscapers. The petunias, peonies and pansies of summer had long wilted away. Stout bunches of purple, magenta and yellow mums stood at attention, braving the cool Midwestern air like a marching band awaiting an October football game. Across the patio the Sky Chief rested at the Centerville Depot

Between long puffs on her cigarette Melba coughed then smiled to herself recalling their college days. Mitchell had been so dynamic when they'd met, in public and in bed. But after his paintings began to sell he changed. He would paint well into the night and crawl into bed, press his warm fanny against hers and fall asleep. Mitchell had become successful as she knew he would one day. He was so prolific that yet unsold works overflowed their basement and cluttered the attic. They had a beautiful home, a Lexus and a BMW, a summer home in Lake Geneva and a nice investment portfolio with Merril Lynch. She had all this with a pinch of golf and a dash of spa treatments and still found the time to go with shopping with her girlfriends. Mitchell had his paintings and his railroad. He rarely left the house.

"Well Ray, has the time come yet?" she asked.

"Oh, I think so, Melba."

She put her finger to her lips signaling whisper mode lest Mitchell hear them. "He was so distraught over the death of that last passenger I thought he was going to do it right there and then."

"That was brilliant the way you tied her death in with the death of that woman in the mall."

Melba exhaled tiny ringlets of smoke that floated up to linger above her head. "Toppled over that railing right there beside me. I got the idea when I saw how upset he became at the last passenger's death when the old fellow at Church died. Mitchell almost didn't take Communion."

"How much do you think?"

"Well, he's gotta have seventy-some unsold paintings that are worth three quarters of a million dollars now. After, he's dead, who knows, they may bring five to six million."

"N-i-c-e," he said removing his red kerchief and wiping his brow. "I put the gun underneath the bridge."

"Thank you sweet." Melba knelt down and bending her head beside the train engine's window kissed Ray on the cheek.

Chapter Five

Mitchell brought his paints and figurines outside on the patio to bask in the sun-drenched crisp autumn air. He could hear the constant drone of the city trucks sucking up curbside leaves, leaves that they used to burn as children but now vacuumed up. He missed flopping in the leaf piles they raked up as much as he enjoyed lighting them on fire. He would stand mesmerized by the flames until the smell of burning leaves was imprinted on his clothing like campfire smoke.

Since the Sky Chief was a passenger short, Mitchell began painting a new female figurine. The train emerged from the Hillard Tunnel and hissed to a stop at the Centerville Train Depot on schedule. Stooping closer to admire his train he noticed red paint on the side of the engine. Upon closer examination it wasn't red paint at all. It was red lipstick, the same shade Melba wore. Inside the engine window he could see the same red paint on the engineer's face. The engineer sat completely still focusing his attention on the tracks before him as if avoiding Mitchell's fierce glare.

Mitchell sank into his chair staring at the unpainted female figurine before him. It was obvious why Melba was seldom home. His painting had suffered. He'd not finished a work in months.

He began painting the figurine before him. As he worked he thought of all the little innocuous things Melba had said to him recently. They seemed to change in light of her infidelity and took on a life of their own. Some rang untrue and fell upon ears deafened by his disappointment. Others grew more menacing, further fueling the furor within him.

When finished he had painted a fair-skinned woman with reddish hair and crimson painted lips. He had crafted a figurine bearing an amazing resemblance to—Melba!

She rolled her eyes and without the flair of gesticulating with her usual long cigarette, her missing conductor's baton, commanded Mitchell's attention. "So, the once great artist now paints figurines for a living, how lovely." The once alluring freckles on her neck had in her older age migrated to form a constellation resembling a winged bat.

Without hesitation and with the Sky Chief still at rest in the Depot he went to the model railroad and plunged Melba into the mountaintop lake.

"You bastard, don't you dare," she screamed.

"I'm sorry Melba, I know I'm not everything you expected. But this…," he shook his head unable to understand her affair. She fought and flopped crazily as he submerged her under the rainwater filled lake.

"You can't kill me. I'm not real you simpleton! Seconds later it was over. Mitchell pulled the lifeless body of Melba from the water and towel-dried her limp body.

With his pocketknife he loosened a patio brick, scooped out some dirt and laid his cheating wife to rest. He replaced the cold brick and sealed her grave. She would never bother him again.

A despondent Mitchell sank to his knees over her grave. A single teardrop splashed the brick coffin making a clean wet circle in the loose dirt. Somehow, he'd lost the only friend he'd ever had.

"Look under the bridge, Mitchell," Ray's little voice could be heard down below him somewhere.

Spotting a glint of metal underneath the railroad bridge he removed a shiny handgun.

"Do it, do it now. After all, what have you got left? Go ahead and join the entombed," he pleaded.

A deafening explosion rang out. Passengers at the Depot wavered like bowling pins. The echo cascaded down the railroad tracks for miles.

Chapter Six

Mitchell's paintings did indeed bring millions. According to his will, Mitchell Mannion Studios created a special art school for the developmentally disabled. His fame became even more everlasting, mentioned with the likes of Whistler and Rockwell.

Melba, unfortunately, met her end at their summer home in Lake Geneva. She had been cruising the lake in a powerboat celebrating with a male friend that day. A collision with a sailboat sent them both overboard. Melba's drowned body wasn't found until early the next day.

Thanks to an endowment fund established by Mitchell, his original studio home is now available for tours. The Sky Chief is still running right on time. Although Ray's body was never found, a certain barrel-chested, fully-bearded man wearing a hat over thinning hair, leans out the window, waves his hand and with a booming voice yells, "All aboard".

Second Hand Rose

The silver cars of the Metra trains reflected the lines of passengers awaiting like a fun house mirror. Across from the train station sat a quaint resale shop run by the local hospital guild. The mannequins in the window often dressed in clothes from a bygone era and sat in tired furniture. Heirloom teacups were arranged neatly as if the stiff figures were expecting company. In the background, a cackling hi-fi played the tantalizing tunes of Mitch Miller and his band.

The Second Hand Rose resale shop had been a fixture in Hilldale for over two decades. Its current location across from the Metra Station brought in many curious browsers from older folks wishing to reminisce a little to young people interested in the museum-like artifacts.

The 4:35 Metra train steamed into the Hilldale station with its usual bluster of puffy hoses exhaling and dry wheels screeching. A woman in a neat blue suit and clad in pink and white cross trainer shoes departed the train, her brownish hair hiding her face as she remained attentive to the platform steps.

"Good day, Ms. Livingston," the Conductor said, offering his hand.

"Why thank you, Roger. Your wife is lucky to have such a gallant man for a husband," Ms. Angela Livingston replied.

"I remind her of that all the time," he chuckled releasing his hold.

"Are there any more of you around?" she inquired.

"Last of a dying breed, Ms. Livingston."

"Then I shall have to savor this moment."

They both chuckled heartily as Angie bounded across the bricked platform and down the station stairs to the street below. It had been a long day for Angie Livingston. She had started her day in the law offices of Preston, Wallace and McGowan at 7:00 a.m. to prepare for a trial at 1:00 that afternoon. At 11:00 a.m. a belated birthday card from her ex-husband, David, had arrived in the morning mail. They had been divorced over two years now. When they met David had been an assistant district attorney then and Angie a rookie lawyer with her current firm. They had been adversaries on many a case in the beginning. Then a mutual respect for each other had led to lunch which led to dinner which led to bed. They had had a uneventful seven year marriage before she'd found out about David's affair. Soon they were before a judge and unmarried unceremoniously and left to follow their separate careers. It wasn't sad, it wasn't bad, it's just the way it is, she figured. Nothing lasted forever. Most of her married girlfriends were just staying in their relationships for fear of the unknown. It's a jungle out there and with AIDS and everything…they rationalized. Life went on— somehow.

Why had he sent her a birthday card? She had celebrated her birthday alone in her condominium with a bottle of cabernet last weekend. Must he torment me on my most vulnerable of days, she sighed. Birthdays had stopped being fun for Angie long ago. David had been five years younger than she and that fact often pained her.

She threw her attaché over her shoulder and purse on top of it as she stepped to the street. Schiller Street was one of the narrower streets in downtown Hilldale. It was squeezed between the overhanging roof of the train station and the green canopies of the little shops on the sidewalk allowing for diagonal parking on the shop side and only a slight lane for one-way traffic to edge by. Little sunlight ever reached the skinny street even at midday.

Angie swept by the Red Dragon Mandarin Restaurant she liked and managed to avoid her favorite stop, Katrina's Bakery, before coming to a pause in front of the teaparty in the window of Second Hand Rose. Something queer struck her as if perhaps she saw her mother and her club sitting down to tea. Mrs. Audy and Mrs. O'Connell were there and of course, the obsequious Mrs. MacCormack and her haughty pearl necklace where there too. Others knocked on the door and entered to the din of chatter and laughter.

Curiosity amid a fog of nostalgia made her open the heavy glass door and enter the store for the first time. Weary antique furniture stood guard over numerous sets of wine glasses, dinner plates and dessert dishes. Clothing once worn by live people waited anxiously to be adopted and taken home. Wood grained television sets that had once ushered in the advent of game shows and soap operas stood finely polished if nothing else to make good end tables should a graying doily cover the circular stain left by a forgotten manhattan glass. Saddest of all were all the empty shoes. Some had tread many miles in pursuit of happiness. Others had found it and danced long into the night. Many appeared at a wedding or anniversary party or some gala event and were never worn again, their one fleeting shot at fame disappearing.

It was here that Angie stopped to pause. A pair of black Angeloni pumps had caught her eye. She'd always been partial to alligator design. The pumps suited her figure better, high heels made her appear too tall. And the alligator lent a sort of wild outdoorsy look to her long thin ankles and strong calves. Wiping off the dust with a tissue from her purse she wondered if they would fit the size number having long ago worn off.

She slipped the Angeloni alligator pumps on thrilled to find they fit perfectly. What were the chances of that? A warm sensation emanated from her feet up through her legs.

"Where did you find those?" asked the clerk behind the counter. She squinted at the alligator shoes through a pair of horn-rimmed glasses that tapered up and out in the corners like old movie star glasses. The rhinestones on the side glinted brightly despite poor light of the store. Obviously she shopped at her own store, Angie thought to herself.

"Oh, with the other shoes, under a layer of dust."

"I'm sorry dearie, there's only the two of us here." She bobbed her blackish grey hair in the direction of a woman stooped over a Zenith radio attempting to tune in a station but mostly tuning in loud static.

"Not to worry. You have to find treasure. It doesn't come delivered."

"Honey, when you get to be my age, nothin' comes delivered."

They laughed at their own humor amid smiles and pleasantries like folks do who share dreams of treasures found and treasures lost.

Angie slung her attaché and purse over her shoulder and carried the bag with her newfound shoes carefully in her free arm.

Once at home in her condominium she dumped her attaché and purse on the sofa table, turned off her cell phone and checked her answering machine. As she always did Angie sat on the end of the couch that afforded her a view out the balcony windows of her second floor unit and propped her feet up on a small ottoman. A cool breeze floated in and ran along the floor.

She just had to try the alligator pumps on. They looked good in the natural light she thought. Her toes tingled with warmth. Perhaps they were a half size too small she considered. The warmth rose up through her calves and deep into her slender thighs. She hadn't remembered a pair of shoes ever being so comfortable.

Angie closed her eyes momentarily. She began to think of David. David hadn't been a bad husband, but he hadn't been a terrific one either. They hadn't been real close but they were good friends. He had a good job, treated her well and always brought home a cheerful disposition no matter what case he was working on that day. He'd always been quiet around the home preferring to read rather than engage in conversation. She'd endeavored at first to talk to him more thinking if she got him to talk it would be good therapy. But she finally gave up and was happy to sit with him through the evenings in friendly silence. Sometimes silence spoke volumes.

Chapter Two

"Well hello, kind sir," she said dumping her overloaded satchel on a nearby desk.

"Sir?" David replied inquisitively looking around behind him as if there were others in the room.

"That would be you, sir. Maureen. Maureen Wilkins at your service. I'm the new Assistant D.A."

Maureen Wilkins was the newest assistant district attorney for the county. She had just graduated from law school and gotten her position due to a kind word from an uncle who was an appellate court judge.

Maureen extended her hand and David shook it politely. Bright red hair framed a swarthy complexion. A thin patrician nose lay hidden behind studious, thinly framed glasses. David felt the glasses got in the way of her sharp, almost masculine facial features. When she spoke her thin red lips stretched tightly across her perfectly shaped teeth. He'd always admired perfect teeth. It indicated to him a noble upbringing.

"Sir David, if you insist."

They worked a large caseload together often helping each other out when a trial date loomed near. Maureen enjoyed working with David and as senior D.A., looked up to him.

She and her husband Mark had been over to the Livingston home for barbecue dinners frequently the first year she worked in the D.A.'s office. Mark was an advertising executive with a large firm in the city. He had a vast array of jokes with which to entertain the four of them and seemed never to run out of material. Angie in particular laughed for hours on end at Mark's own brand of humor.

When Angie left the patio to prepare coffee Mark offered his assistance in cleaning up. She rested her hips on the kitchen sink to fill the coffee pot with water. Mark set a pile of dishes in the sink and brushed up against her.

"You look positively gorgeous tonight, my dear."

"Why thank you Mark."

"No I mean really sharp, really happy. What has David been feeding you?" Angie felt his hip against hers. Was it just the wine or was it intended.

"Mango and other exotic fruits," she teased.

"Tango? Its my favorite," he said placing a nearby rose in his teeth. "Shall we?" Mark placed his arm around her slender hips and with his free hand raised Angie's other hand high in the air. She giggled coyly as Mark pressed closer. She could smell the warm, sweet fruitiness of wine on his vapory breath as he delicately placed the rose stem into her mouth. She felt the intoxicating mixture of wine and laughter awash inside her like a powerful aphrodisiac.

"Oh Zorro, I've heard so much about you."

They spun out onto the patio and made a grand appearance to the hoots and hollers of David and Maureen.

"David, I believe your wife just called me a Zero."

"Nonsense Mark, surely you're a Ten," David assured him.

The four of them toasted Mark as a ten while the flicker of candles swayed in the night breeze. The awkward light reflecting at all angles illuminated their smiles like painted stage faces. With empty wine bottles underfoot David and Mark cradled their arms around each other's neck and sung their college fight songs making up their own hilarious, inebriated verses as they went along. Angie and Maureen shed tears of laughter at the two men acting like boys.

Angie liked Mark, who wouldn't, he was the life of the party. He was warm and romantic and unlike David, outgoing and fun. These were evenings not spent in friendly silence.

It was sometime during this first year that the Mark and Maureen stopped coming over as much. David and Maureen had both been working late hours with the county's budgetary problems spilling over into the judicial system. Mark also had been working on a high priority project at the agency for months on end.

Chapter Three

The next day Angie departed her train and again found herself staring blankly in the window of Second Hand Rose. She felt herself pulled into the shop my some unimaginable force propelling her with passion beyond restraint. The shop's musty odors greeted her at the door. Wine glasses clanged in toast to each other. Antique mirrors reflected past visitors dressed in funny, quaint clothes.

Angie drifted over to a nearby clothing rack looking through a variety of empty dresses neatly arranged for display. Most of the dresses lay flat against one another as if the body that once lived inside was insignificant. Others stood out happily separated from those near it as if recently worn. She found a couple she liked and tried them on in a poorly lit dressing room. One in particular looked very smart on her. It was a sexy, strapless black chiffon cocktail dress which gave her a sophisticated party look. It fit her just perfectly. How unique that people in another life could be so similar in size. Well, that was her good fortune. And it would go nicely with her Angeloni pumps.

A wheezy man with disheveled grey hair boxed her new dress behind the counter. "Very pretty. A new dress has a way of changing a person wouldn't you agree? Gift wrap for this ma'am?"

"Oh no, thank you. It's for me."

"All the more reason to gift wrap it. It's not often we find something we like. Kind of makes it special," he looked up at her with his head cocked sideways and smiled wryly at Angie. Although the store light fixtures were old and yellowed she thought she saw a glint of light reflected in the man's eye.

"That's so kind of you, sir. But please do hurry, I've got to run." The clerk made her nervous.

"Oh, nothing at all. I used to be in a hurry too." Angie looked at the queer man sidling around the boxed dress, taping and cutting.

Angie left Second Hand Rose cheerfully cognizant of having angled another nice deal for herself. The boxed dress swung in arcs as she skipped toward her car. Although it was a sunny day, she removed her sunglasses so as to see better on the shady street. She tossed her bags and boxed dress into the backseat and drove out into the bright afternoon sun. Soon Angie drifted off into the post work oblivion that idle time behind the windshield gives birth to.

A silver four door sedan swerved in front of her, braked and made an abrupt right hand turn. She swung her SUV to the left just missing the rear bumper of the silver car. Her attaché, purse and shoe bag in the back careened forward striking the back of her seat.

"Asshole!" she screamed at the sedan through her open passenger window. She followed that with a ubiquitous hand signal of her own. "Dammit, is everyone in a hurry to die?"

Chapter Four

Success! Angie spun triumphantly in the full-length mirror before her. The alligator pumps and black chiffon dress went together perfectly! It would be just the thing for the firm's cocktail party next Saturday evening. She turned sideways and lifted her bare shoulder slightly higher and with her other arm raised her hand to push her long straight hair upwards off her neck. She looked smart and sexy.

Feeling good about herself Angie opened the refrigerator and poured a glass of chardonnay. She relaxed on the couch and fixed her gaze out the sliding glass doors. The wine cooled her sensations subtly. Soon a warm glow emanated from her feet through her legs and washed over her entire body pouring down her arms and out her fingertips. Perhaps she should turn on the air conditioning. She fidgeted in her seat pulling and tugging at the dress as if maybe it was too confining. Her bare arms felt clammy. The chardonnay, she wondered. Angie found herself unable to think of anything but him again.

When David came home and found her sitting on the couch looking out her favorite window he crept up behind her quietly. He gently lifted the hair on the back of her head and bent down to kiss her neck. Reaching for her wine glass on the endtable, he bent down and touched the cool glass to her bare shoulder and slid it deftly across her neck over to her other shoulder. Angie moaned and rolled her head back over the cool area. She felt his cool wine tongue on her neck. Soon it curved itself around the folds of her burning ear and penetrated inside.

"Whoever you are, don't stop," she pleaded.

"Whoever I am, I'm pretty good," David whispered arousing her with his wickedness.

"Please, have your way with me."

"If I insist," he reached around her from behind and slid his hand down the front of the dress between her breasts. "Your time has come," he warned.

"And come I have," she replied. "Oh my," Angie exclaimed jumping up from her wet seat. She held her wine glass high as it dripped everywhere. There was a puddle on the couch next to her and her lap was wet. Quickly she dabbed up the mess, kicked her shoes off and ran to the bathroom to remove and spot her new dress.

"Damn him!" she said.

Chapter Five

It was Thursday, two days before the firm's cocktail party. The parties were so much fun. All of the firm's big clients would be there and oft times some of the town's more noteworthy politicians and philanthropists attended. David hated the pomp and circumstance of such affairs and always angled to leave early.

Angie had a wonderful outfit picked out now but still needed a finishing touch. A black evening purse would be nice.

"Over there honey, next to the umbrellas," an elderly woman behind the counter at Second Hand Rose pointed. Unlike other items in the store the handbags were piled haphazardly as if dumped on the table by the boxload. This should be much easier than choosing a dress or shoes she thought. Angie rummaged through the pile tossing unlikely candidates aside before finally finding a black patent leather clutch. It was longish in style, longer than it was in height and quite nice. She turned it to and fro trying to see if it was still shiny but the store offered little light.

"Will that be all ma'am," a woman's wrinkled hands pulled the purse across the counter to be bagged.

"Oh, I don't know. I thought that would be all last time I was in here to buy the dress," Angie admitted.

"Once you have the purse, that should be all you'll need," the old woman handed her the bag. The gold fillings in her mouth twinkled along with her smile.

Once home Angie couldn't resist trying on her new outfit. A cup of green tea might be nice. She filled the teapot on the stove and turned on the burner. Quickly she slithered into the chiffon dress and alligator pumps. The patent leather purse reflected brilliantly in the natural light. Surely she would be stunning Saturday evening. She made a mental note to make an appointment to have her hair done Saturday. Something upswept would be appropriate.

Angie poured herself a cup of green tea and sat down. She felt too dressed up for green tea though. Rising, she poured the tea down the drain and opened up a split of champagne from the refrigerator. Ah, much better. Thank you sir, she said raising her glass up for another refill. She batted her long eyelashes twice in thank you and turned to walk away. Angie watched herself glance seductively over her shoulder in a nearby mirror to see if he'd been staring.

Tongues of heat surged through her limbs and into her body. She hadn't felt this way from champagne before. Beadlets of perspiration formed on her arms and forehead. Her fingers tightened their grip on the purse. Placing the champagne glass down she opened the sliding glass doors to cool herself off. It was hard to open with only one hand free. The purse swung wildly as she yanked on the obstinate door. Finally a rush of cool air blew in. Angie walked out onto the small patio and leaned on the railing. She felt warmer now and her head began to spin. Too young for the dreaded hot flashes, wasn't she?

His image pervaded her senses. She found it too strong to ward off. David hadn't been able to make it that evening two years ago she recalled.

Chapter Six

It was a Saturday evening two years ago. The firm's cocktail parties were in their infancy and weren't as leviathan yet as they would become yet they were well attended, fun and usually lasted into the wee hours of the morning. David had begged off attending this time as he was engulfed with work. He'd been working long hours as the courts became backlogged due to recent budget cuts mandated by the county.

"Oh David, must you…" she pleaded.

"Angie, I told you the pressure we're under here."

"Can't you just come for a while."

"I can't come at all. You go and have a good time."

"Okay, I understand;" she didn't really understand. It was the third time this month David had had to work late again. Usually he came home after midnight on those days. She knew because he would kiss her cheek gently before falling fast asleep.

Preston, Wallace and McGowan cocktail parties were the toast of the town. They spared no expense for their clients, partners and staff. Pretty hostesses in short skirts offered trayfuls of hors d'oeuvres and appetizers. Stiff backed waiters carried dozens of fluted glasses filled with champagne to and fro a spectacular champagne fountain. Statuesque ice sculptures shaped like zoo animals sweated amongst their guardians like captured prey.

By the time Angie had made it through the hour long receiving line she was exhausted. Time and time again she had been asked where David was or why he couldn't be there.

He couldn't be there because he and Maureen were working late hours this month she repeated to herself, trying to make it sound plausible. She felt so alone sometimes as if the men avoided her for fear of neglecting their ever vigilant wives while in the company of an attractive single woman. The wives purposely ignored her out of jealousy. This gala evening had been so important to her. She looked marvelous yet felt so lonely.

Not wanting to look alone, Angie got in the buffet line. Two chefs with tall white caps carve up a large beef torso and turkey carcass their sharp shiny knives flashing business under the glare of warming lamps. They chose their weapons from an array of knives. Some were used for thinly slicing the most tender meat while others were better for cutting around the bone and some better for cutting through the bones.

"...working on a Saturday night, tsk—tsk," came the cackle of a gossipy woman somewhere back in the line.

"Oh he's working alright..." she heard the whispering.

The giggling incensed her. Angie circled away from the carving station a couple of steps toward the rear of the line and managed to stumble beside the two figurine women, spilling her whole plate of roast beef and bloody juice all over their flowing dresses. The women shrieked and in backing away knocked over the carving station. Heat lamps, knives and carrion lay astrew on the floor.

"Forgive my clumsiness," Angie said aloud to no one in particular, especially the two women wearing au jus and gravy formals. In a meek effort of assistance, she bent to help the chefs and bustling workers clean up.

But she had heard enough. She'd been deserted by David and now was the laughingstock of the firm's party. With hurried goodbyes to those who mattered, Angie summoned her car and drove off quickly her car engine screaming into the night.

Chapter Seven

Angie pushed her car past the speed limit headed toward David's office. It was still early she thought. He wouldn't expect her.

She slowed her dark SUV to a crawl as she passed the County Building where the District Attorney's office was. All the lights were out. She drove around the back of the building to the parking lot only to find it vacant. Angie sat for a moment. A warm sensation coursed through her veins and circled aimlessly in her body. She began to sweat. Her breaths became shorter and shorter. The face in the rear view mirror which had looked so pretty earlier in the evening was now eerily contorted and menacing. She began to sweat profusely. Strands of her upswept hair had fallen and lay matted to the back of her neck.

Angie gunned the car to its next destination, Mark and Maureen's house. She knew what to expect. After all she had put up with his excuses and stories long enough. She pulled the car into the drive slowly and quietly with the headlights off. Maureen's car was nowhere to be seen but David's silver BMW was parked outside in front of the garage. Angie reached into her long black patent leather purse and removed a carving knife hidden in a white cloth napkin. It hadn't been difficult purloining the weapon in all the confusion she created with her 'accident'. She had simply dropped a the napkin over one of the knives, scooped it up innocently and placed it into her purse.

She knew from many barbecues that Mark and Maureen usually left the sliding glass doors on the deck open for ventilation. Her black chiffon dress and alligator pumps looked so dressy in the reflection of the floor length doors. Usually she would be on the deck drinking and laughing clad in shorts and flip-flops. Like the black robes of justice punishment was best served in one's finest clothes.

Angie crept up the stairs delicately a step at time one hand on the banister for support the other clutching the knife. Upon reaching the closed master bedroom door she drew a deep breath and burst into the room.

The room was lit only by moonlight filtered through vertical blinds striping the room with alternating rays of white light and black bars that made it look like the inside of a cell. David sat up in bed startled by her entrance.

"Angie?" he peered through thin shafts of light.

"Where is she? Where is Maureen?" she asked.

"She's gone for the weekend," he answered meekly. A half empty cocktail glass sat on the opposite nightstand nearest Angie.

"Bullshit!" Angie crossed over to the bed raised the knife above her head. David cowered covering his face with his hands. She plunged the knife deeply into the pile of sheets and pillows beside her husband.

She plunged it again and again.

"For God's sake, Angie," David pleaded.

The sound of tearing sheets were met with a volcanic spewing of white goose feathers high into the air between them. There was no one else in the bed she realized.

The bathroom door swung open. "What's all the commotion?" a figure appeared in the doorway.

Angie gasped and dropped the knife beside her in horror. Before her and larger than life, stood the naked body of Mark. She looked to David in shock.

"Angie, it's nothing…"

"WE'RE NOTHING!"

Mark realizing the awkwardness of the moment took a step forward. "It's just fun, Angie, you understand."

"IT'S NOT ALL FUN, MARK!" She screamed.

Angie covered her mouth and with one long last look at her husband a single tear ran down her cheek and onto her fingers.

That was the last time she had seen David save for the two court appearances necessitated by the divorce proceedings. Now his birthday card to her lay atop a pile of unopened mail.

"Oops," she had caught her foot between the narrow railings on the balcony. One of her pumps had come loose and dangled precariously in the air. She reached over, grabbed the alligator shoe and pulled her leg inside the bars.

Returning to her bedroom she removed the other pump and her dress and slipped into a comfortable flowered top and pair of slacks.

Angie folded the dress up neatly, placed the alligator pumps on top and then with the black evening purse in hand, this time disposed of them properly—in the garbage can.

She recalled seeing an old Raggedy Anne doll similar to the one Mother had given her as a child, in the window of Second Hand Rose. That doll had given her such joy and pleasure as a young girl growing up. Come Monday she would go down there and buy that doll. After all, things are usually better the second time around.

Disappearing

I'd met her in what now has become a quite commonplace way to meet the other sex but a much different way than what I was used to. How do we usually meet people? We tell our friends we are either bored with our current lover or the relationship is headed nowhere or we just don't share the same ideals. Then your friends, either out of sympathy or some abject sense of propriety for those of theirs who are available introduce you to each other. I met her much the same way I did you, my mysterious friend, through a chat room on the internet.

Another message from his mysterious friend flashed before him on the computer screen drawing his attention.

"How nice for you. I'd love to hear more about her."

We met at Rotini's the swanky Italian eatery near the riverwalk. We were able to get a table nearest the window that looked down upon the gurgling river. It had rained all day and the river was swift, carrying with it vestiges of life: paper cups, beer cans and shards of Styrofoam floated down below. I had froglegs. She had angel hair pasta with broccoli. We shared a bottle of Chardonnay and for dessert— creme broule. I watched her delicately raise the spoon to her mouth, wrapping her fine painted lips around each mouthful and removing slowly without a trace of dessert or lipstick on it.

Sure, sure I drink too much. Tell me something new. You're beginning to sound far away. You are beginning to fade away before me. To my surprise she ordered the same after dinner drink I did, a snifter full of Grand Marnier. We toasted to nothing special as we were both lost single souls in a city full of sinners. If not her than another pretty face with a story to tell would be by soon. But she was different. Neither my usual penchant for heavy drinking before dinner or crass humor after could turn her off.

"To our stars," she raised her glass.

She didn't have a particularly notable voice but it began to grow raspy from the orange flavored cognac we shared. Her words seemed barely above a whisper when so guttural as if they were meant for no other ears than mine. I found myself leaning forward across the table to better hear her luscious tones. It was then that I smelled her for the first time. The closer I got, the sweeter she smelled. It wasn't the fruity scent of some cheap perfume but rather flowery and delicate. As she leaned forward to clang our snifters in a silent eye-only toast her tight blouse buckled forward and revealed her the top of her tanned breasts and further down, the milky white skin untouched by sun.

"To all the stars that are ours," I said raising my glass.

I knew she was interested in me but as to why I was confused. Usually these meetings ended about now with me picking up the check and her insisting she had a nice time after a peck on the cheek. I'd call a few days later and some machine would thank me for calling and would never call back. But this one wouldn't let go.

My, oh my, how special we are. Did either of you have any idea at this point?"

Neither of us had any idea. She was my first. We ended up going to an old Irish pub on the other side of the river. We walked slowly, occasionally nudging into each other as if to gauge the response from such an inebriated sashay. By the time we reached the Pub her hand was wrapped in mine. I mentioned the warmth in her fingertips and she spread her hand out making sure I felt each thin bony finger one at a time. In the next hour or so we split a bottle of Merlot and two glasses of champagne. Later that night we ended up at her apartment. Only, it wasn't an apartment at all. It was one of those condos that had been transformed into presumptuous modern living quarters by installing a loft above the living quarters as if one could appraise their lifestyle from above and make smart decisions based on what they saw below.

We made love all night, three or four times I think. I don't remember. She was everything a man could want—tigress enough to challenge even the most creative of men yet able to run her slippery tongue gently through every fold of my ear until hair I didn't even know I had spiked. Finally, we lay exhausted in each other's arms dripping wet, without a breath to give knowing that we each had visited a special place where others only feared to go.

"How romantic. She sounds very special. Some say the first time is the best."

I visited with her many more times that month. Usually at the Pub or her loft or my apartment. We had an affinity that I've never felt before. In a frightening sort of way she seemed to know what I was thinking when she held my hand in hers. I felt her probing intuition as if a palm reader were tracing my hand. Oftentimes not knowing is better. When you can read someone you read all the book, not just the good chapters but those that disturb and keep one from their sleep. She may have felt that reading my book was like reading the Marquis de Sade, a tale told best at night in hushed tones. It was then that I knew she was the one.

She really had no family to speak of. Sometimes it's better that way. She never spoke of any close friends. Even the wheezy bartender from the old Pub who liked watching us fondle each other in the dark corner booth stopped asking about her after a month or two. I can still smell her sometimes when the wind gently brushes the lilac bushes below my apartment window.

"Nice. I always like listening about the first one."

Chapter Two

The small city Makanda police station was serene this particular morning. Gone were the many squad cars and tiny three legged golf carts driven by meter maids. Gone were the swarm of sweaty police officers drenched from the weight of their Kevlar vests and neatly attired attorneys attempting to pry loose an assorted clientele of shoplifters and intoxicated motorists.

The station, built in the early 1920's originally served as a railway station and was easily the largest building in the old part of town. Its red brick and large arched entranceways once welcomed fast-paced commuters and weary travelers from the big city to the east called Brownsville. The Makanda Depot had been the last stop on the line for years until Turner Junction to the west sprung up suddenly years ago.

Twenty seven years on the force had weathered Sergeant Teddie Armstead. He'd seen his share of good men come and go some moving up the ranks eventually promoted and moving on to Brownsville. He'd celebrated their weddings and their kids' birthdays and even tipped a few at Miller's Bar to help celebrate their divorces. He'd lost fine officers in the line of duty only to take the long horse drawn carriage ride down a rose petal littered Main Street to Elm Lawn Cemetery.

The commissioner had told him that funding had finally been approved for a new division. And Makanda was going to be the site of this pilot project. A high tech unit was going to be established and staffed by two highly recommended recent graduates of the Academy.

"Welcome boys. Your office is down the hall first door on the left." Teddie said begrudgingly.

A single light bulb swinging from a frayed cord dimly lit the stairway before them. Two steps down the musty smell of deserted steamer trunks and wooden pushcarts greeted the lads. It was then they realized they were headed down to old Station basement. The laughter of the veteran officers cascaded down behind them punctuated by Teddie Armstead's guffaw.

"Don't come up 'til you catch those dirty rats." Another even louder roar of laughter followed as they swept away the cobwebs in their path.

The next two months saw a remarkable transformation of the old railway station as it was given a new heart surging with electronic energy. Utility trucks parked outside ushered in miles of wires and lines. Cartloads of computers, listening devices and code encrypters paraded by Sergeant Teddie Armstead's desk daily. All the while he struggled with his own budget constraints having had to recently put two of the officers on part-time duty.

Below in the basement two young men barely old enough to be his sons toiled with toys. The two plain-clothed detectives hunched over their computer, their youthful faces bathed in the illumination of a blue screen.

"Nice job, Preston. That's the third one this month you've hooked," said the taller of the two. Brendan McAllister was meant to be a cop. His grandfather had been a policeman during the country's dark Prohibition era. Many a night after the rest of the family had left the dinner table. His grandfather would regale Brendan with tales of the great Elliot Ness and his band of federal agents who became infamously known as the Untouchables. Untouchable because the long fingers of the syndicate could not reach out to bribe or influence them. They were a handpicked crew of dedicated law enforcement professionals in the most violent of times. Brendan, just a young lad then, would listen for hours as his grandfather told his police tales with the greatest of detail as if he were reading from his dog-eared notepad turning each page slowly with fingers rough and cracked from years of handling his service revolver.

"Thanks. Now how do we reel him in?" his partner said. Preston Sheridan was seated in front of the computer rubbing his chin in thought. Not quite as shrewd as his friend and partner, Preston had graduated near the top of this class from the academy and had majored in computer technology. His round wire-rimmed glasses paid testimony to the countless hours spent reading his training manuals which he found boring anyways and myriad of time spent peering into his computer screen for new methods to apprehend criminals. His day was spent searching databases, criminal records and local crime statistics. He had been hand picked by the Commissioner, over the objection of the skeptical Sergeant Armstead and his peers to head up the department's new crime unit, Operation Tech Trap or what the other officers called Operation Rat Trap.

"I believe it's time we convened our first meeting of this exclusive club, don't you think?" Brendan suggested.

"Excellent idea, Watson," Preston replied with a smirk.

Operation Tech Trap had their first real line at cracking a group of individuals who had one thing and only one thing in common—the unique ability to make people disappear, permanently.

Chapter Three

Preston's gaze returned to the computer screen before him as yet another suspicious message appeared. He relished the thought of playing interested listener to another confessor. The unsuspecting feared nothing thinking they were wrapped in the cloak of anonymity and secrecy. As he had hoped their weird tales would become their downfall. His eyes, fish-bowl sized behind thick glasses, riveted on the newly received text.

I do my thing at the health club three days a week. I like to work out after work because I spend a lot of time in my car commuting and the club kind of kills the rush hour. When I work out I try not to dress too hot. I used to wear tight spandex pants, a low-necked top with spaghetti straps and a sport bra but I noticed that within 10 minutes of my usual routine there would always be three or four guys working out right next to me, please. Now I just wear a long t-shirt that hangs down past my butt and a baseball cap with my hair tucked up underneath so I can go about my business without having to make eye contact with the self-infatuated, leering, hard bodies.

"That would certainly make me queasy," Preston egged her on.

This one guy though made me feel more than queasy. He made me feel creepy. He always jogged around the oval track that circled the fitness area slowly enough to stare. Occasionally, I would peep out from underneath my baseball cap and steal a look around the steely machines. He seemed to always be interested in me. Now most men are sneaky when trying to watch you. They are always careful to avert their eyes or smile innocently when caught. Not this guy though. He was damn blatant about it. His face had a faraway, wounded type of look like maybe he'd been in a terrible car accident that left his face permanently tilted sideways. Or perhaps he was just a slow-thinking mouth breather. Whenever I'd catch his furtive glances it made my perspiration smell like sweat.

After finishing my workout I stopped by the tanning place in the strip mall. I find it relaxing after a nice workout to slap on some headphones and treat my bod with some soothing heat while cool jazz floats in my head. Damn if I didn't see this creep from the club in my rearview mirror drive past my car. Could he have been following me? No, the strip mall is a busy place. Lots of people cruise in and out of there all day long.

"So the man from the health club took quite a fancy to you, did he?"

Later on at home I took a quick shower to rinse off the sweat and sun oil. I loved the way the coconut oil covered up the apprehension of my sweat and made what had been the stink of fear into a breezy tropical scent. Soft plushy towels dabbed away the goosebumps raised by the icy air conditioning like cotton balls. I stood in front of the vanity mirror and admired my hard-earned golden body. Long thin arms framed a slender torso outfitted with tight abs and smallish but not too small breasts. Anyhow big breasts got in the way all the time. Some of the bigger breasted women jogged around the track at the club with their boobs bouncing like circus clowns performing a juggling act. No thanks.

I leaned forward into the mirror to study my face. I looked good for my age. Sharp bony features kept my skin stretched tightly. I peered a little closer looking for the first signs of the dreaded wrinkles that had so distinguished my mother's face. But she was a smoker and like most smokers she had the telltale mouth and lip wrinkles that would never disappear. I would never have to worry about that. My tanned legs were long and slender yet muscular from my workouts. I rubbed cream generously over my rough feet calloused by hours of kickboxing class and speedbag drills.

I raised my other foot up on the vanity stool to apply cream and thought I heard a soft rumble like the sliding glass doors of my bedroom opening. Into my bedroom from the outside deck strode the creep from the health club. He peered at me from one side of his face. A slight smiling sneer belied his excitement. His large, big-knuckled hands were trembling.

"How did he find you there? What did you do?"

After I thought I spotted him at the mall I made sure I drove home along the simplest route and made my way nice and slow. It'd taken him a while to find his way to the rear sliding doors outside my bedroom. He'd probably been in his car working up the courage to come in or playing with himself or both all the while his big leathery hands working furiously while I leisurely showered.

"What a delicious situation, do tell me more."

I pirouetted across the room, the leathery feet of my sculpted legs swinging head high in vicious arcs like a helicopter blade. The single eye I could see opened wide in anticipation of my naked arrival. Just like the others who had come, he wouldn't be missed. And we'd all be safer for it.

Chapter Four

People in the small town of Makanda had been quietly disappearing: faceless, nameless individuals who didn't show up for work one day, blank personalities who missed appointments, luncheons and get-togethers, new residents who'd yet to make themselves known, visitors who would never be known. Like pawns in a chess game their disappearance was neither noticed nor recorded.

Those who operate surreptitiously under the cloak of darkness and secrecy all share one mysterious trait. Like stars and all-stars, they all seek attention and acclaim. Like skilled artisans who practice their craft in the lonesome anonymity of their own shop they all want to put their signature on each work of art they create. They drink from the cup of vanity, seduced by immortality.

Detectives Preston Sheridan and Brendan McAllister had pierced this web of danger only to find these creatures stranger than they'd ever expected. Preston had hit on a wonderful scheme of attracting deviate personalities to his website. Get them to talk about themselves and their craft. Develop a relationship with them. Show an appreciation for them and their work. Talk in terms of other's interests.

But it was Brendan who'd hit upon the idea of inviting them to a meeting. A get-together of masters would appeal not only to their professional interest but would also feed their incessant egos. Who knows what could be learned from others of the same craft let alone what delicious stories could be told. None of the suspects had yet incriminated themselves to the detectives. All that was known was that people in town had been disappearing.

The meeting had been set for 7:00 p.m. that evening. They had selected Montana Charlie's, an all night bar and grill on the outskirts of Makanda as the meeting place. It's rough and tumble crowd of pool hustlers and bikers seemed the perfect backdrop to frame their plan. It had rained most of the day and by evening showed no signs of letting up. The faint glow from the red neon sign atop the bar cast an eerie hue across the rain-soaked parking lot. Cars whisked through the gravel lot each puddle pothole shooting sprays of water high in the air. The droplets fell lazily back to the black watery floor once again reflecting the red-lettered sign above, the quiet scene disturbed only by the next motorist, the whole dark picture replaying itself again and again.

Outside the bar and at the far corner of the building the lone figure of a man draped in a dark rain slicker and black hat smoked a cigarette. Across the street and halfway down the block, Preston and Brendan watched closely as the man chain lit another cigarette and rubbed the old butt out with his shoe.

Preston removed his glasses and used his handkerchief to wipe them clean. "I still think we should have let Sergeant Armstead in on this."

"Sure. We'd still be stuck in the basement of the station while Sergeant Armstead took all the credit. This is our case to crack and ours alone," Brendan reminded him.

"Okay, okay."

"The guy outside the bar smoking the cigarette. Do you think he's one of them?"

"I don't know. It could be our Riverwalk Lover. But it's too early. We said 7:00."

"Looks like he's waiting for something. Better check him out."

"I'll take it. I'm the one who communicated with them. It'll be me they look to connect with." Preston said, adjusting his raincoat and stepping from the automobile. He opened his umbrella and proceeded towards the bar feet splashing across the damp street.

Once Preston arrived at the dark figure Brendan saw something that made him very nervous. Both Preston and the man in the raincoat and hat disappeared around the corner of the building out of sight. This had not been part of the plan.

Once around the corner of the building Preston asked the man in what had been a prearranged code, "Are you a stranger in town?"

Preston felt the cold wet steel of a revolver up under his chin. "Do I look like a stranger?" the man replied. This was definitely not the response to the code. "Hands on your head," the gruff voice ordered. Preston's umbrella fell to the ground and began to fill with rain. The man's voice seemed familiar.

With his free hand the man then pushed his collar down slightly and tipped his rain cap back. Sergeant Teddie Armstead pushed his weathered face closer to Preston's. The raindrops on his face and his icy look in his eyes reflected a distant flash of lightning making his contorted face appear grotesque in the moment of light.

Twenty-seven years Teddie Armstead had been on the force. Twenty-seven years he's seen less deserving officers promoted and move on to Brownsville. He'd apprehended con men, killers and worse. Now his men's hours were being cut back and two young detectives were the pride of the force.

"You punk's think you got something on us don't you. Well let me tell you something. My men are apprehending your suspects as we speak. It wasn't hard to locate them. One by one they'll be arrested for their crimes and it'll be me and my force that gets the credit, not you rookie academy boys with all your toys."

Sergeant Armstead pushed the gun harder and Preston felt the back of his head up against the building wall. His wet hair hung over his forehead in his eyes.   The Sergeant frisked him and removed his revolver. With it went Preston's hopes for survival.
"Are you crazy? You can't do this. We're detectives. They'll find you," he stammered.
"Hah! They'll think your group of suspects made you disappear."

Another flash of lightning, closer this time, illuminated a silhouette at the rear of the building. "Drop it Armstead," Teddie Armstead turned and fired his revolver in the direction of the figure but the flash of light had gone. Only the flashes from Teddie's gun lit up the dark night.

Suddenly three blinding flashes from the rear of the building answered the darkness. Teddie Armstead fell to the ground. His revolver splashed nearby. Preston bent over the Sergeant and checked his pulse. The Sergeant had none. Preston looked towards the back of the building. From the darkness emerged a rainsoaked figure with a gun at his side.

"You okay, Preston?" Brendan McAllister said.

"Yeah, thanks. I thought I was...How did you?"

"When I saw you disappear around the corner of the bar I got out and circled the building from the other side. Sergeant's Armstead's squad car was parked out back. I knew something was fishy. And then I saw him with a gun to your head."

"Let's call the commissioner and get this mess cleaned up," Preston said, now clearer of mind. He returned to his car to radio for help while Brendan dismissed the small group of patrons who had gathered outside.

A total of seven suspects had been apprehended and were undergoing intense questioning. Preston and Brendan both received commendations from the Commissioner who was more than happy to increase the funding for Operation Tech Trap. The two detectives had handsome new offices on the second floor of the stationhouse where the new Unit would now operate around the clock.

Months later the sleepy town of Makanda had gone back to its normal ways, free from the darkness that had pervaded their lives. Sergeant Teddie Armstead had been convicted and buried without the usual police honors. All seven suspects had also been convicted and conveniently—disappeared.

Guilty As Sin

There's nothing as invigorating as a five-mile run when the sun first peeks out of the eastern sky. The same snow showers that turned the roads slushy slippery slapped my face awake and fell on my outstretched tongue like manna from heaven. Inhale short breaths in cold weather. Exhale long breaths to purge the lungs of frost. Contrails of faux smoke follow like cartoon dialogue balloons. A couple of left jabs and a right cross precede a pirouette on the slick pavement. Ali's got nothing' on me.

Car zooms past me swerving at the last second and spews gobs of slush the consistency of wet beach sand across my thighs. I memorize the license plate. Few inches of snow and everyone is a rookie driver again. Welcome to the Midwest.

I've been gone an hour, but once home, Crips, my American Bulldog barks and runs at me as if I've been away for months. Her rear end and tail wave in one direction while her massive chest and head the opposite as if she's hinged in the middle. I brace for a collision but she hits the brakes six feet away and slides on the Pergo floor.

I'm thinking I'm in for a knee bending body rub but she prefers the wet snow on my legs and licks my sweatpants top to bottom. I love you too, Crips.

Dean Martin is singing, "When the moon meets the sky…" in my pocket. It's Dina calling on my cellphone. She loves that song so I programmed it in to warn me in advance it's her calling.

"Jack Stack, amateur sleuth." I answer in falsetto.

"I've never thought of you as amateur." She has a way of making me smile.

"Coming by my love?"

"You clean up the beer bottles and pizza cartons?"

Crips barks at me with a menacing stare. Women no matter the species are all jealous. Pointing and stomping my foot at her does nothing.

She barks again.

"You underestimate me. Last night it was red wine and brie cheese."

"Crips knows it's me. Give her a kiss for me. I'll see you shortly."

Give Crips a kiss?! Who could resist that face of hers seemingly formed by pressing up against a department store window and that runny nose… "Dina's on her way."

Crips pins me against the wall in an effort to squeeze by me in the narrow hallway, passes gas and heads anxiously for the front door as paws, rear end and tail all follow in a rumba.

The phone rings again, this time a normal tone.

"Jack, its Allan." Allan Piper was news editor for the Herald. We'd been friends since high school and still played handball together every Wednesday evening.

"Sorry to disturb you so early…"

"Well it is Saturday and Dina is on her way over."

"I've got something you need to see. Just came by e-mail."

"So forward it over."

"Jack, I can't do that. Be here as soon as you can." Allan had been city editor for over five years now. He'd been instrumental in giving me the tips I needed to crack a few tough cases. In return, I'd run down some leads that had given him some exclusive stories he'd run. Knowing Allan and sensing his agitated tone, he was serious. I promised that I'd be over as soon as I could

THE MILTON HERALD'S office building was a sprawling complex that grew slowly with the paper's circulation. Allan had a corner office on the second floor that overlooked the rear of the building. Semi-trailers and straight trucks came and went at all hours of the day and night like mice at work. Never a dull moment in the newspaper business. Today would be no different.

Allan was sitting at his desk back to the door pondering the busy phalanx of loaded trucks below him when I entered. I could see salt and pepper hair sticking up from behind his chair.

"Al, sleeping on the job again?"

He spun around to greet me. His temples and short sideburns had begun to whiten the last year. Al was tall and lean with a long wingspan that helped make him a formidable handball opponent. A shock of white hair fell on his forehead. He brushed it back casually and rose to greet me. "Jack, come in please."

Al looked pale as if he'd been ill. "Al, you look great."

"Bullshit."

"How's Samantha and the kids?"

"Fine. Thanks for asking."

"And Dina?"

"Good. I was going to bring her up with me but she's in the car with Crips. Girl talk."

"I'm glad you didn't bring her. Come and look at this." He sat back down and swiveled his computer monitor so I could see the screen. There in living Technicolor was a ten second video clip straight out of an X-rated movie. A blonde woman lay sprawled on a bed. The camera angle was taken from behind her so you couldn't see her face, only the back of her head and from her waist on down. She was totally naked with legs spread wider than the golden gate bridge. Crawling on his knees between hers was a middle-aged man with a cross-eyed leer.

"Recognize anyone," Al asked.

"Should I? The blonde could be anyone?"

Al enlarged the screen display for a better view. What I saw next shocked even me. Alderman Thomas King, Mayor Schlesser's right hand man, head of the City Council, married and father of three children had come for a taste of honey. "Wow. Where did you get this?"

"That's not all, Jack." Al rubbed his face and chin with a hand as if looking for the right words. "Councilman King was found dead this morning, apparently murdered. There are other details I cannot reveal."

"Do they know about this video? When did you get this?"

"Other than myself, you're the first to see it. Came in last night. Was here when I arrived this morning."

Al squeezed his forehead with his fingertips from side to center.

The creases on his forehead disappeared then slowly came back. He usually got in on Saturdays around 5:30 a.m. The e-mailed video was time stamped at 12:01 a.m. That meant someone had been very busy last night.

"Okay, let's think this out. Where was Councilman King found and at what time?

"Beat officer found him this morning in an alley behind Balducci's, a restaurant he frequented."

"You received the incriminating e-mail at midnight. And Councilman King is found dead at 6:00 a.m. We don't know where the video clip was taken and more importantly when it was taken. All we know is it was taken before the Councilman's death meaning you were being warned about this in advance."

"Why would someone kill him? Why not just blackmail him?"

"Good question."

"You said the video clip came via e-mail? Perhaps we could track it."

"I've got our best tech guy on it as we speak."

Al jammed a sharpened pencil into the cup of pens and pencils on the desk and leaned back in his executive chair. I'd never seen him like this. Even when he was down 19–12 in handball he was as cool, calculating and confident. Next thing I know he'd tied the score up on me.

"That's why I called you, Jack. I don't quite know what to do."

"All right. Copy the videoclip onto a disk so we've got a copy should you lose the original. I'll call Alex Cobb at Police headquarters. He's gonna want to see this…"

Al rose to his feet and turned to looked out the window. "Jack, we can't release this."

Sensing Al's anxiety and out of respect for the Councilman I agreed to wait on going public with the videoclip. But it could hold possible evidence. In the meantime maybe we could trace its origin. Later, I'd need to examine the crime scene and see the body myself. What more do you know about Councilman King?"

He turned to face me. He'd been wringing his hands but now spread them wide, palms open. "What else can I tell you that you don't already know? He was a pillar of the community. He had it all, beautiful wife, nice family, Church every Sunday, political heavy, close with the Mayor."

"Was is right. And pillars of the community don't usually show up on their knees in a steamy video."

DINA PULLED MY car up just as I was leaving. She always looked radiant in the morning especially with the sun reflecting off the morning snow. Her shoulder length sandy hair bounced and followed each turn of her head. Makeup wasn't her thing, which was fine with me. That meant that she usually looked the same, fit, athletic and well, perky. Crips greeted me with squeals of delight and a new rawhide bone in her mouth. A slap on the rump sent her bounding into the back seat.

"You girls out shopping again?"

"Of course, that's what we do. How was your visit with Allan?"

"Not in front of the kids," I nodded toward the backseat.

On the way back, speaking in hushed tones, I filled Dina in. Afterwards there was complete silence in the car save for Crips gnawing noisily on her bone.

Chapter Two

St. Peter's Church is one of the oldest buildings in the Chicago suburb of Milton. Originally built in 1893 it burnt down mysteriously and was rebuilt in its present state in 1925. Some say the fire was caused by a late night petitioner lighting a votive candle while others blamed it on faulty wiring. It towers above all the other structures in town having been built long before local zoning codes limited building heights. It is a magnificent brick structure with a steeple that could be seen for miles. The local parishioners call it the Beacon of St. Peter's.

Louise May sat at her desk fielding telephone calls while logging weddings and baptisms for future mass dates. Her tawny strawberry blonde hair was pinned up haphazardly. Large reading glasses magnified light brown eyes. Tight olive skin belied her mid-forties age. Another telephone call sent her scurrying amidst her paperwork for a lost pen. Finding it somewhere in her tall nest of hair she wonders if that's where her missing notepad might also be. Mondays were hell at St. Peter's. Parishioners fresh from mass the day before and filled with a renewed sense of commitment always flooded the Church with matters of faith the very next day as if the Lord was expecting their call. With over four thousand parishioners and a weekly collection of over $45,000, St. Peter's was the crown jewel of parishes in the diocese.

"Yes, Mrs. Lester. I understand. No problem. Glad to have you." Louise set down the receiver. "Damn, that 's three baptisms for next week's 9:00 a.m. mass. Father White's going to pass out in the holy water."

"Dear Louise," a deep voice resounded from behind her. "I don't think the good Lord will be damning anyone that day."

Louise's face filled slowly with crimson giving her already dark countenance a sort of holy purple hue. She quickly made the sign of

the cross. "Sorry Father Gordon," she called out. "Remember your sermon 'Everyone has their Cross to Bear'? Well mine is Mondays!"
Louise broke her pencil and tossed both halves in the trash can searching
beneath the rubble for another.

Father Gordon Devlin appeared in the doorway of the sacristy. A
man of medium stature, pale white skin and button nose, expressive
blue eyes evidenced his mother's Irish heritage. Just shy of fifty years
old, he'd been at St. Peter's for over twenty years now and Pastor for
the last three. Relatively young to be appointed Pastor of such a prestigious
parish, Father Gordon's good fortune came at the misfortune of its
previous Pastor, Father Dominic. He'd been on leave of absence since
being accused of indecency with a former altar boy a decade ago. Since
then other 'alleged victims' had come forward to join the feeding frenzy
and testify. Father Gordon never forgot the sight of Dominic leaning
precariously on his cane, his hearing aid turned low, crawling into a
taxi. His craggy face and yellow eyes barely high enough to peer out
the window took one long last look at the parish he had built. Bishop
Imell, feeling the Church might benefit from a younger Pastor, gave
Father Gordon the unenviable task of restoring the faith of the faithful.

He walked over to his long time assistant and removed a pencil
from her hair. "Looking for this?"

She took the pencil averting her eyes downward. "I'm sorry Father
Gordon. It's just sometimes I feel so—human."

He threw his head back, laughed and cast his beam on Louise.
"Louise, there is no shame in being human. Most people have a hard
time admitting they're human in my presence. Everyone tries to be so
'perfect' around me."

Louise unpinned her hair and let it fall. A thick lightly reddish
mane enveloped her. She ran her fingers through it twice and shook
her head vigorously like an Irish Setter. She removed the glasses that
hid a thin nose slightly upturned at the tip. Like the mild-mannered
librarian turned starlet, Louise hid her looks well. From the simple
pleasantness of her youth now bloomed a sophisticated attractiveness.
Although she had her share of offers, Louise never married.

"You just bring out the best in people Father Gordon, that's all."

He wasn't swayed by the suddenness of her looks but always appreciated her God-given beauty. "Speaking of which I must be on my way for Reconciliation." He laid his freckled hand on her shoulder. She took comfort in his touch without looking at his firm hand "Why don't you finish up and go home, you look tired." Louise understood and bobbed her head quietly. Father Gordon marched out through the doorway his bright green robes and white undergarments flowing gallantly, sucking the air from the room with them.

HE SAT IN the lonely confessional saying his prayers and waiting, waiting for a repentant sinner to enter the confessional. Years ago he remembered the Church crowded with those awaiting a priest to cleanse their souls, seeking penance for their transgressions—a blessed man that would understand the difficulty of being mortal and able to forgive their mortal sins. Now he'd sit there for the better part of an hour and hear but a few confessions.

He couldn't imagine a dearth of sin amongst his flock for sin knew not famine.

The confessional door creaked open. A whoosh of air went out of the padded kneeler. He slid open a small window covered with cloth and ornate woodwork that leant anonymity to the tiny booth and began with the sign of the cross.

"Father Gordon, is that you?"

"Nicky?" Gordon recognized the high-pitched voice of Nicky Lemontia.

"Yeah Father. Who do you like this weekend?"

"Nicky, your confession first," he reminded him. Nicky was a regular and really wasn't a bad kid but he hung around with a tough crowd that could usually be found playing cards and drinking at Sal's Pizzeria.

"Oh yeah, sorry Father. My last confession was…"

"Two weeks ago."

"Yeah, two weeks ago and I, uh booked some action, like I always do and" he hesitated.

"And?" Father Gordon urged him on.

"And I busted up a few guys who didn't pay what they said they were gonna."

"For Johnny LaRocco, I presume."

"That's right, Father."

"Nicky, the good Lord may turn his head to a little gamblin' but he doesn't like the violence part. You understand."

"Father, you're guy may be the boss up there, but my guy is number one down here."

"I understand. Say three 'Our Fathers' and three 'Hail Marys' for your penance. And give me a hundred on the Bears minus three versus the Packers."

"You got it, Father."

"And remember, the Lord is on your team."

"If only he could play quarterback for the Bears!"

Nicky jumped up out of the confessional, genuflected and sprinted out of the Church.

Father Gordon heard someone new enter. The door groaned as it slowly shut. A petite voice asked for his blessing. "Bless me Father…" a large head of hair dimly backlit framed the silhouette before him, "for I have sinned. My last confession was a week ago." The pungent smell of heavy perfume permeated the cloth screen. Father Gordon closed his eyes and bowed his head. He shifted uneasily, recalling the familiar soft, hesitant tones of the young woman. It had been exactly one week ago since he'd heard her last egregious confession.

Chapter Three

The murder scene in the alley behind Balducci's Restaurant was filled with police, CSI's and unfortunately, ubiquitous white minicam vans of the press. The tall buildings on either side of the alley eclipsed the day's sunshine.

Mucky gray slush mixed with wilted lettuce heads, stale tomatoes and rotten onions awash with dozens of crisscrossed footprints.

My old friend Alex Cobb spotted me and he held up the yellow crime scene tape as I ducked under to get a closer view. Alex and I had been close when I was on the force. He was now the head of homicide and I was a well, private detective, but one with connections.

"Thanks, for holding things up, Alex."

"Can't wait much longer, John. Captain wants the body autopsied asap for possible clues." Always pragmatic, Alex did things by the book, too much so sometimes.

"Cause of death?"

"Throat was sliced from behind. But there's something else you should see."

White cloths the size of bedsheets hung from temporary standards draping the victim's body. This was standard procedure for the most gruesome of crime scenes, those that caused even the most hardnosed cops to lose their lunch. I bent down inside this inner sanctum to examine the secluded body. It was Councilman King all right, a bit bluer then his last screen appearance. Alex loosened the victim's belt, unzipped his zipper and pulled down his tightie whities to reveal the imprint of a black cross, maybe two inches long. I've only smelled it once before on a case many years ago but you never forget the repulsive smell of burnt flesh. It burns the hairs in your nose and makes your eyes tear.

"I thought branding was illegal in this neck of the woods."

Alex rubbed the back of his neck with his large hand. "We're gonna need a posse on this one, Jack.'

It's one thing to track down robbery suspects, jealous husbands or angry business partners but we both knew it could be a long, lonely journey to try to find a deranged psychopath.

"Whoever did this has a lot of balls."

"Not him," Alex said, nodding at the body.

"Excuse me?"

"Take a close look, Jack"

Alex was right. A closer inspection of the Councilman showed he was definitely missing some equipment.

"Testiculus removus," I observed. "Tough to be king without 'em." I rose and stood over the grisly scene for a moment pondering the type of individual capable of such macabre violence. "Looks like the Councilman was sticking his dipstick where he shouldn't have."

Al swore me to secrecy on the evidence we'd witnessed. He was going to need my help on this one. Nevertheless, I decided not to tell him about the x-rated video clip starring the now neutered Councilman King. He wasn't going to be around to collect his Oscar anyway, that was for sure.

I JOGGED THE rest of the way home taking advantage of the bright sun of winter. The snow had stopped falling. I stayed to the plowed streets as many of sidewalks had yet to be shoveled. Cleaning up Milton was a bigger job than it seemed—today.

When I put the key in the front door, Crips signaled her familiar baritone bark. That was followed by the frantic clatter of nails on hardwood. I peeked in the door and waited for her to go into her patented head first slide like she had a stolen base. She saw me peeking but put the brakes on a little too late. At the last instant I threw open the door and Crips slid by me out into the hallway and up against the wall. I ducked inside as fast as I could. But she'd rebounded, tracked me down and tackled me before I'd reached the den. I lay there covering my head as Crips mercilessly scurried about licking me.

I half heard Dina's voice somewhere above us. "Would you two please get a room."

"It's just the papparazi, honey, really."I was getting control of Crips but struggling to stand.

"Papparazi! Looks like an autograph hound to me."

Dina had obviously been working out. She had a white towel slung over her workout bra and shorts. Beads of golden sweat glistened on her flat tummy. I leaned forward to kiss her.

"Yuck," she turned her head away and threw her towel at me. I bobbed and weaved like a prizefighter avoiding the knockout punch. "Shower first, please." I couldn't blame her, thanks to Crips I smelled like an AKC Kennel.

"Together?" I asked.

"Possibly," she peeled a banana, took a bite and washed it down with a squirt of her water bottle. "You go ahead and I'll join you." Dina tipped her head forward and peeked out seductively beneath one eyebrow. 'If I'm a little late, start without me."

"Can I trust you alone?" I said, eyeing her snack.

I turned and headed for the bathroom just as a banana peel hit me in the back of the head. The warm shower water removed the chill I'd gotten at the alley crime scene. Soaping up in all my glory, I couldn't help but feel a twinge of pain down low for the Councilman.

Chapter Four

A cold front swept through Milton overnight leaving behind frozen mounds of dirty slush resembling the surface of the moon, only more slippery. I decided to forgo my morning jog when navigating the slippery terrain in search of my morning paper seemed a dangerous mission. Damn Crips, never could teach that dog to retrieve the morning Herald. As I mounted the stairs with paper in hand I could see her flat nose pressed up against the window. Who had whom trained?

Dina and I had slept well especially since our mutual backrubs in the shower the night before had led to a passionate wrestling match in bed. Strong and assertive when she wanted to be, Dina could easily have her way—when I gave in. She always looked great the morning after, like a finely tuned athlete emerging from the waters of a triathlon. Her sandy hair, still wet and scraggly, almost touched the newspaper she'd buried her nose in. Her square shoulders were bare save for the skinny straps of her nightgown. I came up behind her and rubbed them firmly working up toward her neckline.

"It says here that Councilman King was killed with a…" She rolled her head and moaned.

"Knife," I finished.

"Please, don't…"

I removed my hands.

"Please, don't stop."

I continued, while reading over her shoulders. The article didn't mention the branding nor the fact that the same knife used as the murder weapon was probably used to dismember the unfortunate victim's testicles. Alex Cobb had asked Allan to keep certain details of the murder private, for now at least. I'd hoped that Allan hadn't gone back on our promise of withholding the video clip file while we investigated its relationship to the murder of Councilman King.

Dina had become a pretty good amateur detective herself, so I felt compelled to tell her the gory details of the murder.

"Jack, how could you?" she stood up, crossed over to the sink and tossed her breakfast plate in. From the noise I thought it broke. "Really, you wait until breakfast to tell me this. Why not last night. Why not after breakfast?" She covered her mouth as if to stop the inevitable geyser of toast and orange juice. But in true trooper style she put her hand to her mouth and stifled herself.

"Does Alex know about the videoclip?" she gagged.

"Not, yet."

"You and Allan have an angle then?"

"Uh, not yet."

"Then you two had better get going."

Sometimes a woman's perception is like radar. I didn't even need to tell her where I planned on going this morning. I kissed her goodbye and left abruptly to the tone of Crips' deep-throated bark.

Crips came around the corner dragging her leash in her mouth. Before leaving I cried out through the open door, "Oh, could you take Crips out please, thanks." Funny how that dog could get her leash when she wanted a walk but still couldn't pick up the morning newspaper.

AS SOON AS I got in the car Alex Cobb called. He wanted me to meet him behind the Milton Lanes bowling alley. Another branded body had showed up early this morning.

Two bodies in two days. We had few leads to go on other than the video clip and a mutilated body. Whoever it was behind these killings meant business.

Upon arrival I found Alex along with two black and white squads at the scene. He signaled me over.

"Careful, Jack. Everything's frozen solid around here." He kicked aside a case of empty beer bottles and pulled back a white sheet that lay on the ground covering the dead body. Immediately the repugnant smell of burnt flesh torched my nostrils. I put my handkerchief to my face and knelt down on the slick ice. I looked at the body and then to Alex in astonishment. He nodded, his eyes closed. There lay Reggie Johnson, perennial all-pro running back for the Chicago Bears. I shook my head in disbelief. First Councilman King now Reggie Johnson. This killer just got all the media attention he wanted. The three-ring circus had begun.

"I don't have to tell you that we could have a panic on our hands," Alex said.

"Gonna make the case even tougher now. Cause of death?"

Alex rolled over Reggie's dark, muscular torso and revealed a large knife wound.

"Through clear to the heart. Knife must have been the size of a machete."

Reggie was a twenty-seven year old African-American who'd been with the Bears since he was drafted number one out of Oklahoma four years ago. Last year he led the NFL in rushing.

"The Bears had a Charity Bowl for Cystic Fibrosis last night. They say he left about midnight."

His skin was so dark it was hard to distinguish the branded cross but it was right there in the same place as Councilman King's, right above his genitals, or where it used to be. Alex had pulled the sheet down a little farther to expose the missing piece of genitalia.

"Some message, huh?"

"This isn't a message, it's a sermon."

There was no doubt in our mind now that this was the same person who'd killed Councilman King. The perverted psychopath had run off with Reggie's manhood.

"From the frozen urine on the ground there it seems he stopped to take a leak."

"His last leak." I made a mental note to heed Dina's constant pleadings and use the men's room henceforward.

A ringing cellphone broke my trance. Checking around in my pockets, I found it vibrating like a flopping fish. I turned to walk away so as to get some privacy. It was Allan Piper at the Milton Herald.

"Jack, you've got to see this. I just received another video clip."

"Let me guess, Reggie Johnson?" I whispered.

"Yeah, how did you know?"

"Because he's laying here without his Johnson. I'm on the way."

Detective Cobb had ordered uniformed officers to bag the body. Fortunately the overnight weather had cooperated to give us our first clue. Alex pointed out a couple of footprints frozen in the snow.

"Male shoe, textured bottom with an imprint says Dockers, approximately size 10."

"Great clue. One of the most popular shoes in the most common size."

Alex fixed a perturbed glare on me. "Jack, right now it's our only clue."

I didn't tell him about the other clues, the video clips. Sooner or later, I'd have to.

Chapter Five

Father Gordon watched the young woman's silhouetted head bow. The shadow of her hand crossed her face in the sign of the cross. He sensed the anxiety in her quickened breathing. This wasn't unusual as admissions in the confessional never come easy. But his years of understanding, empathy and cajoling made the process easier for the sinners in his flock.

"Bless me Father for I have sinned. My last confession was a week ago." He knew this and braced himself for the worst.

"I continue to sin against God and Church with my obsessively prurient behavior." A litany of perverse sexual activities followed, each seedier than the next.

"I see. Is that all?"

"I'm afraid that these activities have also," she hesitated and breathed deeply before continuing, "ended up on film."

Twenty years of confessions can steel one's resolve but this young woman's stories tormented Father Gordon like no others before. "The Lord frowns on such behavior. In the future I'd like you to make an appointment to come in for some counseling. Is that all?"

He watched her silhouette change sides as she shifted her weight on the kneeler. "I am responsible for—for murder."

Father Gordon sat back appalled by what he'd just heard. He tried to collect his thoughts quickly to be of some sort of help. Mortal sin was indeed the sin of mortals. Grievous sin required grave measures.

"My child, this is serious. Jesus thanks you for your courage in confessing. You've broken not only the law of God but the law of man. You must do what's right."

"What's right?"

"You must do penance. And I suggest you come forward with this…"

"I can't do that."

"Jesus will strengthen you."

"Father, I cannot and will not come forward. Give me my penance."
She pulled a tissue from her purse and began to dab her eyes.

Father Gordon wiped his brow with the hair of his forearm as the confessional grew warmer and smaller. "But, my child…"

"No, I won't. I knew this was a bad idea." She rose, her eyes still wet and banged about the dark confessional before finding the door handle and leaving.

Whether to avoid the searing heat of the shrinking confessional or to reach out and touch his child, Father Gordon did something he'd never done before. Reaching over to find the doorknob he opened the confessional door. A young woman in a white, spotted fur coat hurried away down the aisle. Long, bright blonde hair slapped her back and shoulders. Her curvaceous figure swayed side to side perched atop six inch high heels clacking on the tile floor until they could be heard no more.

"Damn," he muttered.

A woman seated a few pews away looked at him in surprise, then quickly returned to fingering the beads on her rosary.

MY DAY HAD started nicely with Dina's breakfast but I almost saw it again after viewing the emasculated body of Reggie Johnson. My business was not for the squeamish. Yet that same squeamishness provided me job security.

I headed to the Milton Herald for a meeting with Allan Piper. As usual, I found Allan typing away furiously on his keyboard no doubt under the duress of yet another deadline. Never understood the newspaper business. Deadlines were like cold beer, there'd always be another one coming, so why the sweat?

"Jack, you saw Reggie Johnson dead?"

"Real dead. You saw him alive?"

Allan went to the windows separating his office from the staff writers and drew the blinds. He pushed the button on the doorknob to lock.

"Allan, I didn't know you cared." I couldn't get a laugh out of him. He was dead serious.

"I want you to see this."

Allan's fingers rattled the computer keyboard. There in the living flesh, literally, was Reggie Johnson. The videoclip began to play. A young voluptuous woman was gyrating atop a prone Reggie. Silky blonde hair hung down her tanned backside and in front draped her ample breasts. The white imprint of what had obviously been a skimpy thong danced a relentless salsa beat in unison with her sun-kissed ass cheeks. I asked Allan to zoom in on what looked like red marks. There on her ass were splotchy red imprints the size of a man's hand. Blondie had obviously been a naughty girl. Damp strands of hair began to stick to her. She flipped the hair off her forehead and shoulders with the back of her hand. Her cherubic face was pinker than the rest of tanned body. Nubile but not too shy to wear heavy make-up, especially eye-makeup, she wore eyeliner thick as a crayon and false eyelashes that licked her eyebrows.

"Pretty. And young. Looks like the same girl in the first video." I looked at Allan for confirmation. He was entranced.

"Hey, Allan, it's over." The screen had gone blank.

"Yes she sure is."

"Well thanks to her we've got two dead men, branded like cattle and pieces of their puzzle missing."

Allan rubbed his hand through hair seemingly grayer than the day's before. He looked as if he'd slept in his clothes.

"You get any sleep last night?"

"Some. What has Detective Cobb got so far?"

"Male shoe, Dockers, size 10."

"What did your tech guy find out about the source of the e-mailed videoclips?"

"That's a problem, Jack. We can't lock them down.

They are coming from a series of proxy servers and probably sent through remailers. This guy is smart."

"Dockers aside, I'm still not convinced it's definitely a man. Anyone can wear men's shoes. And how could a man get this close to his victims?" We looked at each other like good friends do who are thinking the same thought. "Allan, we've got to go to Cobb with these videoclips."

"No, we can't do that. What about their families?"

"What about finding out who did this for their families."

Allan rubbed his hand over his chin fingering salt and pepper whiskers. "The videoclips stay here." He rose and turned to face the rear window. I couldn't believe what I was hearing. Allan out of some strange sense of propriety or journalistic confidentiality was withholding evidence that might help the police catch this wretched killer.

I stood to voice my displeasure as I usually do—loud and clear. Allan still hadn't turned around to face me. He continued to stare out the damned window. Then it hit me.

"You're in these videos too, aren't you, Allan?"

Silence followed. Allan Piper was guilty as sin.

Chapter Six

Dina and I usually took turns cooking dinner and since it was my turn I did the honors by ordering out Mandarin. Chopsticks danced in her fingers like a drunk on stilts. Meanwhile, I managed to snare a single broccoli stem that had eluded me for minutes. No wonder she still had a gorgeous figure. No need for fat farms or fad diets like South Beach or Atkins, just pass out chopsticks to everyone.

I relayed the information I'd gleaned about Allan's fear of the video clips being made public.

"Oh, Jack, of all people, Allan."

"I'm sorry too."

"How did he get involved with that…"

"Apparently, through Nicky Lemontia."

"That little sphhtt," Dina made some sort of noise but with a mouthful of chopsticks and Mandarin I couldn't quite make it out.

Crips sat sprawled out on her belly in the kitchen oblivious of our dinner. Usually she'd be underfoot begging scraps but she didn't care for Asian.

"I talked with Alex without telling him about the videos…"

"Jack, you can't withhold the videos…"

"Sorry, Dina. Allan made me promise. Alex says that Nicky Lemontia is Father Gordon's nephew. Says that they know that Nicky has been booking for Father Gordon for a while now but they've been looking the other way ever since the stink with Father Dominic the last couple of years."

"Do you think Nicky could be the killer?"

"That'd be a big step up for Nicky."

"Blackmail isn't that big a step up, Jack."

"No but murder and dismemberment is. No, I don't think Nicky

Lemontia is capable."

We looked at each other across piles of white cartons and soy sauce and dropped our eyes together thinking the same thought.

"Lord save us all if Father Gordon is involved," Dina said.

FATHER GORDON TUGGED at his tight Roman collar. Although St. Peter's had long ago added air conditioning to the Church the heat system was still provided by the radiators that cranked and clunked, hissing out bursts of uneven heat that could melt candles. In between the cacophony of emissions he thought he heard a sob coming from Louise May's office. He found her at her desk with a folded note shaking in her trembling hand.

"Dear Louise, what gives you such pause?"

"It's Abigail. She has written me. All these years and she has found me."

Father Gordon's surprise didn't stop him from trying to console Louise. He stepped behind her and placed both his hands on her shoulders. "Are you sure it's her?"

"Yes, Father. She says here that she was adopted from St. James Orphanage when she was barely three years old. She did the research online through a specialized internet service, one of those 'family tree' searches. Of course, I never had the papers sealed when I went away to have her at St. James. I figured one day if she wanted she should know who her mother was."

Father Gordon stroked her shoulders. "But why now. Why would Abigail contact you now?"

"Her adoptive father got transferred six months ago to California so her parents moved away. Abigail wanted to stay in school here at the university. She rents an apartment in the city and has a roommate. She sounds lonely, Gordon."

"This is not good. What if someone were to find out?"

Louise took Father Gordon's hands off her shoulders and turned to face him. "Is that all you're worried about, yourself?"

"Don't be cross. You've always known the ramifications if she came back."

"Don't worry, Gordon. On the application for her birth certificate I put 'Father Unknown'. No one will ever know you were her father." She returned to the note from Abigail. A tear streamed down her face onto the paper mixing with the ink in a puddle of blue.

He raised her up and pressed her close to himself. Their bodies touched—his firm and warm, hers trembling.

Father Gordon held her head gently in his strong hands. "For twenty years now you have worked here in veiled silence. You have never asked anything of me. You've asked nothing for yourself. All this time I've marveled at your devotion. From your solitude came my strength."

"Oh, Gordon, how did we go so far astray?"

"Wherever we strayed, we strayed together. Ours was a trail less traveled, not without tears and doubt but it led us here to St. Peter's and here we must meet our destiny—together." He gently wiped the tears from her face with the back of his fingers and stroked them dry in her hair.

"She wants to meet with me." With this she reached over to pick up a small photo inside the note and showed it to Father Gordon. "Isn't she beautiful?"

He took the picture in his hands ready to beam proud but instead he closed his eyes and held the photo close to his chest.

"What is it? What's the matter?"

"I believe this Abigail visited my confessional just yesterday."

Chapter Seven

I didn't know where to begin looking for Nicky Lemontia but I knew where I could find his 'uncle' Father Gordon. He liked to book action with Nicky on NFL games. That meant he probably knew what else Nicky was into, namely pornographic films and, God save us, maybe even murder.

Father Gordon had a good reputation about Milton. He'd really helped turn things around at St. Peter's after the departure of Father Dominic. There was a lot of skepticism surrounding the charges against the old priest including questions about the character of those accusing him. But now attendance at Church was up, collections were up and it was chic to be Catholic again.

I found Father Gordon engaged in an animated conversation with a tawny-haired, olive-skinned woman. I couldn't be certain because of the thick glasses she wore but it looked like she'd been crying. Father Gordon's already pink face was as red as the hair on his head.

"Excuse me. Father Gordon."

Startled by the presence of someone in the room, they separated, seemingly embarrassed and probably wondering how much I'd overheard.

"Yes. Oh, Jack Stack. Well it has been a while." He extended his freckled hand and pumped mine vigorously.

"Yes Father Gordon, I must confess it has been a while." Last time I made mass was last Christmas. I didn't know if he really missed me or just my weekly envelope.

"You're always welcome here at the Lord's house."

"As he is at mine, Father."

He chuckled and introduced me to his administrative assistant, Louise May. he shook my hand but averted her eyes. They looked bloodshot.

Father Gordon motioned for me to sit down. Louise began to leave but he encouraged her to stay.

"We have no secrets here that I'm aware of, Jack."

"Would that include putting a hundred on the Bears/Packers game this Sunday?" Out of the corner of my eye I could see Louise squirm in her seat.

Father Gordon's face swelled like a balloon ready to burst. "Is that what this is about?"

"I'd prefer to ask the questions. Where is Nicky Lemontia? I'd like to talk to him."

"I'll call him now if you'd like."

"I'd like."

Father Gordon speed-dialed Nicky on his cellphone and asked him to come right over.

"Five minutes," he said.

"Probably thinks you've got another wager. Is it true that Nicky is also your nephew?"

"Yes. He's a good kid, Jack..."

"Save it, Father. We know he's booking bets for you. So far the police are looking the other way, but they won't any longer. I know Nicky is up to no good. And if anyone knows about it, you do."

NICKY SHOWED UP as promised, right on time and burst into the office.

"Hey Father, you doubling up on the Bears?"

Father Gordon looked Nicky in the eyes and slowly rotated his gaze toward me.

"Say hello to Mr. Stack. He's a private investigator and would like to ask you some questions."

Nicky shrugged the collar of his shirt up on his shoulders like a gangster wannabee, sat down and checked his manicured nails. "It's just little action. You know, a hundred here a hundred there. Nobody gets hurt."

"Like Allan Piper?" Nicky fidgeted in his seat and began rubbing his pretty fingers together.

All this time Louise May sat nearby on a couch listening intently but volunteering little. She removed her glasses and placed them in a case. I did a double take thinking Louise's prettier sister had come in and taken a seat. She ran her hand through her hair and wrapped the bottom curls of her hair around her fingers. Any more tension in the room and it'd implode.

Micky looked sheepishly at Father Gordon who nodded his head and closed his eyes. Father Gordon knew the answer to my question about Allan Piper, but until now had been protecting Nicky given the sanctity of the sacrament of confession.

"So I got Mr. Piper an escort."

"For a price, I presume?"

"Yeah. For a price."

"That's pandering and you're going to jail. Well your 'escort' has graduated. Now she's a porn star. And her clients are showing up dead."

The room went quiet save for Louise's surprised breath as she covered her mouth.

"Mr. Stack, I don't know nothin' about no movies or dead guys."

"Who is she?"

"Abigail Winter. I met her at school. I'm takin' a couple of classes there just to keep my folks happy. She was in one of my classes. Apparently her folks moved away and she needed the extra money. So I set her up with a couple of guys, nothin' special."

"Like Councilman King, Reggie Johnson and Allan Piper?"

"Yeah, that's too bad about Mr. King."

"Yeah, too bad for you. They found Reggie Johnson dead yesterday too. You got alibis for Wednesday morning and Thursday evening?"

"Yessir. Wednesday morning I had class and Thursday evening I was down at Sal's with the boys. They'll vouch for me." Nicky was beginning to sweat. I'd have Alex Cobb check out his alibis. But he didn't seem bright enough nor capable enough of murder.

"Okay, that's all."

"You mean I can go?"

"Not far."

Nicky slinked out of the room without as much as a goodbye. Father Gordon and Louise looked ashen.

"Did you say Abigail Winter?" Louise asked.

"You know her?"

Father Gordon stood up abruptly to intervene. "Sit down Gordon. If Abigail is involved in something this perverted and sinister, I want to know about it." She produced a picture of Abigail from her purse and handed it to me. It was the first time I'd seen her clothed but Abigail Winter was our movie maven.

"There's something else you should know, Jack…" Father Gordon's eyes smoldered with guilt.

"Yes," Louise interrupted, "Abigail has a twin brother named Kane."

Father Gordon looked at her incredulously. "Louise, you never told me…how could you hide…?"

"I didn't tell you because you were so devoted to your calling, Gordon. Your whole life has been devoted to this," she swept her arm around in grand gesture, "that's why I went away to give Abigail up for adoption. I gave her up for you. I gave her up for God. If you knew Abigail had a twin brother, a son to carry on the Devlin name, you would have left the Church and that, Gordon, would have been the worst of our sins."

He wrapped his arms around Louise and held her close to stop her trembling. "My dear Louise, what have we wrought?"

St. Peter's had more secrets than the Vatican had catacombs. Had Louise kept her twin children it would have meant separate lives for them both and she didn't seem the juice box and soccer mom type. I needed to know more about Abigail's movie career, her twin brother Kane and why her clients were turning up dead and branded. One thing was certain, Father Gordon was indeed a father.

Chapter Eight

Three days had passed since the first video murder. My suspicions were we'd get another video clip any time now. Alex Cobb got an address on Abigail Winter and I decided to start with her before someone else showed up under a burning cross.

MacArthur College was located twenty minutes from Milton in downtown Chicago. Abigail lived in an apartment on the south side of the loop near the old Dearborn Train station on Tripp street. I don't always carry 'Lucky' but I figured if things got messy I might need her. She's my lucky revolver and had saved my ass many a time before. I patted my vest and 'Lucky' snarled like a hungry guard dog.

I knocked on apartment #3D and was greeted by a vivacious young college student. She wore a tight grey tight tank top and navy blue short shorts that said 'MacArthur' across her bottom. Her bright blonde hair was pulled up in a ponytail. Thick eyeglasses magnified the surprise in her pale blue eyes. Although she had little if any makeup on and bore little resemblance to the movie Abigail, there was no doubt in my mind she was the star of our video death clips.

When I flashed my private investigator i.d., she dropped her chin to her ample chest and spoke softly. "I thought someone might be coming."

I didn't bother asking if that was the title of her latest video but instead seated myself and immediately began asking questions. Abigail had indeed contacted her mother after all these years.

"I really wanted to meet her. It took me a long time but I found her working at St. Peter's."

I changed the subject. Yes, she had been an 'escort' for men. Yes, Nicky Lemontia set her up at first but it wasn't long before she was able to find her own johns. The money allowed her to quit her waitress job and paid for the plasma television on the wall, home theater system, laptop, and a wardrobe worthy of a diva.

I asked her about the videos. "At first I filmed them for the thrill of it or because they liked to watch. Then as my clients became more noteworthy I did it more for protection or insurance."

"You mean blackmail?"

"Not at all. I had enough money. I was just being cautious." There was something about Abigail that made me want to trust her. She came across as honest and sincere, the makings of a good actress.

When I brought up the subject of a twin brother she fought back a tear. "Kane and I remained close all these years. He never had it as good as I did. I was adopted out of St. James when I was three. My parents were wonderful. I miss them. I wish they were still here."

"What about Kane?"

"He was never adopted. Kane was different. He was a loner, very smart but just didn't fit in with the other children. When the utility shed behind the orphanage burnt down they blamed Kane and sent him to reform school. We kept in touch but over the years his letters got more depressing. I feared he might commit suicide. The only thing that saved him was religion."

"Religion?"

"Yes, he was fanatical about the Bible. He read it all the time. It became his constant companion."

"Abigail, you know that the men in your videos have been turning up dead?" She bit one of her nails and then another like a little girl.

"I know. I feel terrible. I feel responsible."

"I need those video clips now."

"They're gone."

"Gone!"

"My laptop was stolen. All the video clips were saved on it."

"And when was that?"

"About a week ago."

I began to put two and two together but it still wasn't adding up to four. "When did you last see your brother?"

"He visited me last week."

Bingo. Four. This poor little college girl, slump-shouldered and

somber with guilt was a far cry from her former self. She returned my
gaze. She could add too.

I called Alex Cobb and told him about the videos, Abigail and
Kane. He wasn't too pleased with me for holding back evidence but
was happy to finally get something on the case. He would put out an
APB immediately and would talk to me later, in private. That meant I
probably wouldn't get a commendation on this case. As I was talking
with him I got a call-waiting ring, it was Allan Piper.

"Excuse me a moment, Alex. Yes, Allan, I think we may have found…"

"Jack," he spoke over my voice, "I just received another video clip."

I sat back down, looked at Abigail, closed my eyes and just shook
my head.

"Jack, I'm in this one. It's my video!"

Horror of horrors, my best friend Allan, once the victim of
indiscretion was now next on the video murderer's hit list.

"Allan, I'm at Abigail Winter's apartment now."

"Not you too, Jack."

"No, no. But I may have an idea who our murderer is."

"I'll be right over."

"Stay where you are, Allan."

"We've got to catch this guy before he finds me. I'm coming over."

Before I could say another word, Allan hung up and was on his
way. I notified Alex Cobb and tried to figure out my next move.

ALTHOUGH ABIGAIL KNEW of the video clip murders she'd been
spared the gory details of the branding of the cross and the missing
genitalia. Her little game of filmed mating rituals had started out innocent
enough but had quickly gotten deadly. The cross ritual could be the
work of a religious zealot while the dismemberment could be a twisted
form of sibling protection. That a bible-thumping bad boy out to
avenge the sins of his sister could be our murderer turned my stomach.
I couldn't help but see nightmarish scenes of my best friend Allan, the
putrid stench of a branded cross on his abdomen lying dead with parts

of his manhood missing.

The door flew open and Allan rushed in. Eyes wide as pool balls bulged out of his thin face and his unkempt hair looked electrified. Long salt and pepper whiskers hadn't seen a razor in days. Finally, the former copulatory couple meet.

"You little tramp." He advanced on Abigail hands open and fingers clenched. "How could you film us..."

"I did it just for this reason!" She screamed back at him.

"I've got a family," he yelled.

"That's your problem, pal. Don't think you were something special either."

I grabbed Allan by the collar and turned on Abigail. "You shut up, bitch."

"Allan Piper, make your peace," a voice resonating from the doorway sounding like the grim reaper. There stood a young man, tall and thin with angular facial features a bald head and elfin ears. In his hand he waved a steely blue 9 mm gun the size of a pirate ship cannon. He entered the room making a half circle around us.

"Kane, no, don't," Abigail pleaded.

"Who are you?" he said looking at me.

"A friend."

"What kind of friend?"

"Not that kind," Abigail interceded. She had covered for me well. I could feel 'Lucky' growling in my holster. Not yet girl, be still.

Kane turned the gun toward Allan. "So what have we here? Mr. City Editor caught playing doctor with my sister."

"It was nothing, really."

"Your guilty as sin. For your penance..."

"Kane, no," Abigail said.

"In God's name don't do it, Kane." A deep voice boomed from behind him. Father Gordon, accompanied by Louise, stood in the doorway dressed in black save for the white of his Roman collar.

"Come to save a sinner, Father?" Kane asked.

"I've come to save you, son."

The room was getting a little crowded for a family reunion to break out. 'Lucky' still growled but I couldn't get a clean shot off without nicking someone.

"Kane, this is our mother," Abigail said.

"And I am your father," Father Gordon put his arm around Louise and stared at both his children sternly.

Abigail sighed, "Oh my, God."

"He's telling the truth," Louise said.

Kane looked at Father Gordon. "Then you're responsible for this whole mess," Kane waved the gun in Abigail's direction than focused it on Allan Piper. "Sin begets sin." He began to squeeze the trigger.

I pulled 'Lucky' out and warned Kane not to shoot. He looked at me with a sneer while keeping his gun on Allan. "Your penance is death."

Kane pulled the trigger as I pulled mine but not before Father Gordon stepped in front of Allan. He fell to the ground with a bullet in his heart. Allan slumped backwards in shock, then realized he wasn't hit. Kane wasn't so fortunate. 'Lucky' blew off the side of his head. His head lay on the ground in a circle of blood resembling a scarlet halo. Abigail threw herself on him and screamed. Louise knelt over Father Gordon sobbing and praying. I reached down to Kane and yanked a small cross from his neck. It smelled of burnt flesh.

Alex Cobb and his force stormed the room while our guns were still smoking. I pointed to Kane lying prone.

"There's your video murderer." Alex looked at Father Gordon and then at me. "Father Gordon saved Allan's life."

The others in the room waited for me to tell the rest of the story but I figured two deaths said enough. As far as I was concerned they were all guilty as sin. But their secrets, and their sins, died with them.

DINA AND I opened up a chilled bottle of Pinot Grigio and toasted each other.

"I feel bad for Abigail and Louise, after all those years for one to lose a brother and the other a lover."

"It's a shame but now they have something they never had before

—each other."

Somewhere down below the table Crips chewed on a hambone I'd picked up at the meat market. She kept pushing it up against my foot for licking leverage. I reached down and threw the sloppy thing across the kitchen floor. All four paws moved at superspeed like a cartoon dog and she was on it in seconds.

"Beat it, Crips. We're trying to have a romantic moment here."

"Oh is that what you call this."

"Well it's a start.

Dina batted her eyelashes at me as she rose and headed toward our bedroom. "So let's start."

"You first," I followed.

End of the Line

Many residents of the Chicago suburbs spend a good portion of their valuable time involuntarily contemplating their busy, stressful lives in a sort of forced yoga exercise while stopped at one of the many railroad crossings that dot the metropolitan area. Freight trains loaded with mysterious cargo, its cars marked with ornate graffiti courtesy of Latin 1 or Chi Kings, grunt by slowly gathering steam for their trek to the end of the line in Geneva. Passengers in their autos, anxiously awaiting the crossing gates to rise, keep their even more impatient children busy by asking them to count the number of freight cars rumbling by while they mark the number of engines towing the long line of cars, fully knowing each engine means another five minutes of waiting. But its good luck when a commuter train passes. The gates are rarely down longer than a couple of minutes, even if it makes a quick pit stop at the station. Commuter trains whistle by your windshield too fast to count cars. And if it is evening time, an eerie green glow emanates from the rows of windows whizzing by so quickly they become a dreamy filmstrip of motionless faces inside an aquarium like sleeping fish, the turning of a newspaper or book page the wavering fin that keeps them in place.

One such fish inside is William McBride, known as 'Mac' to his fellow workers. Bill labors, pencil in hand, for Grant Thomas, an international accounting firm. He spends most of his time peering into his computer screen and checking the figures propped up on his easel. Then like clockwork he takes the floating aquarium home. Oftentimes he naps until a conductor wakes him and tells him he's reached the end of the line, Geneva. He stirs, grabs his briefcase, departs and drives home in his silver BMW to his wife of ten years, Diana, a pretty woman he met at Northern Illinois University where they were in Accounting School together.

This Friday evening as he frequently does, Mac went out to

Muldoon's with a few of the other accountants for their famous beer-battered fish fry accompanied, of course, by numerous pitchers of beer. The oily smelling eatery was crowded Fridays and filled with the din of loop office workers laughing and toasting each other while they forgot about their jobs, their commute and sometimes, their families.

"End of the line, sir." A tall man in a blue conductor suit and signature matching blue flat cap, jostled his shoulder then shuffled by him into the next car. Mac rose groggy with cheer and peered out the window for the familiar white 'Geneva' sign atop the train station. The sign wasn't there. Must be dark tonight he figured. He reached for his briefcase on the seat beside him but the seat was empty. A search of the floor and seat in front of and behind him produced nothing. Someone had stolen his briefcase! As if that wasn't bad enough, his cell phone was inside. Instinctively, he patted his pocket for his wallet and keys. To his relief, both were there. At least the thief hadn't gotten everything. Upset with himself that his 'napping' habit had cost him his briefcase and cell phone, Mac combed his disheveled hair in the reflection of the window and made a mental note to call the train station tomorrow and file a report. He climbed down from the train watching the stairs closely and stepped onto not the familiar brick walkway of the Geneva train station, but a loose mix of fine white pea gravel. Looking about in the dark night, he saw nothing familiar, no station, no cars, no people. He'd awakened in a fog but remembered the conductor had indeed told him this was the end of the line, but this was not Geneva.

Chapter Two

The train eased to a stop and with one last tired lurch finally stopped. The absence of motion woke up the car's last passenger. Jackson jumped out of his seat shocked to see that the all the other passengers had already departed. He wrestled his backpack on and hurried outside wondering just how long he'd been sleeping. It was a long ride from downtown where his father lived to Geneva and oftentimes in returning home to his Mother's home he'd find himself lulled to sleep by the incessant rocking of the train. When you're ten years old, naps are kind of special. They give you time to daydream the life you wish you really had. Like when Mom and Dad were married and they'd take you to the restaurant for lunch and you could order a hamburger just the way you wanted it piled high with pickles and bacon and cheese, so big it hurt your mouth to open it that wide. He loved visiting his father because it gave them a chance to do 'guy' things together, like going to the health club or spending an afternoon at Wrigley Field. Sometimes Dad even let him tag along when he went down to Casey's Tap for a beer with the fellas. Patrick the bartender would give him a flashlight and Jackson would comb the dimly lit pub for quarters, usually finding enough to play the shuffleboard bowling game where you sprinkled sawdust from a can all over before scooting the puck down the alley.

Where was the train station? The train usually stopped at the end of the line in Geneva. Nothing here looked familiar. Had he gotten on the wrong train downtown? He felt the fine limestone gravel grinding under his shoes. This didn't even look like a railroad stop. No pay phone, no station. Where was he?

"You lost too?" Jackson looked up at the stranger dressed in a suit and tie. He felt relieved to see another passenger.

"I was headed to Geneva, sir," he shifted his backpack unconsciously in embarrassment.

"Don't feel bad, so was I." Mac looked down on the boy. A cowlick on the back of his blonde head stood up like a rooster's comb.

"Where are we?" he asked. The man had taken a handkerchief from his back pocket and was busily wiping his wire-framed glasses.

"Elburn, son."

"Elburn?"

"Yes, it's about twenty minutes west of Geneva. One of the departing conductors told me it's the new end of the line stop. Just opened today."

"Where's the station?"

"See that trailer over there," Mac pointed to a small construction trailer down the ways a bit on the other side of the tracks.

Jackson saw the dark trailer and his mouth dropped.

"I'm supposed to call my mom to pick me up."

"What's your name?"

"Jackson, Jackson Crawford."

"Call me Mac.' Mac sensed the boy's uneasiness. "Don't worry son, the conductor offered to call someone at their headquarters on his two-way radio and have them make a call for me while he waited for his wife to pick him up. But he said Caboose's is still open and its only four blocks into town. So I'm headed that way if you'd like to join me."

There was something about this bespectacled stranger that Jackson liked. He had been taught to fear strangers but this small man with his wire rimmed glasses and honest face resembled his math teacher, Mr. Summerville, in a way. Mr. Summerville's voice was much deeper and louder. But this man that called himself 'Mac' seemed nice and what other choices did he have out here in the dark.

The two strangers in a strange town headed down a dusty footpath together their way lit by only the faded edges of a half moon. They pushed away branches and kicked small rocks in their way. The path ran somewhat parallel to the tracks. The smell of creosote soaked railroad timbers guided their way. In the distance, the muffled hoots of a lone barn owl could be heard above a cacophony of busy crickets.

Chapter Three

Mac reached into the breast pocket of his suit and retrieved a small shiny flask from which he sipped.

"What's that?" Jackson asked.

"Bourbon." Mac replied, swallowing like he was gargling.

"What's it taste like?"

"Gasoline," he answered hoping to curtail any more questions.

Jackson marched forward trying to keep up with his guide, puzzled as to why adults drank anything that tasted like something you put in your car.

Ahead of them just a few steps they noticed a small commotion on the path. A lone sparrow lay flapping one wing wildly and circling about itself kicking up a small cloud of dust. It threw its tiny head back and beat and beat its one wing to no avail only to find itself back where it started time and time again. The two sojourners looked at each other. Mac started towards the bird and moved his foot sideways as if to push the little bird off to the side of the path.

"Wait," Jackson implored. He bent down, cupped his hands and lifted the bird up to examine it. "Bad wing, nothing serious," he reported.

"So put it in the sawgrass over there, it'll be fine," Mac instructed.

"He's exhausted. He'll be fine in a while. Do you have a handkerchief?"

Mac reluctantly produced a white cotton handkerchief and handed it over with hesitation. Jackson wrapped the handkerchief around the bird securely but not too tightly, so as to restrict the bird's wings. Then he tied a small knot in the front and flipped the loose corner on top over the bird's head.

"There, that should hold the little fella still until he regains his strength."

Mac peered at the young boy incredulously. He removed his glasses to wipe them clean. Realizing he'd given away his handkerchief he pulled the shirttail out from his trousers and busily tended to the glasses. At the same time Jackson placed the white package in the side pocket of Mac's suit.

"What are you doing?"Mac asked perturbed. "This is an expensive wool suit."

"My pockets are too small for him," he pulled his little boy jacket pockets inside out to show Mac. "Anyway, birds are cleaner than boogers and snot."

They resumed their march with Mac every once in while checking his pocket for what he feared an imminent attack from the hitchhiker bird. But the little package slept noiselessly.

Jackson shifted the heavy backpack so the straps wouldn't bite into his shoulders so badly.

"What you got in there, bricks?" Mac asked noticing his discomfort.

"Books mostly. Homework books and folders and my Harry Potter novel I read on the train."

"Harry Potter, huh."

"Yeah. My mom always says 'Readers are Leaders'."

"I guess I'd agree with your mother, Jackson. Best books I ever read were those on Poker and Blackjack. Provided me spending money in college."

"Where's your books? Or don't you read on the train?" Jackson asked.

"My briefcase was stolen, along with my cell phone."

"Cell phone would've been nice. How did your briefcase get stolen?"

Mac stopped to take another pull of bourbon. As he raised it high a moonbeam reflected off the metal flask giving it the appearance of a magic elixir with strange powers.

"Fell asleep," Mac offered sheepishly. "Gosh, you ask a lot of questions, let's go."

"That's why I carry this backpack, too heavy to steal." He readjusted the load on his back and attempted to keep up with the steps of the older man. Whenever Mac took a swig of the magic elixir he made a sour face. Why do people drink things that taste so bad he wondered?

But he thought better of asking Mac.

The saw grass on the side of the path gave way to thicket as they got further away from the train stop. The glint of the moon off the silvery railroad tracks was almost blinding compared to the dark thicket alongside them. Mac stopped and placed his hand across Jackson's chest for him to stop also. A strange low, deep-throated rumbling emanated from behind them. He listened intently and heard again what he thought to be the grumble of a distant train engine. This time Jackson heard the noise too. It came from behind them.

They wheeled around to see a lone coyote in the middle of the path. The animal's head hung low with upraised eyes. A sneer began to form on one side of its' mouth exposing sharp yellowed teeth. A thin filament of saliva hung from its mouth dripping like an icicle.

They turned and ran as fast as they could but the coyote was upon them in a matter of yards. It knocked Mac to the ground and swirled around him in a frenzy biting and tearing. Jackson looked back in horror as it attacked Mac while he lay in a fetal position protecting himself. His sleeved arm was in the dog's jaws. The dog shook its head vigorously from side to side. Mac was screaming something but Jackson couldn't understand him. The coyote backed up with its' hind end high in the air and tore at the sleeve. Then it dove back on the helpless man with a growling fervor, circling and biting. Suddenly, the coyote flew off Mac and landed on the ground with a loud yelp. Jackson's backpack had descended from on high and this time struck the coyote's ribcage. Another yelp followed the sound of a rib snapping under the tremendous weight. The coyote rose and scurried into the thicket wailing and braying like a wounded buffalo.

Jackson bent over a still terrified Mac. "Are you okay, Mac?"

"I think so," he gasped checking his arm. It was red and sore, but there was no blood. "My gosh, that bloody beast almost killed me. How did you drive him off?"

Jackson retrieved his backpack and rolled it over to reveal a patch of wet, shiny blood on the side where the coyote's broken rib had punctured its skin.

"Thank you, Jackson," Mac tried to catch his breath. "You saved my ass." He rose stiffly and dusted off the whitish limestone that covered him head to toe. To young Jackson he seemed quite a sight. Loose shirttails hung out from his suitpants and the knees were chalk white from the trail dust. His hair stuck up in the most unusual of places and his face was dangerously red. He looked different but Jackson couldn't place it until Mac said "My glasses. I lost my glasses." They searched up and down the trail for his spectacles but couldn't find them. Finally Mac gave up and decided to move on. He picked up his crumpled suitcoat, examined the tattered, torn sleeve and slid it back on. Together they brushed off the white dust.

"Where'd he go?" Mac asked.

"He ran off into the bushes when I…"

"No, our bird. Where'd it go, its missing." He patted his pocket but the little package was indeed gone. Again, they searched the trail and found the handkerchief not far away. It was empty.

"It flew away. See, it was all right."

"Or got eaten."

Jackson looked up at Mac with dampened eyes and the sternest look a boy of ten years could muster.

"Okay, okay. It flew away."

They continued on the moonlit path Jackson's backpack swaying with each step only now it was on Mac's back. He had offered to carry the heavy load, adjusted the straps and slung it over his dusty, torn jacket.

Mac needed another pull off his flask but that too had disappeared in the melee. His thirst faded reluctantly as he replayed the recent events in his mind. It had been a long day and an even longer evening. He replaced the handkerchief in his pocket, swung his arm around and placed it on Jackson's shoulder. The two of them walked in step and closer now.

From deep within the thicket the deep-throated croaking of a somnolent frog serenaded his mate. Far away, alley cats screeched and fought over remnants of food spilled from a solitary garbage can noisily rolling back and forth in the evening breeze. Like jungle drums, the muffled hoots of an owl, the sentinel of the night, continued to announce their imminent arrival. Somewhere above them a tiny sparrow flew in erratic looping circles taking a circuitous route back to its nest.

Chapter Four

A legion of silver edged clouds marched across the sky hiding the faded half moon. They surrounded the incandescent orb and swallowed it whole. Soon the light of night was extinguished.

"Isn't someone going to be missing you?" Mac asked.

"Not really," Jackson answered evasively.

"Your mother wasn't supposed to pick you up?" Mac probed.

"I was supposed to be at my dad's for the weekend."

"I see."

"Bud dad's girlfriend was there again and I asked to go back home after dinner."

"You don't like her?"

"She's okay. But she's just there all the time and she's just…"

"Not your mom."

"I guess." Jackson seemed relieved that Mac had said for him what he found so hard to say. He wished he could spend more time alone with his father. But that didn't seem likely, for now at least.

"Well, we're going to have to call your mom when we get to this Caboose's. If your dad hasn't already." Jackson hadn't thought of that. Quietly, he played out his mother's possible reactions. Most were not good.

"What about you Mac. Don't you have someone to pick you up?"

Mac chuckled to himself. "Unfortunately no. My wife's car is parked at the Geneva station. She took my BMW when she left me last month." Mac waited for a response from his companion. When none came he tried to make light of his situation. "I snore at night."

Jackson kicked a pebble down the trail ahead of them. "I remember the day dad left."

"We'd better hurry up, sonny, it's getting so dark it's hard to see."

The dusty white trail and the shiny railroad tracks faded away without the night light of the moon. Blackness was all about them. The heavy scent of oil and grease drippings on the creosote railroad ties signaled that they were still on the trail. A lone bat swooped down low, quickly rose and shot past them into the fields. Not faraway the bright lights of the little town of Elburn still burned for them.

Chapter Five

The streetlights of town were a welcome sight. Once on Main Street they headed north uptown toward a large yellow sign atop Caboose's. The only other businesses open were a late night gas station and a twenty-four hour convenient mart.

After their trek from the train station-to-be outside town the one block walk to Caboose's seemed easy. The cloud cover had brought with it exhortations. A stiff wind blew about the town and rushed down the main street whipping up wrappers and dust from the curbs. Street signs on poles shuddered nervously. The only stoplight in town bobbed and strained against its tethered lines.

Caboose's was the oldest building in town. It was the only two-story brick structure. Originally it had been the Elburn bank. Now the new bank was on the outskirts of town near the mall. A neon sign flashed in the window—'Food Served 24 Hours'. Mac threw open the heavy front door and Jackson followed him into the tavern. They got more than their share of stares from the locals. It wasn't every day that a man in a suitcoat, let alone one dusty and torn, with a backpack accompanied by a youngster, frequented the speakeasy.

'Cold beer," Mack ordered from the bartender while removing his backpack and placing it on the stool, "and a coke."

A tall, fierce looking woman with bleach blonde hair placed their drinks on the bar. They both swigged their drinks down and placed the glasses back on the bar.

"My we're thirsty aren't we?" She filled their glasses again. Mac noticed when she placed the glasses on the bar this time that the pinkie finger on her left hand was only a half a finger.

"Hold your horses," she bellowed over her shoulder to a group of men leaning on a pool table reminding her that it was her turn to shoot.

"Thank you miss," Mac said.

"Annie. What's your name stranger?

"Mac. And this here is Jackson. We walked in from the train stop."

"From the train stop. That's a long walk."

"Longer than you think."

"Some other train folks came in earlier. Missed their stop in Geneva."

Mac and Jackson looked at each other relieved that they weren't the only ones.

"Well you got here just in time. Weather is getting nasty out there. S'posed to be a storm headed our way." Annie leaned over to whisper something in Mac's ear. Jackson watched her purple painted eyes shift to him and back. Her large red smeared lips moved up and down and then stretched back toward her cheeks. He thought he noticed a spot in the back of her mouth where a tooth should have been. When Mac said something to her she threw her large blonde head back revealing a set of creases in her throat and laughed like aloud like a man. As if to remind herself she was a lady, Annie covered her mouth and the hole in her teeth with her hand.

"No problem, we'll sit over at a booth if you'd like," Mac acquiesced.

He swept his change off the bar and held it in his hand.

"Now, the first thing I'm going to do is call your mother to pick you up." Jackson fidgeted in his seat knowing the inevitable was coming. He gave Mac his phone number and watched him disappear down a hallway. A loud crash at the front door startled him. The swirling wind outside had opened and slammed the front door shut. A few of the customers peeked out the windows into the eerie night.

Jackson rested his arm on his backpack and leaned his head against the back of the booth. He'd had a long strange journey since leaving his dad's. And what a strange place this was. Perhaps he'd wake up and find himself aboard the train woken out of a Harry Potter dream and all that seemed would turn into all that was.

Chapter Six

When Mac returned he found his little companion slouched over his backpack sound asleep. He slid into the booth and jostled Jackson gently.

"Your mother is on the way."

Jackson rubbed his eyes. "Did she sound mad?"

"Concerned. Apparently your father called her shortly after you left and she's been waiting for your call. I explained that we both missed our stop and wound up at the new end of the line."

A loud shrill whistle from the fire station down the block pierced the night air. The bar patrons looked at one another and then toward the television screen behind the bar. The national weather service interrupted local programming for an emergency storm warning. A paramedic from the fire station stuck his head in the front door just long enough to make an announcement and disappeared.

"There's a twister been spotted thirteen miles southwest of here!"

Those at the bar swilled their drinks quickly. The pool game broke up as the players tossed their sticks on the table. Annie leapt into action. She dried her hands on her apron and bellowed out orders to the two dozen people left in the bar.

"Get away from the windows, now!" Everyone crowded the center of the room. Annie ran to the end of the bar and opened a door. "Into the cellar, quickly." Some of the patrons shuffled past the large woman down the stairs while others hid underneath their tables. A violent wind rushed the building. Floorboards swayed and creaked. Then the full force of the twister banged up against the building. The angry giant beat relentlessly on the south wall making the bricks chafe like sandpaper.

A swell of bodies were locked hopelessly in an attempt to get down the narrow doorway to the cellar. Mac grabbed Jackson's arm, ran toward the pool table and dove underneath leaving his backpack behind. The brick wall finally relented against the wind's incessant pounding and began to weaken. The last thing anyone heard was a loud rumble as the south wall of the bar toppled head over heels inward.

HOURS LATER FIRETRUCKS and ambulances swarmed over Caboose's. Flashing red emergency lights and bright white searchlights cast a pale glow into the black night. Countless volunteers formed a bucket brigade and passed single bricks from the crushed building down the line away from the scene. Paramedics pulled lifeless bodies out from the dusty building and covered them with white sheets. German shepherds rummaged through stacks of bricks sniffing for signs of life.

The same paramedic that had stuck his head in the door of Caboose's to warn everyone mopped his brow with the back of his forearm. A layer of gray mortar dust covered his body. He tried to spit out the chalky powder but only coughed. A tiny sparrow sat on a pile of rubble near him. Exhausted he sat to catch his breath.

"You're a long way from home, little fella, aren't you?"

The small bird flapped a wing wildly and bounced up and down. Its high-pitched chirping alerted the German Shepherds' sensitive ears. They ran to the scene dragging their handlers with them. Once there they began nosing about the pile of rubble and barking loudly. The paramedic jumped up and began tossing bricks aside.

"Over here!" he screamed. Volunteers hearing the dogs' barking had already begun to arrive to help remove debris. After fifteen minutes of frenzied digging they found a man and a boy alive inside the pile. Minutes later Mac and Jackson crawled out from underneath the shelter of the pool table that had saved their lives. A loud cheer went up. Survivors had been found!

Two paramedics rushed a white-sheeted gurney by them quickly. They hit a small hole in the ground and the heavy body lurched. A long fleshy arm fell out from underneath the sheet. There was only a half pinkie finger on the dangling hand. Jackson held tightly onto Mac. Annie had saved many lives in those last frantic seconds.

They drank heartily from the bottled water given them and thanked the paramedic who found them.

"Wouldn't have found you had it not been for that little bird. Gave you away."

The two survivors looked at each other. Mac turned to the paramedic. "Little bird?"

"Little sparrow. Sat on that pile and made a racket so loud the dogs came runnin'. Like he knew you were in there."

Mac smiled down on Jackson whose look said 'I told you so'.

FINALLY OUTSIDE THE yellow-taped disaster area Jackson was reunited with his mother. She hugged him and cried and made such a big fuss over him that he was embarrassed in front of Mac. Just as he feared, she said something about having a little talk with him when they got home. Jackson introduced Mac to his mother and told her that Mac saved his life in the tornado.

"Mac. What kind of name is that?"

"Short for McBride. They call me Mac. Irish."

"And the luck of the Irish was with you then. Thank you so much for taking care of my son," she said squeezing Mac's hand in both of hers.

"I'm not so sure that it was I who did all the taking care of..." he offered. Mrs. Crawford was short with blonde hair like Jackson's and pretty he thought. Her soft blue eyes were the same shade as Jackson's. "In fact it was more like..."

"Teamwork," Jackson said.

"Your son is an exceptional young man."

"Well thank you Mac. He certainly can be," she said, combing her son's hair with her fingers. May I give you a ride to your car in Geneva?"

"Oh no, Mrs. Crawford. I can get a taxi."

"Don't be silly. It's the least I can offer. And please call me, Jean"

The three of them piled in the front seat and pulled out of the little end of the line town of Elburn. When they arrived in Geneva Jackson's mother insisted that Mac come for Sunday dinner.

"On no, I couldn't impose, Mrs., er. Jean."

Mac felt Jackson's sharp elbow in the side of his already sore ribs. "On second thought, that sounds good to me."

Jackson shot Mac a wink. Mack smiled and returned the favor.

Trumpeteer

In a sleepy bedroom community just outside of town, a docile retirement home lies nestled between a shady, tree-lined street and an overgrown forest. Behind the Alden Home tall oak trees rise from the elephant grass and when a breeze blows their gnarly limbs tremble like arthritic fingers. Butterflies flutter about, not the dark orange ones with black specks but the pure white ones that bounce lively and are easy to catch with a net. Rabbits peek out from behind drapes of high grass awaiting their chance to make a beeline for a quick snack of pansies planted under a magnolia tree.

It is here that every Tuesday morning, Michal Levy, musician par excellence warms up his shiny trumpet, 'Ol Sugar. In little less than an hour from now he will perform for the residents of Alden Home. But for now this is the concert before the concert. From the homes surrounding the grounds sashes and sliding glass doors swoosh open almost on cue as the Trumpeteer primes his brass prize. Some come out on their patios, roll up their umbrellas and take their morning coffee to the beat of Ol' Sugar's luscious tones. An army of landscapers scurry about the properties smiling and whistling as they work.

He presses his moist lips to the mouthpiece, puffs hard and beautiful notes fill the forest audience. Michal wonders if this might be the day. Each week he comes dutifully, faithfully hoping that this will be the day she remembers him.

From the second floor of the Alden Home, Berna Levy cracks her window open, just enough to hear the brassy tones she remembers so well. A tear slides down her cheek into the coffee cup she stirs aimlessly but she cannot taste it. The mystical music floats through the crack of the window while his fingers work like pistons atop Ol'Sugar. Berna closes her eyes. The Trumpeteer's fingers are pale and soft like that of a physician's. Like those of her husband's, Gustav.

Chapter Two

"Berna, I have made arrangements for you and Michal to go to my uncle's in Paris," Gustav said.

"Please Gustav, not tonight. One more night won't hurt," Berna pleaded wiping her powdered hands on her apron.

Gustav drew his wife close, squeezing her affectionately. Little clouds of flour puffed from her ample figure, enveloping them in a fog.

"You need to go tonight. The soldiers come closer each day. I will join you later this week. I must help the Liebermans make haste and see to it that my instruments are safe."

Gustav Levy was the finest music teacher in Strasbourg, perhaps in all of France and Germany. He taught piano at the University but when at home played mostly the trumpet and saxophone. His collection of brass instruments was the finest in all of Europe. Auction houses and antique dealers came from all over the continent to view his prizes. In a small shop in the basement he restored dented or twisted pieces of metal into sirens of the gods. Soon his instruments multiplied and he outgrew the shop. Then the second floor studio where he gave private lessons filled quickly also. Finally he bought his own studio in the heart of Strasbourg on a winding street next to a bakery. Each day the sweet smell of early morning pastries would greet him.

But Bernadette Levy worried about the safety of her husband and their young son, Michal. Just outside Strasbourg in Germany, the soldiers had rounded up other Jewish families then transferred them to ghettos on the outskirts of town. Things had begun to change in Germany since Adolf Hitler had come to power. They scared poor Mrs. Lieberman half to death when they visited her house last week and asked for identification.

Michal was almost seven years old now. A handsome boy resembling his father more so than Berna but still he had her piercing gray eyes. She sat him on her lap to inform him they would be leaving that night.

"When will Poppa come, Mother?"

"Soon, Michal. Soon." She stroked his smooth hair watching a reflection of her sad eyes in his.

Berna never saw Gustav again. He like many other Jews had been banished to the ghetto. Later, he met his fate at one of Hitler's concentration camps. She had barely enough time to tell Gustav she loved him before fleeing. All she had left of her life in Strasbourg was her son, Michal.

HITLER AND HIS war followed them to the uncle's house in France. So from there they fled to America, first New York and then later, Chicago where they met many Jewish friends who shared the same fate. Berna missed the old country and her friends but most of all her beloved Gustav. It was a terrible time to be Jewish. It was a terrible time to be.

Michal eventually married, not to a nice Jewish girl, but to Berna's chagrin, a Catholic. He became a successful banker and raised his own family. Michal shared his father's affinity for music and often played organ in the Church choir. One day word came from a friend in the neighborhood that Gustav's fine collection of musical instruments had shown up in a deserted castle outside Munich. The German government had laid claim to the whole collection. Berna had grown old in the decades since the war but was incensed that Gustav's prizes had been taken. Michal hired a European law firm skilled in the retrieval of stolen artwork from the Nazi era. After nearly two years of expensive legal machinations the high court deemed Berna and Michal the rightful owners of the priceless Levy Collection.

The last few years of legal battles had taken their toll on Berna. Her health worsened and she had trouble remembering her grandchildren's names when they came to visit. When Michal recommended she move into the local retirement home she reluctantly agreed.

"Fine, but I am not staying there," she informed Michal. "That place is a death sentence." But stay she did. And in time she grew comfortable there. Michal was distressed that Berna didn't return his phone calls but it was only because she forgot. She made new friends and forgot about Hitler's war, her homeland and Gustav. Forgotten too were Michal and her grandchildren.

Chapter Three

Michal sold most of his father's instruments to the Strasbourg University School of Music. The remainder of the collection he had shipped home. When the shipment arrived his two daughters circled the roughhewn crates with curiosity. Marta, the oldest at eight dutifully informed her six year old sister, Gwen, which crate was hers.

"This one shall be mine," she declared placing her hand atop the larger one.

"What about me?" asked Gwen.

"Yours is over here," she said smiling widely, to encourage her sister to do the same while pointing at a smaller crate.

Gwen rushed up to the crate and placed her ear alongside it.

"It's not a sea shell silly," Marta laughed.

Gwen tipped it back and forth. "Daddy please open them up. Please."

"Okay, but don't be disappointed if they're not toys," Michal warned. He removed the steel bands with wire cutters and used a hammer to pop open the tops. Inside were numerous instruments packed in wads of strange, stringy hair-like material the color of wood shavings.

"That's excelsior," Michal explained. "It protects the instruments."

"It protects the instruments," Marta echoed in a falsetto voice wagging her finger in the air for emphasis.

Michal and Gwen turned toward the strange voice. Behind them Marta stood adorned in a curly wig of excelsior, giggling. Gwen grabbed a handful to imitate her older sister.

"Okay you two, here are Grandpapa's instruments," he exclaimed.

"These belonged to Grandpapa?" They asked in unison of the man they'd only seen in old, cracked photographs.

Meanwhile Michal handled each instrument carefully examining fingerprints once left by his Poppa. He recalled how big his father's eyes got when he pursed his lips and filled his lungs with air to play. His bushy mustache hung over the mouthpiece and flickered side to side as his cheeks filled like sails from the wind.

"Daddy, this one is no good. It has a dent in it." Gwen handed him an old trumpet. Michal recalled seeing that particular trumpet long ago. Poppa had worked hours restoring the damaged instrument. Each time he took a dent out or replaced a part it sounded better. "Alt zuker, I shall call this one, for its sweet, luscious notes are music to my ears."

"Alt zuker?" Marta repeated, scrunching her face inquisitively. "What is alt zuker?"

"That is German for Ol' Sugar," he explained

Michal picked up the trumpet and played for the girls. They laughed and giggled making him play until his cheeks were fire engine red just like they were when he filled balloons for them.

Then he had a wonderful idea. His mother would love to hear Ol' Sugar again. He contacted the retirement home and offered his services. They loved the idea and it was decided that he would play late morning mini-concerts for the residents every Tuesday. Michal couldn't imagine a better gift for his mother than the familiar tones his father used to coax out of Ol' Sugar. Perhaps then she would remember her son.

Chapter Four

The Pavilion room offered a resplendent view of the shaggy green forest behind the home. The mid-morning sun had just begun to peek around the southern windows illuminating the room with yolk-yellow ribbons of radiance. Michal greeted each resident as they entered. Berna had dabbed away her tears and come downstairs with her friend, Agnes.

"Say hello to our Trumpeteer, Berna," Agnes said.

Berna looked up at Michal. He saw in her his own pale gray eyes. Her eyes looked tired. Thin black lines of eyeliner stopped short of meeting at the insides of her eyes. The lipstick covering her cracked lips never reached the corners of the mouth. She smiled politely. "Good morning, young man."

Michal squeezed her hand in his. "Always glad to see you, Mrs. Levy."

Berna shuffled by him and Agnes whispered in his ear.
"I'm so sorry, Michal. Perhaps later then."

"Perhaps later, Agnes. Please, don't be sorry. Be happy we are together." Her hand slipped out of his and the two friends took a seat near the back of the room.

Michal pointed his instrument skyward. Soon the room dripped of richly textured notes seemingly heaven sent. A thin white-haired man hunched at the waist suddenly sat erect in his chair and began to tap his foot in rhythm to the music. A frail woman next to him clasped her once trembling hands as if in prayer and began to clap lightly. The sea of white before him swayed in unison like rolling clouds.

Michal had Ol' Sugar all warmed up and he launched into a couple of the old tunes his father would play for him when he was a young lad. These were his mother's favorites. Ol' Sugar poured forth the enchanting songs.

Berna sat motionless, eyes closed, swept away to a different time, a different land. Deep within their Strasbourg basement she heard tapping and banging as Gustav brought to life injured instruments. Each note he played grew in richness and texture as he pounded out their nicks and dents. The fresh smell of warm bakery bread wafted by. She could taste the sweet white icing atop the strudel as it melted on her tongue.

Berna opened her eyes and leaned over to Agnes. "He reminds me of my dear Gustav."

"He reminds me of your son, Michal," Agnes prompted her.

Berna frowned at Agnes. "Michal married a Catholic girl."

Agnes squeezed Berna's hand tightly. Before them Michal had 'Ol Sugar in full bloom dancing and swaying, following the lead of his busy fingertips. Beadlets of sweat formed on his brow. A drop ran down his now rosy cheek. He sought out his mother in the crowd. She had that distant look he'd seen before. Far from the Alden Home, Berna saw herself sitting in her favorite stuffed chair at their Strasbourg home.

The freshly-baked dark bread was his favorite. Michal would dip the warm bread into his mother's tea so as to melt the butter she'd swirled on it. He took another bite, savored it then dipped it again.

Gustav's voice boomed from the living room. "Berna, you're not spoiling the boy."

"Oh no, Poppa. He's just hungry."

She buttered another piece of bread, dipped it into the tea and gave it to her son. A moment later he implored her, "One more, Mama. Please."

She laughed aloud and put her finger on her son's tummy. "One more and we'll have to roll you out."

Chapter Five

After the concert the crowd exited the room in high spirits. Each and every resident shook hands with the Trumpeteer. They thanked him for brightening their day. As he looked about the room for his Mother and Agnes he noticed that amongst the chairs two canes and a walker had been left behind, no longer of use this day.

Michal wiped the sweat from his brow with a handkerchief and dabbed at his moist eyes. His mother shuffled by him then turned to raise her eyes to his. They looked at each other for a long moment before she spoke.

"When you play, you remind me of—of my late husband, Gustav," she placed her hand over his heart. "He was a hero, that man." Berna lowered her head and ambled away.

Someone tugged at his arm. It was Agnes.

"She is very proud of you, Michal."

He smiled politely. The two women shuffled down the long hallway until out of sight. Ol' Sugar was cool now and nestled comfortably in its velvet-lined case. Michal closed the lid patting it gently. *Perhaps next week, Ol' Sugar.*

Fit for Death

O n approach it can be somewhat intimidating knowing that everyone inside is watching you not out of pure interest but because they are either bored with their monotonous routine or there isn't much to watch on the six overhead television sets. The windows that overlook the parking lot and entrance walk provide beyond that a view of what is usually a very busy scene including a playpark for toddlers, a high school football field and two softball diamonds. Further in the distance freight trains chug by on elevated railroad tracks splitting the horizon, spewing puffs of white smoke that touch the clouds. Since the parking lot is at the far end one must follow the entrance walk past this monstrous bank of long, two-story windows that cover over half the building. If it's a sunny day you can see reflected in the long windows the same scene they see although you can't see them watching you. Because of the walk's proximity to the windows you're the principal player on this crowded stage. Once inside the club you become the audience watching a silent movie of actors who continually enter stage left and exit stage right.

"Hi Jimmy."

"Hello, Mr. Stack."

"Sleep here again last night?"

Jimmy broke into a wide grin. He liked being kidded.

"No sir, but I ought to. I'm here enough." He reaches under the counter and hands me a fluffy white cotton towel. "Have a good work-out, Mr. Stack."

"Thanks, Jimmy. You're the best." He smiles again. 'Jimmy Towels' is a friendly college student who's been working the front desk since high school. He is tall and lean with ears that stick out from his head like large potato chips. A mop of sandy, unkempt hair looks as though his mother cut it at home, months ago. No matter how bad your day has been, it's over once Jimmy smiles that big-toothed smile of his and plops your towel on the counter.

The fitness area is packed with post work patrons mounting raw steel machines busily going nowhere. It's bright and sunny outside the bank of long windows, a great day to be alive, so I thought.

The Clifton Courts health club is located on the western edge of Clifton situated between the Burlington Northern and Northwestern train tracks just south of the two stone quarry pits dotting either side of Route 83. The Courts has been there since 1971 and has undergone two extensive expansions to now serve over three thousand members a week while open twenty-four hours a day. When you pack that many frenetic bodies close together something is bound to happen. Last week it did.

Late Friday evening the body of Gina Garrison, head racquet sports coordinator, was found dead in racquetball court #6 at the far end of the building. Her neck had been broken as if from a fall. And that's what the Clifton Police were calling it, for the moment. Having lived in Clifton all of my forty-two years of life, and being a private investigator, I was asked to look into Gina's death. Of course it didn't hurt that I was already a member of Clifton Courts. Tom Monaghan, club director, hired me for the usual fee plus expenses. Jack Stack, local private investigator, had a case right in his own backyard. I'd have taken it anyway, but it came with a free membership and a little paunch had begun to form down in the area where my stomach used to be, so I figured it couldn't hurt.

Chapter Two

I'd played tennis in college but little since. If I were to find out something about the doings at the Club then signing up for private lessons with Guy Atkins, head tennis pro was a must. We worked relentlessly every day at 4:00 p.m. sharp. He controlled my movements by moving me side to side with his crisp volleys, testing my forehand and then my backhand. Afterwards while I was sucking wind and mopping my brow he would carefully critique my strengths while making sure I realized my weaknesses.

"Your forehand is very good for not having played," he said. "But we're going to have to work on that backhand a little." Guy smiled as I struggled to catch my breath. He waited patiently for me to reply.

"Thanks for the backhanded compliment."

Guy had an easygoing demeanor, nice wide-eyed smile and a big head. Not the kind you get from being good and knowing it but literally a big head.

He was an excellent athlete who kept himself in top shape. I found out that he had gone to college on a baseball scholarship and played a little semipro ball. Like most frustrated major sport athletes who didn't have the size or speed, he found another sport that didn't require either but played to other strengths, like agility and coordination—tennis. And he was easily the best in the Club. He spent most of his time giving private lessons to young developing players, mostly those whose parents could afford him. And most of those were from the girls' tennis team at Clifton High. They would bang volley after volley until the court was littered lime green with tennis balls while a vigilant father watched from the bench. Afterwards he would always give them a pep talk and then offer a briefing with the parent. His passion for the game and affable personality endeared him to his pupils and their parents.

But get him in a competitive match with guys of his talent level and Guy was a different, well, guy. One afternoon in a tough doubles match with two 'A' players and another instructor from the club, he really let loose on his partner with a string of profanities when missing an easy volley for match point. Competitive juices die hard. As do tempers.

"That's too bad about, Gina," I fished around.

Guy bent down to stuff his racquet into an enormous tennis bag that held three or four extra racquets. "She was my direct supervisor. As Racquet Sports Coordinator, I mean. Great person. Been here a long time. Everybody liked Gina."

Everyone but one, I thought. I wondered who would replace her in the hierarchy.

"Were you close?"

"Close?" he rose to look me in the eye.

"Did you get along well?"

"Certainly."

"You going to be next Racquet Sports Coordinator?"

Guy smiled like the mouse that'd been through the maze one too many times. "I see where you're going with this, Jack. No, I'm not interested. I make too much money from lessons to give up that time just to do something I don't want to do—be an administrator. I like playing—and teaching tennis."

"Where were you last Friday evening?"

"Had a lesson from eight to nine and then played a match from nine to ten. Left the club after that. Gina was friend of mine, don't even go there, Jack."

"Somebody went there, Guy."

I left the court and headed for the showers. Guy's next lesson was already warming up.

Chapter Three

I sat in the steam room soothing my aching body with the hot, wet vapor isolating me in my pain. The close air made it tough and difficult to breathe. Prior to joining the Club, I stayed in shape but mostly by walking my Jack Russell terrier, Ajax or beating the speed bag in my garage twice a week. Still had that golden gloves form twenty years later. Working out was one thing but being worked out by someone else was cruel and inhuman torture.

I already knew Frederick Piper III from the Chamber of Commerce. A successful real estate agent by the age of forty, he had made most of his money buying and selling local properties in Clifton. His wife, Katrina, was a former 'hands' model whose lovely hands adorned various jewelry and other highbrow magazines. They had founded their own real estate firm and together bought, sold and either lived in or ran their business at one time out of all of them. Fred had been divorced twice with three young children by the time he'd met Katrina. She was very active in the community having served on the Chamber of Commerce and various other charitable organizations in town. The daughter of Pat and Terri Hamilton, she inherited her height from her mother who played volleyball at Northwestern and her wealth from her father, who owned the Clifton National Bank. Katrina had never been married before. Together their buying power was unrivaled and so had been their manner of doing business. If they bought from you or retained your services and didn't get a lead or referral in return they soon found someone else to replace you.

A muffled voice pierced the dampness.

"Hey, Jack, that you?" Fred Piper was seated right across from me. With the steam valve hissing and filling the room with dewy clouds I hadn't noticed him.

"Fred?"

"Yeah. How the hell are you?"

"Fine, Fred," I deadpanned. He was not one of my favorite people.

"Put that little place of yours up for sale yet?"

It wasn't little and it certainly wasn't for sale. "Not yet, Fred."

"Let me know when you do. We have some very interested buyers…"

"I'll let you know, Fred."

We sat in silence for moments. Funny how some people whose life is their business run out of things to say once bizspeak is dead.

"Too bad about Gina Garrison," he said.

"Real bad for Gina Garrison."

"That why you're here?"

"Yep."

"I can't imagine her falling like that. She was in such great shape, a real fitness nut."

Fit for death, I thought. I wondered why Fred had mentioned her name. He had a reputation before marrying Katrina Hamilton of being a real ladies' man about town. Why the sudden interest? People have a way of talking to me about death. Part of the job, I guess—me and morticians.

"You know her?"

"Come on, Jack. Everyone knew Gina. How could you not know her?" Fred leaned forward through the hot mist. I could see his round, chubby face. He had gained quite a bit of weight since I'd seen him last. Looked like Cupid in the clouds.

"Now if you meant 'knew' her in the Biblical sense, I resent that question."

I leaned forward and tilted my head slightly so he could see the angular features of the Jack Stack boxer's nose and infamous glass jaw.

"How well did you know her?" I repeated.

"Sold her home to her this year. She was really in love with this three bedroom Tudor over on Larch street. Thought she got a good deal." The only good deal anyone got was also a good deal for Fred.

"Heard she beat you in racquetball."

"Well, word does travel. She beat me one out of three games we played." Nobody beat Fred.

"You at the club last Friday evening?"

"Yeah. Played racquetball from seven to eight. After that I took a steam and whirlpool and went home. Were you aware that Gina Garrison was having an affair, Jack?"

"No," I said, surprised.

"You might want to check that out. I didn't kill Gina. I liked her."

If Fred Piper liked someone they were in trouble.

"You let her win?"

He let out a big grunt and climbed down from his perch. Wafts of billowy moisture curled behind his large, rotund body as he moved. The door opened and the vapors rushed to escape.

"No," he mumbled.

If Gina Garrison was indeed having an affair then I had a new angle to work and possible motivation for her murder—or fall as it was being called.

Chapter Four

The class was tough at first, the footwork being so different from that in boxing, so I hid in the back like the poor student until I learned the steps. After a few classes I got the hang of it enough to move forward nearer the instructor. Aerobics classes were not my favorite but in my business you do a lot of things you don't like.

Our instructor was full of energy today and I was paying the price. My cotton tee shirt was wetter than any of the tight, shiny, stretch danskins the ladies in the class wore and my new Reebok cross trainers began to hurt so much I'd swear they were a size too small. I'll never understand why women can workout for an hour and not sweat while I work up a sweat putting my shoes on.

She wore a headset over her bright, short blonde hair and barked orders into our brains while deafening disco music inspired our rapid foot movements across the stepper, a little platform designed to make the workout even harder as you stepped up and over and around the nuisance. High cheekbones and a strong jaw that jutted out to touch the microphone on the headset gave her a commanding presence. A thin strapped, black tank top showed off her strong, well-rounded shoulders and narrow waistline. Tight black leotards accentuated her muscular legs and severely protruding gluteus maximus.

Every once in a while I'd mess up a step and could feel the drill sergeant's tone rise an octave as if everyone was being punished for my shortcomings. Pat Fagan's dance aerobic class was the most crowded offering at the club. If you didn't get there early and grab your stepper, you didn't dance. Her dances were original and the music fun. She had the figure of a bodybuilder but moved like a gazelle. Afterwards, I introduced myself. Keeping my distance so as to not drip on her, I explained my reason for being at the club.

"Jack you didn't have to take my class just to question me." Her voice was very pleasant now.

"When's the next class start?" my face was red and I couldn't stop dripping.

Pat took my hand turned it over and put two fingers on my wrist. A few seconds later she removed them. "No more class for you. Your heart rate is through the roof. Let's walk and cool down a bit."

As we walked I talked.

"Obviously you knew Gina Garrison."

"Yes, I'd known Gina from another club we used to belong to. It was on her referral I was hired here." She handed me a water bottle from her bag.

"Straight water?"

"Follow orders and you might make it through this week."

I listened and drank. "Where were you Friday evening, if I may ask?"

"Here at the club. My last class was over at eight and then I worked out upstairs in the fitness area until nine or so and left. You can check my time card," she smiled. Pat Fagan for all her intimidating presence was very attractive, when smiling.

"I will." I'd finally stopped sweating. "Oh, you know anything about her having an affair?"

"What kind of affair?"

"An affair affair, why"

"Gina was gay, you know."

"Oh." A person's sexual orientation certainly wouldn't preclude one from having an affair. But it sure could shrink the playing field of suspects.

Chapter Five

Rick Cannon watched me intently as I worked my way through the various weight machines. He charted the pounds and repetitions in a small notebook so as to record my progress. Every once in a while I could see him shaking his head. Now I am not a weightlifter but I'm no weakling either. Obviously my boxing skills and walking regimen didn't translate into success in the fitness area.

Rick was the senior personal trainer at the club. He could usually be found in the fitness area walking around the track with newer members, breaking them in slowly or encouraging them to their limits on the weight and cardio machines. A popular trainer with all members Rick was of average height and somewhat older than most of the other employees, mid-fifties maybe, but still fit. You could tell his tan came from a salon but it looked better than some of the bottle tans that ranged from Indian red to Mayan bronze. His hair was suspiciously blonde. Nevertheless, it looked good with his tan.

He always had an encouraging word for those around him and seemed to genuinely care about his clients—most of which were women, housewives usually—with money to burn, each trying to outdo the other. Rick had what I call, job security.

I'd been on the treadmill for fifteen minutes already and was beginning to work up a thirst.

"Don't forget to drink your water," Rick pointed to the bottle in the cupholder.

"Yessir," I saluted. I was sick of water. It lacked the refreshment of a cold beer and tasted like plastic when lukewarm. A quick swig kept him happy.

Finally he mercifully slowed the treadmill to 'cool down'. I wrapped a towel around my neck and I began a nice walking pace.

"Rick, you've been here a long time. What did you think of Gina Garrison?" My words were spliced between desperate breaths for air.

"I heard through the grapevine that you were asking a lot of questions, Jack." Rick made sure his surfer's smile wasn't lost on me.

"Good, then you won't mind answering a few. Gina?"

"Gina was great. She got along with everyone. She could be tough though.

"Tough how?"

"Controlling, manipulative. She wielded a lot of power around here as second in charge. I didn't have a problem with her like some."

"Some?" Whenever I see someone deflect attention and raise a shield I raise an eyebrow.

"Well, I know Guy wasn't pleased with her. She kept shifting a lot of his team tennis pupils to other instructors and cutting his lesson hours."

"Why would she do that?" I could breathe again and took pleasure in that simple task.

"There were rumors about Guy and one of his students from the Girls' Tennis Team at Clifton High."

This was the first I'd heard of this. "Was it true?"

"Truth and rumor dress alike at this club, Jack. You should know that."

"Yeah. So you liked Gina."

"I didn't say I 'liked' her. I got along with her. Please don't put words in my mouth." All of a sudden Rick seemed defensive.

"You here Friday evening?"

"Taught a spinning class from eight to nine that evening. Punched out and left shortly afterward. You can verify that."

"I will," I said, stepping off the treadmill and drinking the last of my plastic water.

"That all?"

"For now."

"I've got it good here, Jack. I'd never murder anyone," Rick left me alone in the fitness area, a duck out of water.

Rick Cannon had it good here all right, maybe a bit too good.

Chapter Six

My interviews had been more productive than I'd expected these last couple days. Guy Atkins was allegedly mixed up with one of his girls' tennis team members. Gina Garrison was having an affair—a gay affair at that. And I was beginning to lose the paunch above my belt. Not a bad week's work. Yet some loose ends bothered me. How could Fred Piper know of Gina's affair and not know the specifics—that it was probably with another woman. How did Pat Fagan know Gina was gay? Did she have firsthand knowledge? And why was Rick Cannon the only one who knew of Guy's possible involvement with a member of the Girls' Tennis Team? By the time I found the answers to these questions and the true cause of Gina's 'fall', I might be ready for the Club's upcoming 5K run. I wasn't sure how long a 'K' was but I was glad to hear it was less than a mile.

The fact that Fred Piper had just sold Gina a home in Clifton seemed interesting. The Dupage County Courthouse seemed a good place to start. All real estate transactions were kept on file in the basement of the annex building. Fred Piper's real estate agency was listing agent and selling agent on the Garrison property that had sold three months ago. Fred had made a nice commission on the deal but it all seemed legit. Before leaving, I decided to check the court records just in case. Court records were kept on touch screen computer on each floor of the Courthouse building itself. By just entering a name you could pull up any past or pending court cases. Gina Garrison's name was listed. First entry was Gina Garrison vs. Eric Garrison—her divorce proceeding two years ago. Next was a DUI conviction just a couple of months ago. That didn't seem to go with a woman who was all about fitness. Last was the entry Ms. Gina Garrison vs. Classic Real Estate. Classic Real Estate was owned by Fred and Katrina Piper. The case was still pending.

I called in a marker with a longtime friend in the Courthouse filings area and found out that Gina Garrison was suing Classic over the property she had recently purchased. Apparently there were some severe structural problems that had showed up after a period of rainstorms. One corner of the foundation had sunk some thirteen inches. Gina had been suing to rescind the deal. Classic was countering that the home passed inspection at time of sale. At question was a $300,000 property. Classic's commission, $15,000, had been escrowed pending judgement.

"HI, MR. S. How are you today?"

"Fine, Jimmy. Two please." Jimmy Towels stacked two white fluffy cotton ones on the counter for me. "Big workout today?"

"Lookin' good, Mr. S." He was right. I was beginning to look pretty good, almost back to fightin' shape. I nodded for Jimmy to meet me at the end of the counter.

"Jimmy, I need your help."

"Sure, Mr. S. Anything I can do. Is this about Ms. G.?"

"I'm afraid it is. What do you know about Guy Atkins and…" I hesitated hoping Jimmy could finish my thought.

"Carla Edwards, number one girls' singles player at Clifton High. We actually dated a few times. She liked me, I think, until…" he hesitated before speaking in a whisper, "I'm not supposed to be telling you this, I promised Ms. G."

"That's all right, Jimmy. That's why Mr. M. hired me." I was speaking Jimmy's lingo now, making him feel like he was in a James Bond movie.

He looked around and leaned forward. "Ms. G. caught Guy and Carla sitting in Guy's car out in the south lot one evening after lessons. She never let on as to what exactly she saw. I never saw her so angry. Said Guy told her he was just giving Carla a ride home."

"When was this?"

"Couple of months ago."

Coincidentally, that was about the same time as Gina's DUI. For my money, coincidence is evidence.

Jimmy Towels had given me some timely information. So Guy was coaching and poaching the Clifton High Girls' Tennis Team star. Carla Edwards was good, real good. She only played against men at the club and beat most of them. Her two-handed backhand just exploded. It was more powerful than most opponent's forehand. Next year she'd be playing for the University of Illinois on scholarship. Heck, she could probably go now. She already looked college age. Tall and lanky with arms that could reach any alley shot, she wore her blonde hair back in a ponytail that bobbed like a whitetail deer when she played. I always wondered how she got around on her shots being so big-breasted, but it didn't seem to bother her, just put more thunder behind the ball—and other things.

Guy was coaching an adult beginners' group when I found him and waved him over. He instructed his charges to continue drilling and walked behind the court to see me. He leaned forward inquisitively. A bright red Wilson racquet was in his hands. He kept one eye on me and the other trained eye on the drills. His face waggled like a bobble head doll or someone who'd watched too many tennis matches.

"Jack, what is it? I've got a class."

"Don't worry, Guy. It'll just take a minute. Two words."

"Go ahead."

"Carla Edwards." A warm red glow percolated up from his neck and filled his face.

"Screw her," he said through clenched teeth.

"Did you?"

"Screw you."

"Don't dare." I got right in his face, or forehead, my being a few inches taller.

"Nothing happened. I gave her a ride home one evening."

Who gave whom a ride was a matter of debate. He grasped the racquet tightly like a weapon. I didn't back off an inch.

"Gina Garrison caught you two, didn't she?"

"There was nothing to catch."

"Too bad Gina isn't here to confirm that."

Guy relaxed his grip on the racquet. He seemed to melt into his coaching mode.

"Gina didn't see shit, Jack. Gina was stressed out anyway."

"Oh?"

"Yeah, early last week she caught Pat Fagan shooting up in bathroom of the ladies locker room."

"Heroin?"

"Jack, this is a health club not a crack house. Steroids. How the hell do you think Pat got that big? Now I've got to get back to my lesson."

Pat Fagan on steroids? Her body was developed like a body builder's. And whatever happened between Guy Atkins and Carla Edwards had incensed Gina Garrison enough that she was visibly upset. I wondered how Carla Edwards father would feel about all of this.

TOM MONAGHAN CALLED me into his office. Forensics had come back clean on Gina Garrison's body. No telltale fingerprints or bruises other than the trauma to the head from the fall could be found. Fingerprints had been found on the viewing ledge above the court. After the crime scene had been secured all Club employees were required to submit fingerprints to the Clifton police. Those on the ledge had belonged to Rick Cannon.

Tom had more news for me. He unlocked the top drawer of a file cabinet along the wall and pulled out a file marked 'Employee Reports'. Last month Gina had written up Rick Cannon. 'Write Ups' were like Club report cards. One could affect your annual review. Raises and overtime were doled out sparingly by Mr. Monaghan on the basis of Gina's reports. More than one violation could mean immediate dismissal.

I pressed Tom for this confidential information. Apparently, Rick had been censured by Gina for "conducting Club activity off premises for profit". I asked what this meant in Clubspeak. He informed me that Rick Cannon had been found doing personal training at his home with Mrs. Alicia Silvers, a Club member. Not only was this against Club policy but it also affected the Club's bottom line. And Tom Monaghan was all about the bottom line. More importantly, it didn't look good if Club members, especially married ones, were keeping up their fitness with Club staff off premises. Now Rick Cannon had two strikes against him. I found Rick in the trainer's office munching down a tuna fish on whole wheat.

"Rick, Rick, Rick." this was my way of starting in on someone when I had them dead to rights.

"Hi Jack, yogurt for you?" He handed me a small container.

"No, thanks, just had a bacon double cheeseburger. I thought you told me you didn't have a problem with Gina?"

"Not at all."

"Mrs. Silvers ring a bell?"

"Oh that," he paused to lick his lips.

"That was my bad. Mrs. Silvers had been pestering me for weeks to do some home sessions at a reduced price. Have you met, Mrs. Silvers?" *I hadn't.* "Alicia can be very persuasive." *I bet.* "Anyhow, I did. And she told one of her girlfriends who told one of her girlfriends who told… you know how Clifton is, Jack."

"Good thing nobody told her husband."

"Jack, Jack, Jack. You don't think that I…" that movie star smile might have worked on Alicia Silvers but it wasn't working on me.

"Wanna tell me about your fingerprints on the viewing ledge above the racquetball court where Gina was found." His smile became a smirk.

"I watch matches all the time up there between sessions. We all do."

I knew he was right but sometimes push leads to shove. Rick wasn't shoving back. I rose to leave.

"Oh and Jack, skip the burger next time. Have a salad."

I hoped he liked his tuna fish on whole wheat sandwich. They serve it every Wednesday on white toast, in prison.

So Guy Atkins was giving 'private lessons' after hours with the star player of Clifton High Girls' Tennis Team. Rick Cannon whose prints were found on the viewing ledge of the racquetball court where Gina was found dead had also been 'written up' by Gina for conducting personal trainer lessons off premises with Mrs. Silvers. If Rick Cannon was my man then he was cooler than the cucumbers in his salad. Gina sure was upset with Guy Atkins for his dalliance with Carla Edwards but why hadn't she written him up like she did Rick? Fred Piper III's firm Classic Real Estate was being sued by Gina and Pat Fagan had been caught shooting steroids by Gina yet she wasn't written up either. I needed to talk with Fred and Pat soon. Where emotions still ran hot —so did leads.

Chapter Seven

The next day around lunchtime I caught up with Fred Piper in the whirlpool. The sea otter was lounging lazily, his massive body hidden underneath the bubbling waters like the iceberg that sunk the Titanic. Thick black hair soaked with foam covered his chest, shoulders and arms. The water level was precariously close to overflow.

"Hey, Fred," I said carefully stepping into the cauldron.

"Jack, I've missed you. Reconsider selling the little place yet?"

"I wouldn't get a good recommendation from Gina Garrsion on your firm would I. Of course, she's not around anymore either." I love myself when I'm subtle.

"So you know about the lawsuit."

"I do. Did you think I wouldn't."

"Gina didn't stand a chance in court. Home passed inspection prior to sale."

"Funny how the foundation sank so soon after the sale. How many home inspections does that outfit do a year for Classic?"

"Home inspections are done by an independent third party, Jack. That's mandated by law." Fred shifted uneasily. The water in the spa sloshed over the edges.

I stared at him for moments without saying a word. This worked well in boxing matches usually drawing my opponent out of their strategy and creating an opening for my lethal uppercut.

"Whatever. If you did your homework you'd find out that the commission has been escrowed until court proceedings have been determined. You'd have also found out that the amount escrowed is a whopping $15,000. Not enough to kill for, Jack."

I wanted to ask Fred at what amount he set the killing price but bit my tongue. Something I don't do often because I prefer to save my tongue for other pleasures. Fred was right though. As disagreeable and dishonest as he might be, I couldn't see him risking everything for a measly $15 grand. That was pocket change to Fred Piper III.

PAT FAGAN WAS in the aerobics room practicing her routine in the full-length mirrors that covered each wall and reflected the gleam of the shiny hardwood floor. Loud dance craze music boomed throughout the room echoing off empty walls and reverberating enough to shake the glass walled entrance. She didn't notice me enter the room until I reached over and turned off the stereo.

"Hey pal…" she wheeled around in a perfect pirouette with her outstretched leg just missing my face.

"Whoa, whoa there girl."

"What the hell do you think you're doing," she snapped through clenched teeth. The muscles in her face twitched. "I'm in the middle of a routine, here." Her muscular arm shot by me and I ducked as she reached out and pushed the power button on again. I reached down and yanked out the power cord holding it up for her to see.

"Show's over." Pat Fagan stiffened and calmed herself by breathing slowly and deeply. I reached over, grabbed the water bottle on the tall speaker and handed it to her. "Cool down, Pat. I've got a few questions for you." Realizing that I wasn't scared, she acquiesced and raised the bottle to her mouth. Before she could take a swig I grabbed her hand.

"That water clean?"

"Of course, what are you implying."

"You're not taking steroids?"

With this Pat broke out in a loud laugh, pulled the bottle away and slugged it down like a dockworker at a bar. "So you heard. Word travels fast."

"Where there's thunder, there's lightning. What's so damn funny?"

"You don't drink steroids, Jack. Get with the times."

"I'd rather not. Why don't you tell me about Gina catching you doing steroids."

"It's no big deal. I was pumping up for a bodybuilding contest last month. Everyone does it." she recapped the bottle and offered me some. I didn't trust her.

"Why didn't Gina write you up?"

"We lived together."

"You what?"

"You heard me. She held onto her house as long as she could after the divorce then it got too expensive for one person to afford. I let her stay with me until she found something. Then she bought that dump from Classic."

"You two were roommates?"

"You could say that."

"Could I say you were something other than roommates?"

"I don't kiss and tell, Jack." A wry smile formed across her strong face. Her punky blonde hair stood up in gelled spikes.

"Well seeing as Gina's dead, I think you're off the hook."

"Your could say we were an item. For a while."

"A while?"

"Yes, when she moved out and got her own place she found someone else."

"Guy Atkins," I surmised.

"Yes, how did you know?"

"Never mind. I thought you said Gina was gay."

"I thought so myself after the divorce. Some swing both ways. Her loss."

She plugged her music in and began swinging her muscle bound body around the stepper in rhythmic fashion pumping her knees high in the air and clapping her hands. I turned to leave thankful I'd never met anyone in the ring like Pat Fagan.

"Oh, and Jack," I turned around looked back knowing I shouldn't for fear of turning to stone, "don't ever turn my music off again." I left Pat Fagan spinning in her own drug-crazed, fantasy world. She may have been pissed off at Gina for leaving her for Guy Atkins but the fact that she wasn't written up over a surefire violation of club policy meant that the two still had a healthy respect, or fear, for each other.

Chapter Eight

I'd been at this for days now and was running out of suspects. First Rick Cannon had fallen off the radar screen and now Fred Piper III and Pat Fagan seemed unlikely murderers. A quick glance in the mirrors of the fitness area gave me a smile. The paunch around my waistline had shrunk. Unfortunately, I was always hungry. I bought a power bar from the snack counter and headed for Tom Monaghan's office. There was one piece missing from this puzzle and I figured I'd start at the top.

"What have you got for me, Jack?" Tom rubbed his fleshy face. I couldn't blame him. He was anxious to solve Gina's death and put the Club back on pace.

"Nothing yet." He wasn't pleased but tried not to show it. "Tom, who found Gina's body Friday night?"

"Jimmy from the front desk." Jimmy hadn't told me that he found Gina's body. "That hour of night I usually have one of the young people patrol the back halls by the racquetball courts. They're dimly lit at that hour as most matches are over by nine and we try to conserve on electricity. When Jimmy reports back which courts are empty we turn the lights off at the front desk for those courts."

"Can I assume that the light were out at nine o'clock Friday evening?"

"No, Jimmy did his last sweep around ten minutes after nine. That's when he found Gina's body." Tom looked like hell. If I didn't find Gina's killer soon, I was afraid he'd have a breakdown.

IT WAS FIVE o'clock, rush hour at the Club and Jimmy Towels was hurriedly signing members in and issuing them their white fluffies. I waited until he had a break.

"Jimmy, over here." I motioned for him to come over by the side counter.

"Sure Mr. S. Any breaks yet?"

"Jimmy, why didn't you tell me you were the one that found Gina Garrison's body?"

"Gee, Mr. S. It's not something I brag about. And you didn't ask."

"Never mind. We need a break in this case desperately. Mr. M. is losing patience and I'm running out of suspects. Did you see anything, hear anything, find anything that might help?"

"Not really, Mr. S. . . ." I could tell Jimmy was hesitating. He looked nervously around him. His large ears peaked through his straight hair as he swung back to face me.

"Jimmy, this is important." He reached under the counter and pulled out an envelope not sealed but closed with a rubber band and pushed it across the counter behind a stack of white towels. I removed the rubber band and peered in the envelope. Inside was a rubbery stretch sport bracelet. It was kelly green in color.

"What's this?"

"A sports bracelet."

"I know that." Yellow was the color of the Lance Armstrong bracelet for cancer that started the whole craze. Pink was for breast cancer awareness. But I didn't realize the significance of the green bracelet. "What's it for?"

"That's the colors of Clifton High, kelly green and white. All of the Girls' Tennis Team members wear one. Won't take it off until they win State." I couldn't believe what I had in my hand. Jimmy had had the bracelet the whole time. When I asked him why he didn't produce it earlier he just hunched his bony shoulders up sheepishly until they touched his mop of hair and said 'I dunno'. It was time to call Guy Atkins and Carla Edwards on the carpet and stir things up until the dust settled, just my type of housecleaning.

Chapter Nine

Tom Monaghan's sleeves were rolled up and his tie was loosened.
He kept twirling his pen in his fingers. He was nervous. Not as nervous
as Guy and Carla though. They sat across the desk from us in Tom's
small office to the side of the front desk. I let them squirm a little
before letting them know that we knew about their little affair. Guy
began to protest his innocence but I cut him off. Carla hung her head,
stared at the floor and said nothing. Now it was time to divide and
conquer. I threw the Kelly green sport bracelet on the desk.

"We found this on the floor where Gina Garrison fell. Look familiar?"

It got a reaction. Carla raised her head and appeared shocked to
see the bracelet. She pushed her blonde hair behind her ear and looked
at Guy in surprise.

"I lost my bracelet that night in your car. How did it get here?" I
had a feeling that wasn't the only thing she lost.

"Guy put it there to deflect suspicion from himself to you, Carla.
He had a lover's quarrel upstairs on the viewing floor with Gina. She
was furious with jealousy about his relationship with you. They had
been having an affair for months. That's why she didn't write Guy up
when she caught you two in the parking lot together."

Carla stood up in horror. Guy rose at the same time. She reached
back and slapped him with as good a forehand as I'd seen yet at the Club.

"You bastard…trying to frame me…" Carla began to sob.

"Atkins, you're fired." Even Tom got his two cents in.

Guy pulled a .38 special out of his pocket. Carla gasped. I stood up
immediately but Guy would have none of it.

"Sit down, Stack. I'm sorry, Carla. But Gina threatened to expose
us. You were my protégé. Had I gotten you into the University as their
number one player I could've opened up my own clinic around here.

You were my best shot in years. Once Gina started screaming and hitting me, I pushed back and she went over the ledge. It was an accident."

"Like the accident of leaving the bracelet behind to frame Carla."

"Shut up, Stack." he looked down at Carla. "Sorry, baby. You understand."

"Son of a bitch," she muttered.

Guy waved the gun around a little like an inexperienced gunhand would and then pulled Tom's phone cord out of the wall. He ordered us to stay seated and was out the door in a flash. Tom rose quickly. I put my hand across his chest to hold him back.

"He's got a gun, Tom."

The gun exploded like a cannon shot. A loud thud of bodies pounded up against the wall. I ran outside the office to find Guy slumped on the floor near the outside office wall. The gun lay nearby. Lying underneath him bleeding was Pat Fagan.

LATER THAT YEAR, Guy Atkins would be teaching tennis for the next fifteen to twenty years—at the state penitentiary. Carla Edwards went on to the University of Illinois and as a Freshman became their number one singles player. Rick Cannon now charges obscene hourly fees for his in-your-home Personal Training and has many wealthy Clifton housewives as clients including Mrs. Katrina Piper who along with her husband Fred, settled out of court with Gina's estate on the tainted home they sold her. Pat Fagan, after tackling an armed Guy Atkins, recovered nicely in the hospital for a few months with a punctured lung and broken rib. During that time she shed her steroids and her attitude. She still teaches aerobics at the Club but looks like a fit and trim athlete now—not a tight end.

I found out that Jimmy Towels was sweet on Carla Edwards. They had dated a couple of times. She was impressed to be going out with a college boy, until she graduated to Guy Atkins. That was why Jimmy Towels slipped me the information on Carla and Guy. He was jealous of Guy and knew that Guy was already on thin ice. Any light he could cast on Guy might help sink the surly tennis instructor. He kept the bracelet to protect Carla. Jimmy still works the front desk and dates the pretty coed that works behind the juice bar.

In Gina's memory the Club established the annual Gina Garrison Sportsmanship Award for the person most exemplifying great attitude, energy and decorum on the courts.

Now that I knew what a 'K' was, I was gearing up to run my second 5K race in the Clifton Courts Autumn Run. I still love the Club and work out there more than I ever did before. It's funny how when you put three—four thousand people, twenty-four hours a day, seven days a week, together what you get. It's all about fitness—until things go wrong.

The Empty Cup

s coffee shop goes it wasn't trendy, didn't offer lattes or a drive-thru but it served a piping hot, original home-brewed blend that kept its customers coming and the tip jar full. The Empty Cup coffee house sat at the end of Park street in a quiet Chicago suburb, Turner Junction, so-called for the numerous trains that crisscrossed the town eventually emptying into the massive rail complex on its west side. Park street at one time had been a busy thoroughfare that climbed a hill and crossed the railroad tracks a story above street level. Turner Junction's red brick train station loomed precariously above, its age reflected in a tired tilt caused by the settling foundation. As a result the The Empty Cup was forever engulfed in perpetual shade only to be devoured one inevitable day by the station as it slid downhill to its final resting place.

Years ago the railroad gates were removed and the street was blocked off to create a dead end. A wall of glass windows afforded the coffee-sipping patrons a view of passengers floating by like a busy aquarium. They carried heavy satchels in one hand with the other arm askew for balance as if carrying a bowling bag. Others bore loaded backpacks which bent them over at the shoulders affording a nice view of the tips of their shoes or loose change on the sidewalk. It was the perfect location for a coffee shop and The Empty Cup was always at least half-full, or half-empty depending on who was counting.

The young woman behind the counter spun around nimbly with a full cup of coffee and smiling, placed it directly on the sports page laid out on the counter.

"Hey, now how can I read about the Cubs game?" He frowned back at her his hazel eyes afire, adroitly lifted the cup while whisking the sports page out from underneath, replaced the cup and folded the paper beside it. The whole matador maneuver appeared graceful save for the shaky cup which threatened to spill the high seas of coffee inside.

"There's more to life than sports," she said.

"That's why I read the sports section, honey." He loved to call her honey. 'Bees come to honey' his mother used to say. "Rest of the world will just have to wait until I'm finished."

"Out late last night again, huh Dad?" While Vin relished his daughter's company he thought he could hear the seldom faint tones of her mother echoing somewhere in the deep repressed, recesses of his mind. Oh he'd been out late last night again. But to look at Vin Mcfinn you'd think he'd had ten hours of sleep. Sitting at the counter hid his true height. A pinkish face belied his years and a strict workout regimen kept his body trim. Truth be told it was the fine blend of not coffee but beer and bourbon that stretched his puffy facial skin tight. By day the health club he just about lived at helped purge the routine ingestion of nighttime toxins. Save for the occasional hand tremors he was a man who had successfully vanquished his own devils—for now.

"No later than any other evening. And I was up at the crack of dawn this morning writing while you were probably sleeping away your dreamy life. Then you broke the sound of light to get here while applying your mascara at each redlight and some quick eyeliner at the stop signs."

She turned back, her long blonde ponytail whipping off her square shoulders, kissed her fingertips and blew softly in Vin's direction.

"Love you too, Dad."

They got along well and truly sparkled in each other's company, much like he and her mother had some twenty years before.

A DEPARTING PATRON opened the door and an elderly woman in a wheelchair clamored in. She paused once inside to catch her breath and with both hands pushed back the beehive of wispy white hair swirling about her head. The Empty Coffee Cup like many of the dining establishments in town had been forced to succumb to federal handicap guidelines. Due to the extreme cost of remodeling they'd become compliant via a small envelope deposited in the back pocket of a city inspector; the coffee house had simply removed a stool at the counter. Maggie, seeing Esther in disarray, emerged from behind the counter and swiveled her way past some tables toward her wheelchair. Her out-of-the-bottle, in-the-sink-shiny red hair was pinned up loosely and bobbed as she talked. A low cut tight white blouse with a button conveniently missing revealed end of the alphabet cup sized breasts that would cause most to tip over but Maggie's ample backside served as a complementary counterweight giving her perfect posture. As she bent down to help the woman her double vision derriere set against a patron's backside inadvertently pushing his chair in for him. "Can I help you, Esther?"

"Thank you, Maggie," she said as she caught her breath. "Could you push me up to my usual spot, please."

Esther's head snapped back as the powerful woman navigated the wheelchair through the tables and up to the counter with a bang.

"I said 'up to the counter', not 'into it', godammit!"

"Sorry, Esther. It's crowded this morning," she apologized while laying a menu and full cup of coffee in front of her then hurried off to deliver an order.

Maggie was the whirling dervish that made The Empty Cup work. When she took over the little coffee shop four years ago there was seldom more than a handful of people inside. For the first few weeks she spent most of her time reading old newspapers the train passengers had left behind. Then she changed coffee vendors opting for a richer, premium blend to compete with the big name brands and began serving breakfast and lunch.

Maggie was a local girl, one of the few who stayed. Her senior year at Turner Junction High, or The Junk, as it was appropriately nicknamed, she was captain of the cheerleading squad. Now in her mid-forties and five years off her divorce she just didn't really care anymore. That coupled with a penchant for her own cooking meant the doorbell wasn't ringing for Maggie any longer, or was it the other way around.

When she returned Esther peered intently through thick reading glasses perched unevenly on the tip of her nose.

"Ahem," she cleared her throat. "Is there a problem?"

"Just looking for lipstick. Last cup I was served wore the mark."

"That was your lipstick, Esther."

"Wrong, dearie. I'm not wearing any..."

"Well you are now," she said planting a kiss from her ruby red-caked mouth on Esther's lips. Esther blushed a painted smile, "The usual, please."

"Crepes Suzette with extra whip cream, for the queen, please."

Maggie may have given up on herself but not others. She had a way of making them all feel like royalty.

Chapter Two

An athletic young man with a crew cut blew in the door swung his leg wide and mounted a stool near the window. He spun around on the stool full circle, smiling playfully. Vin noticed Blair followed his every move. He thought he heard the fellow wish her a good morning softly, almost privately. As Blair approached him his smile widened. His dark eyes mirrored the myriad of lights inside the coffee house.

"Good morning Car," she said placing a steaming cup of black coffee before him.

"Good morning, Blair Baby. How's your day so far?" His blonde crew cut and square jaw gave him an almost military look and made him appear older than her. Blair absentmindedly placed the scalding coffee pot on the counter as she chatted.

"Blair, don't scorch the counter with that pot!" Maggie yelled from the far end of the counter. Blair jumped, startled by the early morning shrill of her voice. Down went the coffee pot crashing into pieces leaving a shimmering river of black glass running through her legs. A few feet away a drain swallowed the swirling mess. Vin jumped out of his seat to see if she was hurt but the young man had already leaned over the counter pulling her aside.

"Are you okay?" he asked.

Maggie arrived and instant later. The rest of the patrons rose at once from their seats as if at church service only except they were more interested. Seeing no one maimed, the crowd sat back down on queue disappointed they weren't witness to some great catastrophe. But then again the patrons at The Empty Cup were a different breed altogether.

Blair had escaped most of the damage as the scalding coffee pot had narrowly missed her. Maggie raised her voice above the din of the diner and two busboys appeared out of nowhere scurrying around in a blur, a mixmaster of arms, elbows, dishrags and mops. Blair introduced the young man she'd been talking with to her father.

"Dad this is Carson." They shook hands cordially. Carson or 'Car' as Blair referred to him except for the short haircut reminded Vin of himself as a young man—all angles, from his powerful jaw to his square shoulders, broad chest, and long, lean arms. Their eyes locked as they shook hands each trying to out-squeeze the other. Somewhere along that icy link of vision a tremor of mutual dislike vibrated like a tuning fork.

"Pleasure, sir," Carson intimated.

"Likewise," Vin returned.

They were still shaking when Maggie intervened. "Okay boys, how about some coffee, on me, instead of Blair this time."

VIN KNEW THIS was his second chance. He'd only met Blair two years ago on her nineteenth birthday. Her mother, Rosa, knowing Vin would come whenever she called had contacted him.

"Vin, it's Rosa." He never tired of hearing her chanteuse voice, a result of having polyps removed from her throat as a teenager.

"I'm getting divorced." Vin fumbled for the right thing to say.

"I'm sorry," he lied. *What were you thinking marrying him instead of me?*

"Paul left me for another woman."

"Another woman…?"

"Yes. Apparently they've been seeing each other for a while now." *Probably longer than you think.*

"I found condoms in his ditty bag." *So, old Paul was dumber than the button down, corporate image he portrayed.* Vin couldn't comprehend anyone in their right mind giving up on the woman he'd desired so badly for so long, yet had such a short time. Her image pervaded his thoughts as he recalled her solid facial features, high cheekbones, bony jawline and prominent chin. Her nose was slightly crooked but not out of place with the strong almost masculine lines of her face was the result of too many backhands by her abusive father having returned home from

Kelly's Pub. Too many nights his heavy clump on the stairs leading to her and her sister, Sarah's bedroom meant having to fend him off halfway up before he'd get to the top and have his way. Sometimes, but not often enough to be without blame herself, her mother would pull him back down. As Blair grew older she understood and forgave her mother as she surely suffered her own end for the intercessions.

The handsome looks had come from her grandfather on her father's side. Her toughness came from her father. She grew up a tomboy, the son her parents never had.

What a fool, Paul. What were you thinking? Clear thinking came easy to Vin when it came to other's decision making. "I'm sorry, Rosa."

A STORYBOOK ROMANCE it wasn't. They were high school lovers that kept in touch when he went off to college and she to get married. When he graduated, secret liaisons led to Rosa becoming pregnant with Blair while married to another man. A painful, guilt-ridden divorce followed. Vin's offer of marriage did little to console her. Confused and wanting to rid herself of the source of this dilemma she avoided him and left for St. Mary's, a home for unwed mothers. There she planned to give her baby up for adoption.

Vin stopped hearing from Rosa. He couldn't blame her as he himself was as much to blame for their transgressions. Later he found out that Rosa had a change of heart and kept the baby. By then they'd each had enough of shame and blame, so they moved on with their separate lives.

They kept in touch sporadically. When they did Vin felt the pain of closeness never rewarded as if they were reaching out for each other their fingertips almost touching yet separated by sin never cleansed and the fearful specter of temptation for more. Vin married, had children and got divorced well over a decade ago, never remarrying. Rosa remarried, her husband adopting her first-born child. She named her Blair, after one of the midwives at St. Marys who had been kind to her. Her husband adopted Blair and they had two more children together.

Vin feared he'd never see Rosa again. He and his own blood would wander the earth never knowing each other, never laughing, never hugging, always wondering.

Then came the eventful call from Rosa.

Chapter Three

"Who's the soldier boy?" Vin asked Maggie.

"He's not a soldier boy," she spoke softly so only he could hear. "Carson is from the young people's church group. They met on a mission to Louisiana last year to aid the victims of that Katrina storm. Nice young man."

Vin sipped his coffee. It tasted bitter. Maggie casually dropped a half teaspoon sugar into his cup.

"My coffee's not that bad. Why the long face?"

"Can't imagine what she sees in him."

"Vin, look at me." He moved his eyes from the coffee cup to Maggie. Her eyes were a moist-soft blue like the bottom of the health club pool. Most of the time she made sense. But now he prepared himself for one of those mother-like advice intonations you don't want to hear but know you're going to.

"Those Church people are good people, like you and me. Just, they don't swear, don't drink…"

"Don't tell me what they don't, tell me what they do."

"They go to Church, go on missions to help others and convert those without. What's wrong with that? Lord knows at least they're not writing graffiti on the railroad underpass walls at night like some of those worthless dropouts from the Junk. Good kids like them are welcome in The Empty Cup anytime. They're just different, that's all."

Vin swirled the dark contents of his cup as she talked hoping she'd run out of steam.

"Has Blair talked to you about joining the All Lives congregation?"

"No, You?"

"Oh sure. But sugar, my time is past I'm afraid. There was a time when maybe…" Maggie paused to recall those days when she didn't color her hair or watch what she ate and ohhhh, the stream of gentleman callers she thought would never end, "ahh forget it. What about you?"

"No," he said shaking his head. "I'm Catholic, a former altar boy. I'm not going anywhere."

"A former altar boy, you don't say."Maggie raised her penciled eyebrows in a wide arc trying to imagine the cherub-faced Vin in black robes and white frock.

"Yeah, I drank my share of altar wine in the sacristy before Father arrived for Mass," he let it be known. "Remember, Billy Wigler?"

"Didn't he graduate the Junk a couple years ahead of us?"

"Yeah, that's him. Well Billy drank a little too much and threw up all over himself. We cleaned him up fast as we could, got another smock and stashed the dirty one in the dumpster behind the church. But that foul smell of cheap wine puke lingered like mustard gas so we had to light the benediction charcoal and sprinkle it with the incense powder. Father Mac came in just then and told us there was no High Mass today and please put it out this minute."

"Didn't he end up in a wheelchair?"

"Yeah, went to Vietnam to be a hero, stepped on a land mine and came home a paraplegic. By then his parents had divorced. He lived with his mother in small apartment behind the Washrag Laundromat over by the car wash. I used to see him in the bars around town for a while, begging beers—he was always three sheets to the wind. Things just never went right for Billy, like from that day on he was cursed or something."

"My how the mighty have fallen," Maggie finished drying a coffee cup and placed it atop a pyramid of others.

Vin taken aback retorted, "Excuse me but I still go to Church."

"Then say a prayer or two for me, will ya?"

"Maggie, you've got all you need right here."

"Honey, either you're not prayin' hard enough or your Guy's hard of hearin'."

AT ROSA'S INVITATION, Vin had stopped over at her home. After meeting her two younger children, he uncorked a bottle of Merlot and poured them both a glass. They sat at the kitchen table talking while the kids sat in the front room playing video games on the television set. It had been a long, long time for both of them. Rosa hadn't changed a bit, still lovely as ever and forever youthful, the blessing of a swarthy complexion from the Sicilian side of her Italian-Polish heritage. Only when she batted her eyelids did he see the years of motherhood and a stressful marriage. The lines of fatigue, where the makeup caked were those of an woman who raised three children, worked part time and spent many a night alone in a wintry bed as her husband travelled, slowly climbing the corporate ladder. Her dark brown eyes sparkled in his presence but when she closed her eyes he could see the pain of years of tears. They toasted each other happily but with reservation, wary of crossing paths again, knowing full well that having the courage was easy but what followed might not be.

"Rosa, about..."

She lifted her hand to stop him mid-sentence. "Please, let me apologize first. I was wrong for running away from you, us."

"But, why?"

Rosa spoke slowly as if laboring for air, "I was confused. I felt guilty. I was pregnant. My husband was divorcing me." She talked into her wine glass not looking at Vin.

"I'm sorry," he reached across to cover her bony hand with his. All these years all he could think of was how he'd been wronged. He never understood, but now felt Rosa's pain. The long sad suffering only a woman could know. They both stared at the strange sight of their hands together. In the quiet that followed only their hearts spoke.

The front door opened and two teenage girls burst into the room giggling. They swept by with quick hellos and headed to the downstairs den, their long hair flopping and bouncing like wild horses as they bounded down the steps.

One of the girls had long blonde hair that reached her square shoulders, a broad Irish face and athletic build.

"Was that Blair?" he asked.

"Yes," Rosa smiled.

"Don't you think you should introduce us?"

Rosa walked to the top of the stairs and called for her daughter, "Blair come up please, I have someone I'd like you to meet."

Vin rose from his chair when Rosa introduced Blair. He reached his hand out to her. She swept by his outstretched hand into his arms and gave him a long, warm hug. When she raised her head he kissed her gently on the forehead. "Hello, sweetheart." They hugged for what seemed minutes before Rosa intervened.

"Okay you two, Blair you have company and Vin and I are talking. Perhaps you two could get together for dinner tomorrow evening." The arrangements were made and Blair skipped back downstairs.

They sat back down. Two glasses of red wine separated them. Rosa sipped from her glass slowly eyeing Vin. "Well?"

Vin finished the remainder of his glass, exhaled a long breath and collected his thoughts. He'd been awash in Blair's warm acceptance of him and mesmerized by her beauty. The resemblance surprised him. It was as if he were looking at himself in a mirror when he spoke to her.

"Well…I think I just met the love of my life."

"Me too," Rosa smiled.

Chapter Four

The weather was always the same at The Empty Cup. Dwarfed by the shadow of the tilted train station looming eerily above, the little coffeehouse seldom saw a ray of sun, felt the chill of snow or the slap of rain. It was difficult to tell night from day. But the gloom didn't stop the bustle outside the shop. Fridays were hectic in Turner Junction. Passengers lighted from the station at all different hours filtering down the stairs, swinging into The Empty Cup. Maggie never disappointed. She played waitress, maître d, and emcee to perfection. As a result, dead presidents overflowed the register and tip jar.

"Here you go Lucky," she said, scraping an unfinished plate of scrambled eggs into a bucket-sized bowl. Lucky had been saved from the Pet Rescue pound some four years ago shortly after Maggie opened shop. He was only a year old then, scraggy, neglected and missing a piece of his tail. One eyelid drooped heavily, covering half his eye, giving him the appearance of an aged prizefighter. Both ears stood up pointy, but the left one had a chunk missing, the result of a predatory bite. The good people at Pet Rescue gave him the prescribed shots and started him on a protein rich diet.

Maggie felt for him. He had such sad eyes. "What's his name? She pointed to the cage with the German Shepherd inside.

"Him?! The young female volunteer seemed surprised by her interest. "Oh he's been here a while. Doesn't have a name."

"Come on Lucky, let's take you home." With that the two became fast friends and forever inseparable. Thanks in part to Maggie's loving care but moreso her cooking, Lucky had grown to a hundred and forty pounds. He spent most of his time lying around behind the counter scarfing up leftover omelets and grilled cheese sandwiches, letting the waitresses pet him and always keeping an eye on the clientele.

Up at the register a tall man of color was gesticulating wildly. Apparently, he'd had one too many on the train ride from downtown, probably stopping in for a cup of coffee before returning home to the missus. Disheveled and malodorous, his scent resembled that of burnt flowers like those smoked through an octopus pipe, cleansed only by the copious steam baths people from that region of the world frequented.

"Excuse me ma'am but I gave you a ten," he said in an accent that was high pitched and very insistent.

"Sir, you gave me a five," she said backing away from his offensive odor.

"No, no, no. I'm sure it was a ten." He swayed slightly as he talked.

"SIR, YOU GAVE ME A FIVE DOLLAR BILL," Maggie raised her voice. With this Lucky began to stir from his nap.

"I gave you a ten," he repeated looking into his wallet. "It's the only one I had, I know," he said raising his curious voice to match Maggie's. Lucky sat up at full attention not happy to have been awakened from his nap. He was head and shoulders above the counter.

The man of color took note of Lucky but insisted he was right. He made the mistake of pressing closer toward Maggie thereby involuntarily leaning over the counter. "I am positively sure..."

Lucky began a deep growl that sounded as though it came from the belly of the devil. His lips shrunk back in a sneer revealing long pointy teeth resembling those of a wild boar.

The man looked at Maggie then to Lucky then back at Maggie. "Maybe it was a five," he said placing the bills in his wallet, turning to leave.

Vin watched the scenario play out in slow motion as if underwater. Their words seemed elongated like a cheap toy running out of batteries. He'd hoped to be a man of action like the dynamic characters he wrote about in his stories but he wasn't those characters. Instead, each time he had an opportunity to shine a perverse sense of paralysis enveloped and immobilized him.

Car who'd been cannoodling with Blair rose from his stool to address the stranger, "Aren't you forgetting something?"

"What's that?" the man asked.

"An apology, you owe her an apology."

Blair tried to drag Car down to his stool. "Car don't start..." Lucky continued his sandpaper growl. Even Esther further down the counter hard of hearing as she was had taken notice.

"You're right young man. I am sorry." The stranger tipped his head in Maggie's direction all the time keeping a wary eye on the German Shepherd behind the counter. With that he backed his way toward the door in a roundabout manner like a rudderless ship.

"Don't forget the tip jar," Esther called out after him.

IT'S NOT OFTEN one is given the chance to atone for the sins of their past. Vin felt that his reunion with Rosa along with the beautiful Blair was his chance for redemption. On Sundays he gave thanks for his cherished gifts. Recalling Maggie's comments about the All Lives congregation Vin always made sure to note the priest's homily that Sunday should Rosa inevitably mention her church. They talked every day and met as often as their schedules permitted, he busy with his writing and civic volunteer work and she with her church work and raising three children. Rosa was unsure about having relations at first but Vin's passion and charm won her over. He was convinced that this affair was not only too long in coming but ordained from above.

"What are you doing under there?" he asked Rosa as she scrambled around on her knees beneath the sheets like a ghost arising from a heavy sleep.

"You smell like a brewery! Where have you been?"

He pulled the sheet up to see his love and she pulled it back down scrambling around in her lion's den. This wasn't exactly his idea of making love. "Ohhh myy," he groaned, succumbing to her ways.

He recalled their younger years when they first made love. They'd steal away to secret spots and share moments too brief. Vin never forgot looking down into her deep brown eyes, so dark they were almost black—a tunnel to her soul, apprehensive but enticing. When they kissed she never closed her eyes, caverns of intrigue kept open for only him to explore.

When Rosa emerged from under the sheets she had already mounted him. He squirmed a little in an effort to assume the missionary position but there was little he could do. Rosa was petite but lithe and strong, especially of will. When she bent to kiss him her hair covered their faces. The world went dark. Her moist tongue entered his mouth not leaving until he was panting for air. Closing her eyes, she stuck her tongue in his mouth once more, rose up on his body and back down slowly. Vin watched Rosa bounce, knees bent forward like a jockey while he desperately gasped for air now in the final stretch run. Then the finish line.

They lay next to each other entwined, their clammy bodies heaving together.

"God, I love you Rosa," he offered between shortened breaths.

"Thank you, Vin, me too," she whispered, falling asleep in his arms.

Chapter Five

Blair teetered for a moment, wavered and finally stumbled against Vin. He chuckled at the sight of his daughter trying to negotiate her way through the crowd in new high heels.

"Oh my gosh, how does Mom wear these things?"

"Practice, sweetheart. Practice." He offered the crook of his arm. She clutched it like a life preserver.

"Oh thank you, Dad. That's better."

Blair looked resplendent with her upswept hairdo, black evening gown and trainer high heels. This was just many of the fundraisers Vin attended as an active member of the community. Lately, he'd often been seen around town with Rosa on his arm. And the small community of Turner Junction took note. *Didn't they go together in high school. Wasn't there a rumor they had a child. Never married did they? Gosh they look happy, like they were meant to be a couple.*

It was Rosa's suggestion that Vin escort Blair to one of the functions. She'd bought her new shoes, which after hours of practice, Blair finally agreed to wear. She found a lovely evening gown at the Second Chance resale store downtown that fit her daughter's athletic build perfectly giving her a more lady-like appearance. Rosa did her hair and makeup herself, Blair fidgeting the whole time like a fussy child. "Oh, mother, please."

"Hold still, Blair. My goodness you're impatient. Life is not always spandex and Nikes." Blair sighed, putout and pouting.

Rosa opened the front door for Vin. He looked dashing in suit and tie. They chatted while waiting patiently for Blair. When Blair finally appeared—her mother had instructed her perfectly in the importance of just such a delay tactic—Vin couldn't believe it was his daughter he was seeing. She was positively radiant. The upswept hairdo accentuated rosy cheekbones and a strong jawline. The sheen of the dress accentuated the curves of her frame honed by hours of workouts. Her steely blue eyes sparkled with delight.

"Excuse me miss, but could you tell Blair I'm here," he panned.

Vin wanted to hug his daughter in the worst way but fearful of messing her up took her white hand, lifted it to his mouth and kissed it gently. "To the Belle of the Ball."

As she did when not knowing what to say, Blair, giggled nervously. "Oh Dad, you're so silly."

"Okay you two, you'll be late," Rosa said.

They departed arm in arm she almost skipping to the car, Vin literally walking on air. Rosa leaned against the open doorway, smiling, watching the love of her life leaving.

"SO TELL ME about this new interest in your life," Vin quizzed his daughter.

"Car? Oh, Dad. He is so nice. I've never known a guy like him before. He's not from Turner Junction, you know."

"So I guessed."

"His father is chief of police in Watertown. They just moved there from Plain Ridge where his father was chief there also. Apparently he had some 'trouble' there and transferred to Watertown."

"Trouble—like criminal type trouble?"

"No not like that. All Car would tell me was that it was some kind of domestic dispute. He's a recovering alcoholic. He goes to A.A. meetings, you know. They just figured a change of scenery would be best."

Nice family. First Rosa's father now this boy's father too. These poor women are surrounded by demons. They are both so beautiful yet tragedy shadows them. How ironic that the ocean's most majestic ships filled with riches, their sails billowed proudly by warm trade winds, carry the heaviest of anchors.

The gala dinner was well-attended. As active as Vin was in the community he was on a first name basis with most of the attendees, including Mayor Samuels who commented on his most attractive date and insisted they both sit at his table. Blair of course was the hit of the table. Young and pretty, all the men asked her of her plans for school and work while their wives made sure to ask if she had a boyfriend, what his name and how serious they were. This had the distinct purpose of throwing a little water on their husbands' campfire of interest.

They ate and danced and danced some more. Blair sipped at her coffee with her pinky finger held high as Rosa instructed while Vin polished off most of the bottled wine on the table. He was the hit of the table with his quick wit, cute jokes and of course, most beautiful of dates.

The night passed quickly but not without father and daughter getting to know each other a little better. It was past midnight when they left the fundraiser. On the ride home Vin offered fatherly advice on love and relationships to Blair and she in turn opened up to her father like she had no man before. Her adoptive father was just that and nothing more, she related. They had never been close. For some strange reason Vin took comfort in that.

He accidentally took a wrong turn on Washington Street but quickly made up for it by taking a shortcut past the junior high and through a nearby alley coming out right on Blair's street.

The hour was late. Rosa's home was dark save for a dim porch light above the front door. Vin escorted Blair up the steps. She put her hand in the crook of his arm not so much for support this time as she had gotten much better on the troublesome high heels. His body generated enough heat to dissipate the coolness of the evening air. When they got to the top of the steps Vin put his arms around her and held her close. Blair let her purse slide from her hand past her wrist to her elbow and wrapped her arms around him. She felt supple in his hands. Vin looked down into her eyes cobalt now that the midnight hour had passed. As he leaned forward Blair dropped her head back and to the side her thin lips offering a wistful smile. She closed her eyes slowly as if slipping off into a dream world. Vin drew close enough to smell her fragrance mix with the sweet dew of her breath, intoxicating and enticing him. He kissed her passionately, on the forehead and whispered softly, "I love you sweetheart."

"I love you too, Dad," she hugged him tightly.

"I'm sorry it's been so long…"

"Shhhh," she hushed him. "We don't apologize in this family."

He turned to leave her, "I hope you had a nice time."

"The best."

Vin descended the steps as Blair entered the doorway. "Oh, Dad."

"Yes, sweetheart."

"One more thing, could you not drink so much next time. I like your better when you're not drinking."

He thought briefly about what she'd said, smiled to himself, turned and left.

Chapter Six

"Well, if it isn't the Cheshire Cat," Maggie welcomed Vin, placing a hot cup of coffee before him. "Was that you I heard whistling on the way in?"

Vin hadn't whistled in years. He used to love to whistle. He wasn't much for remembering the words to songs but could whistle them all from memory. Whistling just seemed to make any task easier. His favorite was the theme song from "Bridge Over the River Kwai", a movie he'd watched with his father as a young boy. Whenever they walked somewhere they'd whistle that song together, stepping their knees high in the air as if marching. "Was I whistling? I didn't notice."

Esther sitting nearby couldn't stop herself from eavesdropping. There were no secrets in The Empty Cup.

"Sounded awfully good to me. Gosh, I loved that movie. Gable, wasn't it."

"William Holden."

"I knew it was some handsome movie star."

Something was amiss in the air. The conversation smelled stale, like burnt toast. Vin looked around for Blair but didn't see her. "Blair sick today?"

Maggie turned to pick up an order of toast. Esther turned her head away. "She quit."

"She what?" he asked in disbelief.

"Just up and quit. No notice or nothing."

"But why?" Maggie kept whisking around appearing busy. Esther stared into the coffee cup she stirred with a spoon.

"Apparently, Car," she emphasized his name by shaking her body at the same time, "didn't approve of her as a waitress," more emphasis on 'waitress' as if it sounded dirty.

"She was the best waitress here," Esther sipped at her coffee sounding as if she'd lost a daughter. "Made the most tips too."

"Why wasn't I told about this?" Maggie turned her head and looked at Vin with one eye peering out from underneath a crooked penciled eyebrow, saying nothing. She didn't have to. Vin had seen that look a thousand times from his own mother. At first he was dumfounded but after seeing it enough he began to know its meaning. It was the dreaded '*You Figure It Out*' look he'd come to know and hate, mostly because he couldn't always figure it out but knew that he should and she had. He looked to Esther but she was busy dipping her toast in her coffee cup.

Lucky tipped his nose up in the air turning and sniffing about. He jumped up and ran around in circles, head raised, barking loudly. Those closest to the counter covered their ears.

"Oh my God!" Maggie yelled. The sprinkler system behind the counter turned on automatically. Flames leapt out from the flat griddle. The sprinklers only spread the fire further. It was a grease fire started when the fryer oil had gotten too hot and sparked out.

Vin watched the whole scene play out before him like an old time silent film where the actors moved in clipped motions. He felt himself go numb. The dreaded paralysis began to creep through his body.

Maggie rushed to the spot of the fire trying to smother it with damp towels. A spark hit her apron and the thin material began to flame. Seeing her in danger, Vin quickly removed his sport jacket, leapt over the counter and adroitly wrapped it around Maggie's waist damping the fire on her skirt. He whisked her away from the hot fryer out of danger.

"Extinguisher?" he yelled.

"Over there," she pointed her skirt still smoldering.

"It's a grease fire," Vin's voice rose, grabbing the extinguisher and aiming it at the base of the flames. "It's gotta be smothered. Turn those damn sprinklers off!" He sprayed the fryer vigorously as he got soaked with water from above. "They'll only spread the fire!" In a matter of moments he'd put out the fire. A number of the patrons had made for the exit. A fire engine pulled up outside courtesy of the sprinkler notification system. Esther casually dipped the last remnant of toast into her coffee.

"Oh, Vin. How can I thank you," Maggie hugged Vin, tears melting eyeliner and mascara. "I could have lost everything."

"Including you," Vin held her until she stopped trembling. Lucky, soaking wet and smelling like an old wool rug, circled them both rubbing his matted fur against their thighs. They were still in each other's embrace when the firefighters burst in. Seeing everything under control they congratulated Vin for his actions but The Empty Cup would have to be closed for the day until inspections were made.

"You're a lucky lady, ma'am," one of them said. "Those grease fires can be deadly." Vin wrapped his jacket over Maggie's shoulders. They were both dripping wet.

Maggie closed the shop while the firemen combed through the mess. Vin caught Esther attempting to wheel herself out, grabbed her chair and assisted her toward the door. Her once wispy grey hair hung down about her face like a wet puppy.

"Put it on my tab, Maggie,"

"Nonsense, Esther. It's on me."

"Young lady, I'm in no mood to argue. My coffee's cold, I didn't get to finish my toast and I look like a drowned rat." She turned around to Vin, "To the Beauty Parlor, young man, if you wouldn't mind."

"Not at all Esther," Vin replied.

When out of earshot from Maggie she whispered to Vin,

"Nice work, never seen you move so fast."

THE MONTHS ROSA and Vin spent with each other were special. He had even taken to writing poetry recently, something he hadn't done since his college days. But he missed seeing Blair at The Empty Cup. The smile and gleam of her youthful innocence radiated through the shop complementing Maggie's well-intentioned but more worldly way of manners.

He called Rosa offering to buy her lunch at the atrium restaurant in her building. It was spur of the moment but Rosa loved Vin's impulsive invitations. But he had other things on his mind.

"Maggie tells me Blair quit The Empty Cup," he said to Rosa, trying to sound matter of fact.

"I understand you got lost taking her home the other night. Had too much of a good time, did we?" A not so faint tone of disapproval lingered in the air like a bad odor. Vin recalled Blair's comment about liking him better when he didn't drink. Rosa didn't pursue the matter, just letting Vin know she knew was enough.

"I took a wrong turn, so what?"

"Blair is working with me now, part-time, while she finishes her schooling." Rosa examined then gnawed at a cuticle on her nail.

"That's too bad, I thought she liked it at The Empty Cup?"

"Vin, do you see a future in The Empty Cup?"

"It's not a future, Rosa. It's a job while she goes to college. Everyone liked her."

"Do you see a future in us?" Rosa stopped chewing her fingers. She toyed with a cherry tomato rolling it around on the salad plate until it disappeared beneath a lettuce leaf.

"I wouldn't be here if I didn't."

"How can we be together if you go to St. Matthews and me to All Lives?" Her voice rose steadily. "You can't raise a family like that, two religions in one house."

Vin was shocked by what he was hearing. "It's not that complicated, Rosa…"

"It is!" She stammered. A couple at a nearby table began to stare at them. Vin felt trapped in the booth like a figure inside a snow globe. He felt that numb feeling envelop him again as if a large shadow had crossed his path, erasing him. But this time the shadow passed him by. Vin collected himself.

"True love trumps all, Rosa. For every problem, there's always a compromise, a solution." Rosa's face was wine red.

"This will never work. It never did work, did it Vin?" Rosa began to compose herself to return to work. A momentary silence drained the fight out of both of them. "I'm sorry, Vin." She batted her eyelashes not seductively but rather out of conviction. They parted without a kiss, only a glance, hers more a glare his a woeful stare.

"What about, Blair?" Vin asked.

"Give her a call anytime. She's old enough to make her own decisions. Good-bye, Vin." Rosa scurried out of the bright light of the glass ceilinged restaurant and disappeared into the distance of a dark elevator. Vin watched her leave as she had so many times before. He expected the doors to open and Rosa come running back to him with tears in her eyes. When it finally opened a carload of passengers lit from the elevator leaving it momentarily suspended, empty. A deafening ding echoed through the atrium. The doors inched closed like the final curtain on a thirty-year play.

First Blair, now Rosa. That old Catholic demon—Guilt—rose up inside him like the fires of hell. *What had he done to deserve this?*

Vin drove around aimlessly for an hour finally parking and entering the confessional, the one place where sins could be washed away, pain melted and sympathy served with humble pie—Kelly's Pub.

Chapter Seven

After the fire The Empty Cup remained closed for a day and a half before reopening to the delight of many sleepy-eyed train passengers now able to get their morning fill of liquid vitamins. This had given Maggie time to hire a new waitress. Dorothy, or Dottie, as she preferred to be called was a former barmaid in her mid-thirties, pleasant and plain-pretty. The patrons were charmed by stories of her wilder 'saloon' days. She could also work the register and open or close the restaurant, giving Maggie some time to herself for a change.

Vin rose around midday, took one look in the mirror and scared himself. His eyes were bloodshot, his lips pale as his face. The clothes he wore had that slept in, on-the-La-Z-Boy-overnight look. A two day-old beard sported the first noticeable signs of grey unlike the dark brown hair that covered his head and hadn't seen a comb in days.

The stranger before him mused.

The loss of one is hard to do. The loss of two is even harder too. It's a strange looking glass we peer through, once you've lost two.

Having seen enough of himself in the mirror, he wandered down to The Empty Cup and plopped himself down on the last stool available, next to Esther.

"Rough day?" Esther asked.

"Rough week," he replied.

"Two," she yelled down the counter to Maggie, pushing her empty cup forward.

"Shhhh. Not so loud," Vin winced in pain.

"I see. That kind of rough, huh?"

"Well," Maggie said noticing Vin. "Look what the cat dragged in. We'd just about given you up for dead."

Lucky woke from his nap, stood tall, wagged his tail and whined a little until Vin reached over the counter to pet him. "Gotta change your name from Lucky to Hero now, boy." He pulled a broken dog biscuit from his jacket. Lucky took it gently from his outstretched hand and began chomping, his lips curled back in a pleased doggie smile.

Dottie brought them both coffee and introduced herself to Vin. He raised one droopy eyelid to say hello. She'd seen his type before plenty of times. "Sure you don't want me spike that coffee for ya? Little hair of the dog, just what the doctor ordered."

"Not yet," he waved her off, his looping hand inadvertently making a circular kind of sign of the cross, above his cup. Dottie retreated leaving them alone.

An awkward silence followed. Maggie and Esther felt Vin's pain. They winced at each other wishing they could help. Moments seemed like minutes before Esther spoke up.

"I survived four husbands. Buried two of 'em, divorced the other two.

"Divorced one myself," Maggie said.

"Used to fight like hell. Those two were real bastards," Esther said.

"Yeah, know what you mean. Screaming like hell, pots and pans flying, the rough make-up sex. He was a real sonofabitch."

Vin was beginning to feel like the fattest man on a leaky lifeboat.

"God, I loved those bastards."

"God, I loved that sonofabitch."

They all chuckled heartily, fortunate enough to be able to laugh at and share their misfortunes with each other. Vin tipped his head back finishing off his cup.

"Can I buy you drink, fella?" Maggie asked.

"I'd like that, Maggie.

"Dottie, take over for a while, please," Maggie said removing her apron.

"What about me?" Esther chimed in.

"Keep an eye on Lucky for me." Then she rethought herself, "Lucky, keep an eye on Esther."

Leaving The Empty Cup in the shadows behind them, they headed north toward Kelly's Pub, awash in the sunlight of a gorgeous afternoon.

Vin's arms swung freely and easily at his side. In the crook of his hand he felt two tender fingers with long nails press against his palm. He squeezed them tightly. They felt good.

Devil Inside Her

"She had the devil inside her." Grandma leaned forward, arching an eyebrow. "Ain't much good ever came from that woman. I warned him."

"Why did Dad marry her?" I asked.

Her eyes nearly crossed the bridge of her nose. "Your father didn't listen. He was smitten with her." Grandma shook a pack of unfiltered cigarettes until one stuck out like a straw in a drink. A picket fence of thin cracks danced about her mouth as she smacked her lips. A furtive glance begged the matches on the table. I understood and held a match near. As she puffed, tall flames flickered from the tip almost singing the wisps of thin hair that fell across her pained eyes.

"Once the devil sets up shop, you need to watch 'em. When she was out of sight—oh, Lord, that woman."

"Was she as pretty as Dad says?"

"It's the pretty ones that's the most trouble. They got the demons others don't." Grandma blew a perfect smoke ring in the air. It hovered above us like a halo. I wonder how different my mother's life would have been had it rested on her head.

Dad said, "She wasn't well". His deep voice could rattle the windowpanes. When he yelled the dog would hide under the kitchen table shivering, whimpering. Afterwards we had to coax her out with treats. She'd slither out on her belly an inch at a time like a salamander.

"Grandma says Mom had the devil inside her."

"I think she had the fever when she was young," he muttered, working a chew of tobacco round his mouth while he worked in his woodshop. Sighting down the length of the board, he ran his plane carefully along the edge stopping only to whisk the curly wood shavings aside. He didn't like to talk about her as much as his mother did.

When Dad screamed at her we would hide under the kitchen table like the dog. Once Amy wet herself there. We all shook and jostled for position trying to avoid the yellow river that snaked its way past us. No one dared come out until his locomotive bark trailed off into the woodshop.

Turk, the oldest, said he thought she went away. But that's what they told him. She just disappeared one day. We all believed she'd be back. That allowed us to play hide and seek, climb the low-limbed apple trees and suck cherry Popsicles 'til our tongues were sore throat red. Summer came and summer went. The apple trees dropped their fruit. The leaves turned a shade of burnt orange, like the tips of a campfire, only to fall to the ground where they were swept up by the cool winds of the north and scattered piecemeal in the fields. Still she didn't return.

I forget how old I was when I realized that she would never return. Our youthful remembrances of her were all we had to hold on to. One time I found her out back behind the shed smoking all by herself. She called me over and swore me to secrecy. "We mustn't tell your Father or Grandmama." Then she let me take a drag off the white stick. It was such fun I asked for another. She pursed her lips to the sky, exhaled gently as little ringlets of smoke floated above us. I tried it too but blew only baby puffs that turned wispy then disappeared.

One day when Dad was in the fields she got behind the wheel of the pickup truck even though she didn't know how to drive. We all hung on to the rear bumper while the truck did circles in the drive until we were dizzy sick and little sister Ellie threw up. Then she let Turk drive the pickup. We had such fun until Billy Boy, disoriented and walking in circles, bumped into the laundry pole, cut his lip and took stitches. Upstairs in the bedroom window a pair of snarling eyes swayed back and forth. The more upset she got the more violently Grandma rocked.

Then the fire came. By the time the neighbors got there the shed was completely engulfed in flames. Tongues of fire licked the nearby barn. The horses and the cows had to be removed lest they burn to death. The neighbor men soaked the barn with endless buckets of water ad it was saved. But the shed had burned to the ground. A few charred pieces of wood stood like blackened tombstones. After that we never saw her again.

I guess I'm lucky to have remembrances of her. I miss her comforting embrace when I cry. I miss the soft songs she'd sing me when I was sick. But most I miss her goodnight kiss. And when I feel compelled to take a chance or do a dare I never hesitate because I feel that just like her, I have 'the devil inside'.

About the Author

Stephen H. Jansen's *Secrets of Mirror Lake* is a fascinating tour de force collection of diverse short stories in the commercial literature and mainstream literary fiction genres. An array of contemporary heroes/heroines struggle to emerge from a morass of moral dilemmas and daunting circumstances. It is seldom an adult reader finds such richly entertaining storytelling and first-rate writing together in a single volume.

A graduate of Southern Illinois University with a degree in English—Creative Writing, Steve has successfully completed all courses toward a Masters in English—Creative Writing at the University of Illinois. He owns his own financial planning firm, Jansen & Jansen Financial Services in Elmhurst, Illinois and is also a freelance fiction writer.

Steve participates in Writer's Workshop courses at the College of Dupage, in Glen Ellyn, Illinois and is a member of the Naperville Writer's Group, Naperville, Illinois. He currently lives in Naperville, Illinois.